Intimate Strangers

Lasairiona E. McMaster

To Jo
Thanks for paying
for my editor!!
with love
Las xxx

ISBN: 978-1-9161784-0-3
Cover Design: Pink Ink Designs
Photo Credit: Bernie McAllister

To Jo of Jo
Thanks for being my editor!
With love
Las xxx

For the real-life 'AJ', thank you for being my muse, for showing me that Disney romances do really exist, for believing I could do anything and for encouraging me to write these words that were in me to write.

Chapter 1

"By the way, classes are boring when there isn't an entertaining Irish lass in a chat window to talk to. Can I book you for every class I have this term?"

And that was it. That was the moment he got her, hook, line and sinker!

Lisa didn't see it coming. She hadn't planned it, or gone searching for it, but that was the moment she fell head-over-heels for a guy she'd never met. A hockey player and musician who was absolutely *gorgeous* – and smart to boot. AJ had appeared as if from nowhere and swept her wholly off her feet.

She hadn't been prepared to be swept any which way and was a little out of her comfort zone to say the least. Lisa was one of those stereotypical curvy-girls: big boobs, big hips, big bum. In a society that deemed you could either be big, or beautiful – never really both – she was always pretty self-conscious of how she looked. She was working on it, it helped having a tribe of supportive and badass friends who wouldn't abide her even thinking the 'F' word (Fat).

She still couldn't take a compliment, though. If someone said something nice about her, she couldn't ever just say “Thank you.” She’d palm it off, or throw it back at whoever had given it in some form of embarrassing, “please don’t call attention to me in any way,” reaction.

Meeting someone online, however, was slightly different. Her words made her first impression. Even so, when he took an interest in her, it was entirely unexpected. But she had rolled with it all the same. On paper, she had met the man of her dreams. He was a man who checked all of her boxes – and more – and before she knew it, she had landed herself a guy on the internet. She didn’t, by any means, feel like she needed a man to complete her or anything. She was a *badass biatch* who could rule the world if she decided that’s what she wanted to do. But she did often dream about a badass husband at her badass side as she ruled the world!

Getting to know each other hadn’t been easy. She was in Newry, Northern Ireland, and he was six hours behind her in Huntsville, Alabama. They were both in college, four thousand miles apart, and working on finishing up their degrees. She had a job and he had hockey – which essentially took up every free moment he had. When he wasn’t playing hockey, he was gigging in coffee houses and bars with his guitar.

Finding time online together was tough. They’d resorted to daily back and forth emails, and she would regularly stay up late to catch his hockey games online, then stay up later still, to try and catch him on Gmail chat after the games. They'd had months of trying to align their schedules to try against the odds, to find some "alone" time, for them to just sit, without having to multitask, or run off, for whatever reason. It was hard, but they stuck at it. Seven months since their introduction in the first group chat with her best friend, Chelsea, and his best friend, Jeremy, she sat staring out the window of the Aer Lingus plane in disbelief of her own spontaneity. Last minute, open-ended flights and playing hooky from university wasn't typical behavior for her, but she'd assured herself that it was necessary and that he was worth it.

Jeremy also played hockey. He used to play for Chelsea's home team in Iowa. He and Chelsea's ex-boyfriend had been team-mates and as Chelsea spent more and more time at the rink over the course of the relationship, she'd grown to be close friends with Jeremy.

The two of them had colluded to bring Lisa and AJ together in a chat window when AJ broke up with his girlfriend, and from everything Chelsea had told him about Lisa, Jeremy thought she'd be a welcome distraction for his friend.

Lisa didn't have much experience with boys. Her dad was strict throughout her teenage years. She was seventeen when she met her first boyfriend, was allowed to see him on Saturday afternoons, and only when her homework was finished. Chelsea was most certainly in favor of introducing her to a new guy, who, according to

Jeremy, was a good one. And so, a Gmail chat window with four participants was created – only two of whom actually knew what was going on. Lisa and AJ had been momentarily confused, but the conversation had flowed easily between the foursome and, before long, the two of them had opened their own private chat-window to get better acquainted.

Her first flight was supposed to be seven hours, then an hour lay-over in Chicago, followed by a shorter three-and-a-half-hour hop to Huntsville. In reality, seven had turned into ten, she had missed her connection, and had wound up spending the last couple hours dozing on chairs while waiting for the only plane the nice guy at the customer service desk could cram her onto. Finally, though, the captain had just announced they were landing. Her phone had died a sudden death as it played Jason Mraz, and she couldn't find her charger, so she'd spent the last few hours flicking through the in-flight entertainment system menu in an attempt to distract herself. She couldn't tell whether it was the change in cabin pressure, or the butterflies in her stomach, but a sudden wave of nausea hit her. In reality, it was probably a combination of both. Part of her couldn't wait to get out of the tin-bird, while the other part kind of wished she could stay in its protective confines and just pretend she'd never left Ireland at all.

This is it, she told herself as she felt the wheels hit the ground.

Disembarking from the plane, she made her way to

baggage reclaim. Her nausea had largely abated, though every now and then she felt the occasional flip-flop in her stomach reminding her of just how nervous she was.

She was already tired. Despite having gained six hours in the time change, she hadn't slept much on the plane and was hoping, likely against hope, they wouldn't expect her to be in any way energized when she landed.

She had that icky feeling you get while travelling and really needed a shower. She collected her cases – largely full of Irish crisps, bread and chocolate (her American bestie had a penchant for all things Irish) and her own tea bags, which she took with her everywhere. Always. She cleared customs but had to dance the "Why are you coming to America?" tango with the humorless immigration officer first, which added another hour to her travel time.

Bursting through the arrivals doors, pushing the precariously stacked Smarte Carte in front of her, she started the search for *the* red coat. She knew it wouldn't take her long to find it in the sea of people waiting to greet their visitors. It was the same red coat she had searched for the previous year, only this time in a different airport, Huntsville International Airport instead of Chicago O'Hare.

"Hey, Irish!" she turned towards the source of the voice and grinned.

"YO, IRISH!" the voice repeated, "Frickin' took ya long enough." Chelsea jabbed playfully as she wrapped her arms around her exhausted friend.

"We were starting to think you weren't coming," added a second voice. This was one of the many moments she was dreading on this trip – the sister. *His* sister.

"Hey there, missy, what's the *craic*?" Lisa asked, as calmly as she could muster, extending her arms for a hug.

Breathe, she reminded herself when she began to feel light-headed. *Breathe again. And again. And once more. Last thing you need is to pass out in front of "the sister", now BREATHE, DAMNIT!*

The stubborn panic was slow to subside.

"Hey yourself," Ana, the sister, grinned, "It's so good to finally meet you, Lisa!" She returned the hug. "How was your flight?" Ana asked politely as they headed for the car park.

"Long, boring, and a screaming child. You'd think after the first few hours they'd exhaust themselves, right?" Not waiting for a reply, she continued, "Wrong! Wrong! Wrong! He screamed in the check-in lounge, and then again while boarding. He screamed again during the delay, and for the entire feckin' duration of the flight. I even heard him screaming in baggage claim after we landed in Chicago – although, by that stage, I was ready for a scream-fest myself, so I can't really blame him there! There was more screaming on the connection – no idea if it was the same child or not, but Christ I am *over* the screaming!"

Stopping, she realized the two girls were staring at her with wide-eyes, and with an expression on their faces that she recognized all too well from her last visit to see Chelsea. “Too fast?” she asked more slowly.

They nodded in unison.

“And you usually understand me so well,” she turned her attention back to her friend in the red jacket, blushing a little. She had known her best friend, Chelsea, for a few years now. They had met on an online journaling website called Live Journal and they’d instantly bonded and became fast friends. They enjoyed making each other’s lives that little bit stranger. Chelsea’s schedule was more flexible than AJ’s, making it much easier for Lisa and Chelsea to speak, in some form or another, every day and they would usually end up giggling uncontrollably together across the Atlantic. And when she was down, or upset, or even when she was happy or excited, or just needed to scream, shout, whine, bitch or just for a regular “Hey, what’s up?” kind of chat, she called Chelsea.

“Yeah,” she paused, “but when you talk like *that*,” she smiled, “I’m surprised even people in Ireland can understand you,” she laughed.

“Hey!” Lisa protested in mock shock, “I’d usually come back with some witty yet cutting retort, y’know, to shut you up and all. However, right now, I’m knackered!”

Turning to Ana, she asked, “Is it far?”

It was the first time either Lisa or Chelsea had met Ana. They’d talked a little online, but they weren’t exactly friends. Chelsea was in town to see Lisa and catch up with Jeremy, and Ana was in town to visit her brother, and to co-ordinate Lisa's secret transatlantic drop-in on him. She seemed a good sport, she didn't know either Lisa or Chelsea well, yet she had agreed to pick them up at the airport and take them where they needed to go. Lisa's delay had meant that Chelsea had gotten some extended one-to-one time with Ana, and Lisa was eagerly looking forward to a debrief later when the two were alone.

Ana shook her head, and said, "Not really, and you can sleep for a while when we get to the hotel." Checking her watch, she added, "We have time, it's only three."

"Does he know?" Lisa asked shakily.

Ana laughed at what must have been clear terror written across her face and replied, "No, he doesn't have a clue."

Not that this made the somersaulting in her stomach lessen.

"When did you arrive?" she asked Chelsea, who had made the trip to Alabama from Iowa to see both Jeremy and Lisa while she was in town.

"Oh, about eleven thirty this morning," she began, "your Irish ass was due in a while ago y'know!"

"Give over your whining already! I'll go back home if you don't shut up!" She huffed as she pretended to walk back towards the airport.

"Yeah, ok. Go on," Chelsea teased, "then you won't meet him," she continued lightly.

Lisa stopped dead. *Him.*

You win, she thought to herself. She could feel both girls looking at her in amusement. Her stomach flipped again and heat rose in her cheeks. Casting her friend a withering look she mumbled something inaudible as she plopped into the car and put her phone on charge.

She was starting to regret giving in to her impulse to book a flight across the world for a guy she had met on the internet.

"We should meet some time."

"I'd like that a lot."

This exchange had become a common theme in her chats with him. They got along great online, and over the occasional phone-call, but one of the joys – and dangers –of the internet is that you can tell anyone, anything, and you may never know if it's true or not. Ultimately, the only true test of whether they were relationship compatible or not, lay in a face to face meeting.

She'd floated the idea to Chelsea, who, in true enabler fashion, encouraged the idea whole-heartedly. But, other than his town, his school and a few places he hung out sometimes, she didn't know where he lived, or how to find him at any given moment.

She needed help. Enter Ana.

Other than chatting online, Lisa had only ever *actually* said 'Hi' to Ana once before, when she was on the phone to him. She'd been in town visiting him for the weekend and had been impatient for him to get off the phone so they could go to dinner. Ana had been good friends with his ex and Lisa was convinced this meant she was destined to be public enemy number one when it came to his sister.

But when she'd emailed asking for some super-secret help in setting up a surprise meeting with Ana's brother, she had been only too happy to help.

It hadn't taken much secret-planning. Ana flew from Michigan to Alabama fairly frequently, and he was so caught up in college and hockey that, even if she didn't, he likely wouldn't have noticed that anything was amiss.

Lisa's nerves were really beginning to overwhelm her, and she was starting to wish she'd waited until Christmas.

Of 20-never.

Chapter 2

When Lisa woke up, they had arrived at the hotel and her nap had perked her up a little.

"We're here!" Ana announced from the driver's seat. *Although, technically, she's in the passenger seat where I'm from,* thought Lisa with a smile. Every time she visited, she was amused at just how different things were this side of the Atlantic. The food tasted funny, the money looked weird and the cars were put together back to front, to name but a few weirdnesses. But she loved it. There was something about this country that kept her coming back, and wanting to come back. Her plan was to see all fifty states, Canada, too and then she'd pick somewhere to settle down for a while. Somewhere she could call home for a few years.

The hotel was massive. *What isn't in this country?* she mused as she gazed around in sheer awe. When they got to the room, she headed straight to the bathroom, where she found not just a shower, but a bath as well.

"Thank Goodness!" she exclaimed as she turned on the taps. As the water ran, she turned her attention to her suitcase. Confusion hit.

What will I wear? She pondered.

“Haha!” she said to Chelsea, “I’m *such* a girl. I'm even nervous about what to wear.”

Smirking, she replied, “You’re only realizing this now?” Coming across the room to join her, the two girls observed the open suitcase, “What’s it gonna be?” Chelsea asked.

No reply.

“Lisa?”

Shrug.

“Ok, close your eyes and pick something random, deal?”

Lisa nodded in reply. Closing her eyes and trying to still her racing mind, she was really going to meet him – the butterflies hadn’t left her stomach. In fact, it felt like they’d been replaced with kangaroos throwing a party.

Letting out a deep breath, she tried to think logically. *It’s a hockey game – wear your hockey jersey, you dumb ass!* She scolded herself silently. *How obvious!* Opening her eyes, she rummaged for the jersey of her local team, the Belfast Giants. Last time she was in the States, she’d worn it and attracted quite a bit of attention as it was different to North American jerseys and tended to stand out, even in a crowd. The Belfast Giants were a largely unknown team in Alabama, save for a few hard-core aficionados, but it was obviously a hockey jersey and it sparked some interest. She lay it on the bed and grabbed her toiletry bag. Glancing at the clock, she saw it was 4.15pm – face-off was at 6pm. *Plenty of time,* she assured herself.

"Ten minutes," she announced to the girls as she turned towards the bathroom.

"Not likely!" joked Chelsea.

Sighing loudly, she shook her head and laughed, "You know me too well," she said as she locked the door behind her.

Sinking into the hot, bubbly water, she felt her muscles relax. She loved baths, *and you could totally fit two people in here,* she thought as she lay still in the water.

When she emerged from the bathroom, the girls were pretending to be asleep, fake-snoring, loudly. It was 5pm!

"Funny bitches," she snapped, taking the damp towel off her head and flinging it at Chelsea – she didn't know if Ana would have taken it in good humor, although if she'd had a second towel to hand, she might have found out.

"Did you shave your legs?"

It was Ana. Her voice was filled with a mocking sarcasm. Not knowing how to reply, she looked at Chelsea for an exit. Her face was hot, her palms were suddenly clammy and her throat was dry.

"Well, she has a point, Lisa. I mean, if you're gonna get busy with her big brother, you gotta be silky smooth!" Chelsea chirped.

"I...uh...er..." she stuttered.

The girls were now laughing so hard they could barely catch a breath.

They've planned this.

"So funny!" she snapped at them both, "reeeeeeal mature." The laughing continued as she dried her hair.

"Straight or curly?" she asked them.

"Curly," they chimed in unison.

"Up or down?" she followed up.

"Down."

When she'd finished doing the bare minimum with her naturally curly hair, she got dressed, stuck on some lip-gloss and was ready to go. 5.35pm? She mentally patted herself on the back as she eyed the clock, *not bad*. Stealing one last glance at herself in the mirror as they headed out the door, she took a deep breath. There was no turning back now.

They were seated just in time for face-off. Lisa didn't have to hide too much; she knew there was little chance he'd see her from the ice. Though she *did* keep the shouting to a minimum as there *was*, however, a chance that he would hear her. It would be pretty easy to pick out her accent in the throng of American and Canadian voices. *It has to stay a surprise,* she reminded herself as the urge to shout hit hard when the referee made some crappy call on Jeremy, captain of the home-team, the University of Alabama Huntsville (UAH) Chargers, and AJ's best friend.

The game was close, the Chargers won by three goals to two. AJ had a good game, with the exception of some stupid high-sticking penalty. *It wasn't even a high stick!* Lisa grumbled to herself. The high-stick call was followed closely by a second penalty, this time for hooking – which, in her opinion, was also a dodgy call. Although, to be completely fair, she was a tad biased!

So much for the nickname 'Pim' becoming retired, she thought wryly, making a mental note to poke fun at him later.

Pim, short for "penalty infraction minutes" or "penalty minutes" as it had become known over the years, was a nickname Ana had taken to calling him when they were younger. It wasn't one of those ironic nicknames where you call a giant guy "Smalls". Instead, considering how often he graced the bench in the box, it was factually accurate and had stuck around, mostly for Ana, but occasionally for Jeremy and increasingly for Lisa, too, though she found it funny that *her* AJ and the on-ice AJ were often seemingly so different.

When the final buzzer went, the kangaroos in her tummy did a crazy Mexican-wave and her heart leapt into her throat. She tried to swallow, but her throat was dry. Ana had told him to come out the front door. She said he'd had a string of objections, but he'd still agreed to it. He hadn't been very suspicious, and probably just figured she'd have someone with her to fend off the sixteen-year-old puck bunny invasion that awaited the players after every game.

As soon as he stepped out of the locker room AJ looked around for his sister. Watching him from her hidden position, Lisa was mildly amused at the obvious irritation the bunnies were causing him – he had barely stepped two feet before he was nabbed by a giddy bunch of girls, wearing what could not *possibly* be considered clothing.

They can't be more than fourteen! she thought, her mouth agape. He tried to hide that it bothered him and just be polite, but despite never having met him face to face, she could still tell that he was getting steadily more annoyed. He looked good. *Damn, he looks really good. That suit! Oh, I just love game night,* she thought as she eyed up her boyfriend.

My boyfriend.

Are we there yet? Can I call him my boyfriend?

You kinda just did.

I don't think we're there yet.

The kangaroos waved again.

We definitely aren't there yet, Lisa.

He was clearly itching to get out of the suit; he tugged at his collar and loosened his tie...*maybe I could help you with that, Pim,* she thought coyly as her cheeks flushed pink and her heart beat a little faster. He turned behind him to sign an autograph for a little boy, no older than five years old. His smile was genuine and reached all the way to his eyes. *So cute!* He was great with kids, he took a bunch of them for practice regularly, and clearly had a way with them.

I wonder how many kids we'll have together? We could maybe have a family hockey team.

Lisa! But look how cute he is with that little one, my ovaries just may explode. Focus!

Chapter 3

Taking a deep breath, Lisa stepped out from behind the pillar. She counted silently to three, closed her eyes,

"Hey, hockey boy!" she called confidently and loudly enough to be heard. She prayed her voice wasn't as shaky as she thought it was.

Shit, she thought, *now everyone's looking at me!*

AJ froze. Realization struck. She could see the side of his face and his jaw was hard-set. It flinched.

"Holy shit," she heard to her left. Glancing without turning her head, she saw that it was Jeremy. Having only spoken to him in chat-windows, she recognized him from the team pictures she'd seen. She smiled at him slightly as he stood with the same dumb-founded look that AJ was turning to reveal.

Don't fall to pieces.

Don't fall over, period.

He's staring. Speak, woman!

"Any chance of an autograph?" she asked full of faux nonchalance, still smiling, moving slowly toward him. His cheeks were flushing slightly and the people standing around looked somewhat confused. Chelsea and Ana were standing nearby with grins on their faces as he stood in shock for a moment, seemingly deciding what the hell to do. Their eyes met and she held his gaze. What felt like only a second later, she was wrapped in his arms.

Finally! she thought, enjoying the warmth of his embrace. The moment seemed to last forever and, as they pulled apart slightly, he brushed her cheek with his lips, and smiled. She could tell he was still confused. When he opened his mouth to speak, his voice sounded hoarse and a little shaky,

"What – How? I – uh—" She put her finger to his lips and shushed him. They weren't alone. His team, his sister, Chelsea, fans and bunnies? This wasn't a conversation either of them wanted to have in front of an audience, so she said lightly,

"Good game, mister – shoulda dropped your gloves once or twice and shown that number twenty-eight who's boss, but not altogether a complete disaster." She smiled at him.

"You watched the game?" he asked, suddenly self-conscious that people were staring. She nodded twice, once answering his question and once toward the people staring.

"It's the accent – they're not used to it!"

Returning her smile, he turned to Chelsea.

"Chelsea, right?"

"Yessir, that would be me," she replied, taking his outstretched hand and shaking it.

He threw his sister a look that said, "I'm going to kick

your ass," and asked,

"Have you guys eaten? The guys were gonna grab some food and a beer-" his sentence stopped short as he saw her try, unsuccessfully, to stifle a yawn, "unless you're too tired?" he asked her, smiling as she slipped her arm through his.

"Actually, I'm famished!"

They headed for the car park, and Ana and Chelsea headed for Ana's car.

"Lisa, you can keep Pim company," Chelsea called in that knowing, sarcastic sweet-way only best friends can.

This was the moment she'd been dreading. Not in a *dread* dread kinda way. But her tummy was in knots, her cheeks were still pink and both her heart and mind raced. She had to spend time with him, alone. *What if he's angry I didn't tell him I was coming?* She hesitated for a nanosecond and then realized she was being insane and over-thinking things as usual.

You're worrying way too much, Lis.

"Sure," she replied, matching her friend's tone and flashing a wide smile as she climbed into the car.

Oh my gosh.

Lisa heard Chelsea giggling and AJ was offering her the keys, "Were you planning on driving?" he asked.

Climbing out of the car, her face hot, "Stupid American cars," she grumbled as she walked around to the correct side.

"See you there!" he said, grinning to the others and getting into the car. She avoided his glance as the car hummed to life.

"How was your flight?" he asked.

"Ugh. Don't ask," she replied, "If you'd seen me a few hours ago, you'd not have voluntarily put yourself in the position of being alone with me. I was spitting fire! Your sister must think I'm a real nutter for all the ranting I did."

"I doubt it," he replied laughing, "she *is* related to *me* remember?"

"Good point!"

"Hey, that hurts! And as I recall, I didn't actually voluntarily put myself in the position of being alone with you," he answered with a winning grin.

Now it was her turn to pretend to be wounded.

That smile.

The ice was broken – *Wait a minute,* she thought to herself, *there was no ice,* no awkwardness, no banging of heads as they hugged.

No kissing.

Yet, Lis. No kissing, yet. There will be kissing.

With any luck there will be more than kissing.

She glanced at him again.

Definitely more than kissing.

I like that things are so comfortable with him.

She felt totally at ease with him, way too at ease, as though she-

Oh, shit, she thought as she recognized the feeling. *Chelsea is gonna kill me! It was literally the first thing she'd said when she made introductions.* She'd done her best-friend due diligence and warned her of the age-old stereotype. *Never fall for a hockey boy. They're bad news.* And Lisa promptly went and did just that.

***

Uh oh! Too many people! she thought as they stepped inside. Her face must have betrayed her nerves because he leaned towards her and whispered in her ear, "Don't worry, babe. If things get too much, just say you're jetlagged and I'll take you back to your hotel."

She smiled appreciatively as she felt his fingers brush hers. *Babe.* Their eyes met again. *Look away!* she told herself. When he looked at her, she felt him peer into her soul, she felt her cheeks heat up as she forced herself to look away.

Seems my cheeks are going to remain various shades of pink on this trip.

A voice disturbed her thoughts,

"OHMIGOSH it's LISA!"

Turning to face her, she smiled; it was Stephanie.

"Hey you!" she said warmly, "it's been too long." They hugged. "Have you seen Chelsea?"

Stephanie went to UAH like the boys, but she was originally from Iowa, where she and Chelsea had grown up together. Lisa had met her on her previous trip to visit her bestie. In truth, Stephanie was a bit annoying and over-protective of her friendship with Chelsea. One of those, 'She's *my* best friend and she can only have *one* best friend,' types. She spent most of her time trying too hard to fit in with the "in crowd," and trying to find herself a boyfriend, as though her self-worth would improve with the validation of a man by her side. It seemed that none of the "sisters are doing it for themselves" feminista-intervention chats from Chelsea had hit home. Lisa hoped that one day Stephanie would realize she was a goddess who didn't need a man to complete her, but for now Lisa suspected that she was so caught up in her new boyfriend that she was neglecting to find herself first.

"Yeah, she's over there," she gestured. "I'll join you in a few, I've just gotta talk to somebody first." She blushed through her smile. Stephanie and Brian were still trying to get past the "just dating" phase and hit the relationship phase. But she seemed happy.

Stealing a glance at AJ *-sigh-* she led the way to the table; drinks were already waiting. She had told Chelsea no alcohol – tonight at least. And, taking a sip from her diet coke, she checked the time. It was only 9.45pm, the night was technically still young, for someone who wasn't jetlagged, at any rate.

He sat across the table from her and try as she might, she couldn't stop herself from looking at him. She felt like a teenager – trying to stare without getting caught, it wasn't working so well.

He's so friggin' fine.

She was enjoying herself, the rest of the team seemed friendly and they only mocked her accent occasionally – as opposed to AJ and Jeremy who mocked her at least once every time she opened her mouth to speak. It was also great to see Chelsea again; she had missed her best friend a lot.

And him?

Well.

No! She chastised herself. *You can't be in love with a hockey boy – it's the LAW.* She rolled her eyes. She'd heard the spiel countless times. "Rule number one in hockey," Chelsea had told her before making any introductions, "*never* fall for the boys – they're trouble!"

Glancing at Chelsea, she realized she was in for another ear-bending, albeit a semi-light-hearted and only partially-serious ear-bending, but an ear-bending nonetheless. Chelsea had been burned in a relationship with a hockey player a couple of years prior, and, as a result, she was hellbent on reciting the warning frequently to Lisa. Lisa wasn't sure her best friend would ever fully recover from the hockey boy who broke her heart, but she acknowledged that she was doing her best to keep her nose out of her relationship with AJ. She also knew Chelsea, thankfully, wasn't the 'I told you so,' kind of friend, in case there came a point where she was, in fact, proved right about hockey players.

She was sure they both already knew she was done for. Lisa *had*, after all, flown halfway around the world to meet this guy. She'd already caught feelings. It was just a question of how deep they ran for both of them and seeing if they could figure something out.

Could long-distance even work for us?

She had no idea.

It already wasn't easy, and they'd only known each other for a matter of months. How long would they need to do long distance? They were both in college and neither had plans to move country any time soon. But how long could they realistically manage to stand doing long distance? Something would have to give eventually.

Everyone says long-distance relationships are doomed from the start. She'd heard those warnings from her friends, her family, from the lady who cut her hair. They all thought she was crazy getting involved with a boy living thousands of miles away.

But, she thought staring at AJ again, *he's* – his voice broke her thoughts,

"You ok?" he asked, his voice filled with concern.

"Hmm? Oh. Uh. Yeah, I guess I'm just tired," she answered, avoiding his anxious stare.

"Wanna call it a night?" he asked. She nodded and started to stand, checking the time – it was after midnight.

"You're not leaving already, are you?" Jeremy asked.

"Yeah," she replied, smothering a yawn.

"But, it's *early!*" he protested.

"For *you* it's early," she said picking up her bag, "for *me,* however, it's six a.m. and I need some sleep!"

"Ok," he answered, realizing he wasn't getting his way.

That's mature. Are you sad I'm leaving? Or that I'm

taking your bestie away?

"Nice to finally meet you all," she chirped as brightly as she could manage as she hugged Chelsea and Ana goodbye.

"See you in the morning," she told her friends. They didn't offer to leave with her, they trusted AJ to get her home safely. As did she.

"We'll let you sleep in, don't worry!"

"G'night!" she called to them as she headed for the door. She felt a hand at the base of her back, guiding her through the crowd, she felt the warmth through her jersey and couldn't help but smile.

Instinctive protectiveness, I kinda like it.

When they got outside, his hand didn't move.

"You cold?" he asked.

She shook her head in reply, yawned again. As he opened the car door, he asked again, "Are you really ok?"

Nodding, she smiled softly,

"Yeah, I'm ok, I'm just a bit-" she searched for the word, "overwhelmed," she finished.

Smiling, he closed the door with a soft thud, and they sat in silence as he drove to the hotel. A comfortable silence. She knew he understood and didn't feel the need to fill the quiet with unnecessary conversation.

He walked her to her room, his hand had again found its way to her back. *He's probably afraid I'll collapse from tiredness,* she thought to herself.

Or maybe he just wants to be close to you?

I certainly want to be close to him.

She chewed her lip. *Real close.*

She empathized with his desire for closeness. Living with an ocean between them was painful. Right now, though, he was simultaneously keeping his hand on her back and managing to open every door – *just as he said he would.* When they first started talking, he'd warned her that he was pretty old-fashioned when it came to dating.

I really kinda like the chivalry though.

She yawned loudly, too tired to try and race him to open the doors herself – her natural inclination when she wasn't exhausted.

When they arrived at her door, she took his hand and led him inside. He whistled softly as he admired the room. "This is niiiiiice," he exclaimed.

"Yeah, Chelsea is great at picking hotel rooms. Tea?"

"No thanks"

"Water?"

Shaking his head, no, he sat on the sofa as she put the kettle on for herself.

"I know it's not particularly sexy, but I'm completely knackered. Would you mind if I went and stuck some pjs on?" she asked.

"Sure," he replied, kicking his shoes off and swinging his legs up onto the sofa. When she emerged, she was wearing his oversized Alabama t-shirt that he'd sent her in a care package along with a birthday present earlier that year. She wore it with her *Teenage Mutant Ninja*

Turtles pj shorts and some thick slipper socks to warm up her toes.

"My favorite cartoon! And you said it wasn't sexy," he said as she spun around for him to take in the ensemble. "There's not a lot sexier than seeing you in my shirt ... I'd say we could probably lose the furry socks but I know you're prone to cold extremities."

Moving his legs, she sat next to him on the sofa. Not too close, she didn't quite feel at ease within herself to behave as a "regular girlfriend" just yet, but he inched closer to her.

Is he just being nice? Or is this him being 'boyfriendy'? Why isn't Chelsea here to psycho-analyze this for me? I can't ever tell what the signs mean!

It's definitely a good thing, right?

Only one way to find out, I guess...

Setting her mug on the floor, she rested her head on his shoulder, and he slipped his arm around her.

Breathe. He didn't push you away. You didn't read things wrong.

Breathe again. Could you calm down a bit? He is who he says he was, he's gorgeous, his smile could melt butter and he's definitely interested in you enough to sit close to you and put his arm around you. Chill.

She must have fallen asleep, because when she woke, she was lying on his chest. She could feel the sunlight trying to peek through the curtains, she could hear the soft thudding of his heart, and could tell that he was awake. She slid her fingers down the inside of his arm and laced her fingers with his.

"How long have you been watching me sleep?" she asked, tilting her head to find his gaze.

"Long enough," he replied, smiling, "Good morning."

Returning his smile, she answered, "Good morning. And long enough for what, exactly? Did I snore? Did I DROOL?" she asked, raising her eyebrows in horror.

Oh my God Lisa, did you DROOL?

Laughing softly he shook his head. Instinctively, she pecked his lips lightly, and his arms slipped around her waist.

"You hungry?" he enquired.

"Nah," she replied, "not yet. Did the girls come back? I figured they were giving us some space together, but I assumed they'd arrive later and then I guess I fell asleep on you. I'm clearly a very concerned friend."

"I could tell that from the snoring. And the drool. Ana texted to say she and Chelsea had 'made other plans' for the night. Ana stayed at my house and I think Chelsea crashed with Stephanie? Either way, they were both fine last I checked." He paused. "Lis, honestly, you didn't drool. I'm kidding!"

Check your face anyway, she thought as she wiped her mouth with the back of her hand.

Phew.

Checking his watch, he sighed heavily, "Babe, I..." he began.

"Have practice," she finished for him. "Yeah, I know. Were you asking me if I wanted breakfast out of politeness? You really should go though..." Checking her own watch, it was nine a.m. "you're already going to be late!"

"Well, I couldn't really *go* anywhere with you stretched out on me now, could I?" he joked. "Not to mention, I'd have happily gone to practice even later if you'd wanted to grab breakfast."

"Oh, you noticed I was lying on you, did you?" she pouted playfully. "But I don't want to move, you're comfy!" she grumbled, though she was already moving to sit up.

"Hey," he said suddenly.

"Yeah?"

"You got plans for tonight?"

Shaking her head, she told him she hadn't planned on making any until she'd talked to him about his schedule.

"How does dinner sound?"

"Great!" she exclaimed, smiling.

"Great," he echoed as they walked to the door.

"AJ?" she began.

"Yeah?" he paused, reaching for the door handle.

"Is this a non-date, date?"

A little needy, perhaps? But let's hope he found it cute.

Smiling, he reached out and wrapped his arms around her waist. He pulled her gently towards him and shook his head. "No, babe," he answered, kissing her forehead. "It's a date!" he said simply.

She felt her cheeks flush and he smiled at her, "I'll

come get you at five-thirty?"

"Sounds good," she answered, closing the door behind him. Her heart was racing.

Don't fall in love with a hockey boy! She scolded herself again. But she knew it was already too late.

She was a goner.

Chapter 4

The day passed quickly as Lisa and Chelsea went shopping in town. They had lunch and got back to the hotel at four thirty p.m. – in plenty of time to get ready for *it*. *It*. She had been thinking about *it* all day, *the* first date, the big first date – her head felt light just thinking about it.

Dumping all her purchases on the floor, Lisa headed towards the bathroom. She'd accidentally left her mobile on the counter before they went shopping. Lisa knew that Jeremy had Chelsea's number to give to AJ if he needed to contact her. *Quite the game of telephone, really.* Chelsea came into the bathroom to join her. Lisa smiled in confusion, "Chelsea, I know you've missed me, but I'm just about to pee, so could I have some privacy?" Her smile faded as she saw the look on her best friend's face. "What's wrong?"

"Here," she held out her phone. "There's a message for you," she paused heavily, "from AJ,"

"Summarize for me," she said sourly. The look on Chelsea's face told her it wasn't exactly good news.

"I...uh," she started, "please, just listen to it!" she said, trying to hand her friend the phone.

"Just tell me!" She snapped.

"I dunno, really," she replied, "he says something came up with one of the guys on the team and he can't make it, he's sorry and he wants to reschedule," she finished, holding the phone out again.

"Nah," she shook her head, "I don't want to listen to it."

Chelsea put the phone back in her pocket. Lisa closed the toilet and sat down. Sighing deeply, she turned to look at her friend. She didn't have to say anything, Chelsea knew her, she could read her like a book – there was no lying to her. Chelsea immediately saw the hurt in Lisa's eyes and her concern was evident.

Lisa couldn't cope with pity so she stood up and announced that she wanted to get drunk.

"You sure?" Chelsea asked, eyeing her with suspicion.

"Yeah, call Stephanie, Ana, and anyone else you think would like to come. We'll go get dinner and we'll hit the town," she grinned. "After all, it *is* a holiday for me, right? And I *did* come to see you as well – even if you *don't* believe me," she added, sticking out her tongue.

Chelsea returned her smile. She could see Lisa wanted a night out on the town, and she also hadn't had a good night out in a *long* time. She was easily persuaded. "You have thirty minutes to get ready," she told her friend, who was already choosing her outfit.

"Give me ten," came the reply.

She slipped on a pair of jeans and one of the approximately twelve thousand graphic tees she owned.

Tonight's choice? Wonder Woman. *Bet your ass.* She painted some clear lip gloss on, shook her hair loose and glanced at herself in the mirror.

"It'll do," she muttered aloud.

Slipping on some shoes, she called to her friend, "You ready?"

"Yessum."

"Then let's go!" grabbing her coat she headed for the door, leaving her phone behind – deliberately this time. Chelsea followed closely behind and they headed to dinner. When they arrived, Ana was already there, and she looked worried.

"Aren't you supposed to be having a candle-lit, romantic, first-date dinner with Pim right now?" she asked. "Is he ok? He's not sick, is he?"

Shaking her head, Lisa told her what had happened as Stephanie arrived. When Lisa had finished, Ana got up without a word. She returned a few minutes later with a tray of vodka shots, which she passed around, while informing everyone that the night was going to be a wild one. Despite her sadness, Lisa remembered what AJ had told her about Ana's tendency to get others drunk on vodka whilst drinking water herself and so made her trade drinks. True to her word, this time it really was vodka in Ana's glass.

This is going to be one hell of a night. Though I really could do without the sister-pity.

Dinner was a hoot. They laughed, and the drink flowed. When dinner was over, they headed for the bar they'd been to the night before. They could have gone anywhere in the city, but they all liked the atmosphere and it already felt familiar somehow. If she lived locally, she could see this place being her go-to bar on the weekends. There was also a small part of Lisa that hoped they'd 'bump into' one of the players on the team so she could quiz him on where AJ was, who he was with, and why he wasn't wooing her on their first date-date.

Subtle, Lis.

They were tipsy and giddy and, as they looked for a table, Lisa offered to go and get the first round of drinks. Approaching the bar, she saw him, standing talking with one of the guys she recognized from the night before.

Shit.

She groaned.

Frickin' perfect. She almost laughed. *What the actual fuck?* she thought, striding up to the bar and smiling at the bartender when she caught his eye.

"What can I get you?" he asked.

"What cocktails do you have?" she asked, smiling again.

"Huh?" he looked confused.

My bloody accent, she realized. *I only said five words! Though I guess it is fairly loud in here.* She indicated he should give her a pen and his notepad and she wrote,

"I'd like four, nice, large cocktails – as strong as you can make them please!"

She flashed her "bartender smile" as he read it, and he nodded with a wicked grin. Taking the pen from her, he wrote,

"What's your name and where are you from, honey?"

Glancing to her left, she saw Jeremy trying to indicate her presence to AJ. She took the pen from the grinning bar man – who, she had a suspicion, was probably gay, and, feeling the eyes of the guys to her left she quickly jotted down her answer,

"Lisa, Ireland – you?"

"Cool, Brad, NYC – do you know that you have three guys staring at you, to your nine o'clock?" he called loudly to her.

"Yeah, the guy in the middle and I know each other, the other two are his friends."

"Enough said," he nodded, giving her a knowing look. "Go sit down, I'll bring these over," he said indicating the drinks he'd started to pour in front of him. She tried to pay, but he pushed her hand away. "This round is on me," he told her. "Welcome to America."

Blushing, she thanked him and headed back to the table.

"What took you so long?" Stephanie had to yell to be heard, the music was so loud.

"Don't look," she began, "but AJ's up at the bar,"

As if on cue, they all went "Huh?" or "What?" and turned to look at the three guys who were staring back at them, propped up against the bar.

"I SAID DON'T LOOK!" she hissed, "Don't you guys understand English?"

They were giggling, and the cocktail Brad had handed

her as she sat down was disappearing fast. She felt the heat rising in her cheeks. This was bad. This was very bad. She hadn't expected to see him tonight; she'd assumed his friend's crisis didn't involve a bar. She was pretty tipsy, and seeing him made her head spin and her heart lurch. She needed to leave; it was a bad idea to get drunk.

She needed to leave, now.

Chapter 5

Lisa was just about to tell Chelsea she wanted to leave, when Chelsea grabbed her hand under the table. It was now *she* who was hissing, "He's coming over." She didn't need to tell her not to look, nor specify who 'He' was.

"Give me my hand bac-"

"Hey," he began.

"Hey," said Stephanie, glaring.

"Hi," answered Chelsea.

"Pim?" Ana queried, as though she expected him to stand and give them all an explanation right there.

"Hello," Lisa answered, avoiding his eyes.

"Can I talk to you for a minute?" he asked her. Even in the dimmer light, she could tell that he was blushing and looked guilty.

"Actually," she stood up, grabbing her bag in one motion, "I was just going to head back to the hotel, I think my jet-lag is getting the better of me," and with that, she was striding past him. *Just how much did I have to drink again?* she wondered as she headed towards the door.

Focus. Straight line, Lisa, she told herself.

When she got outside, she found a step to sit on and

slowed her breathing. He followed her; she could hear his footsteps coming up behind her.

"Forget the way?" AJ asked her, sounding hurt. Without turning around she replied,

"No, I'm just getting some air before I go back to the hotel."

"Got a minute?" not waiting for a reply, he sat down beside her. "You look good," he said softly.

"Thanks."

He looked good too, but she wasn't going to tell *him* that.

He sat quietly for a moment; he could probably tell that she wasn't going to make this easy for him.

Not my job to make things easy for you, boyo.

Taking a deep breath, he slid closer towards her until they were sitting side by side and their clothes were touching.

Focus. She steadied herself. *It's like an electric jolt, every damn time!*

"I'm sorry," he began quietly, "it was important, he-"

"Important?" she repeated. "Did somebody die?" Her quick breathing was returning. *Steady Lis.*

"No."

"He *obviously* hasn't lost a limb," she paused and pretended to think. "Internal bleeding?"

"No,"

"Terminal disease?"

"Lis-"

"AJ, what was so damned important that it couldn't

wait until tomorrow?" she asked, her voice laced with sadness and disappointment.

"Well, if you'd let me get half a sentence out, I'd tell you," he retorted hotly. "His girlfriend, well, his fiancée, broke up with him earlier. He was with her for six years. She's been seeing someone on the football team behind his back. He was in a bad way, Lis, and I've known him since high school. I couldn't say no to him."

She was still fuming.

"He broke up with his fiancée?" she repeated slowly, struggling to control her temper. *Bloody alcohol! That's what you get for telling your new Barman BFF to make them strong!* She cursed silently. "And you had to babysit him?"

"Lisa, it's not like that. He's a good friend and he needed me!"

"And what about me, hmm? I flew halfway across the planet to see you, AJ. You could have made time for me."

"I-"

Cutting him off, she continued, "It's not like he doesn't have a whole hockey team that can take him out and get him drunk. He's so plastered he doesn't even know who he's talking to. Jeremy could have handled it, or anyone that wasn't you. You could have gone to see him tomorrow, or worked around him and slotted me in *somewhere*. But you flat-out cancelled our first date, AJ, and not even *to* me. To Chelsea's answering machine, which you knew she'd pick up first!" Somewhere during this rant, she felt tears well up in her eyes, but she didn't fight them. She continued,

"I'm not here forever, AJ," her voice cracked. She turned to look at him, her eyes glistening. She could see fear beneath the calm surface as he tentatively slipped his arm around her shoulders. He didn't interrupt, there was really nothing he could say. He'd made the wrong choice and hurt her; he didn't want to say something stupid and make the situation any worse.

"I have to go home at some point, it's taken us seven months to meet for the first time, and God knows how many more it'll be before we find a second time." She tried to stop herself crying, and, between heaving, choked sobs, she continued, "I'm overwhelmed, AJ. I've met your sister, your best friend, I've met your teammates... I want to find a place in your life while I'm here! I want to spend time with you. I could have come out with you. I'm not expecting you to share every minute of every day with me...but...I..."

Her voice trailed off and she turned her head away from him. Day two and she was already feeling like a controlling, crying maniac. This was not how things were supposed to go. She was drunk and crying. She was embarrassed and hurting. He pulled her closer, wrapped his arms around her and said quietly,

"I'm sorry."

She nodded slightly, and they sat still for a few minutes, in silence. She felt safe there. She calmed herself and her tears stopped, but his arms stayed around her.

"Our first fight," he began, breaking the silence, "does that mean we get to make up now?"

She smiled despite herself, *damnit.* She mentally kicked herself. He could always make her smile, through emails, and now in reality too. She lifted her head slightly to look at him, he tilted her chin and she closed her eyes. She felt him move towards her. *Our first proper kiss!*

"There you are!"

Stephanie. Lisa groaned. Audibly. AJ smiled.

And Chelsea. And Ana. *Friggin' wonderful.*

Her pink cheeks returned. Ana had a small grin on her face, Chelsea looked guilty, and Stephanie was laughing. Clearly now wasn't the time for their first kiss, especially now they had an audience.

***

"Let me take you out tomorrow," he pleaded as she turned the key in her hotel room door. He had taken her back, shortly after they were interrupted by the three friends. She turned to give him her best, "yeah right," look.

"Really!" he continued, not deterred in the slightest by the look of disbelief on her face, "please?"

She looked at him intently. She should have put up more of a fight, or at least have pretended to be deciding, hesitating, *something!* Instead, she just said, "Fine."

Opening the door, she turned to say goodbye. He

kissed her softly on the cheek, "Does six suit?" She nodded.

"See you then," he smiled.

"Don't be late!" she called after him as he headed for the stairs. "And please don't kill yourself on those stairs!" she hollered louder as the door closed. He always took the stairs over the elevator wherever he could. *Athletes.* She sighed loudly, *he's going to try to make me exercise on this trip, isn't he?* She was already dreading it.

Chapter 6

Someone knocked on Lisa's door at 5.45pm.

He's here! At least it better be him. Maybe you should start googling how to hide your dead boyfriend's body when he stands you up for the second time in two days, Lis.

Give the boy a chance...

then Google.

She was ready, mostly. Her hair was loose over her shoulders, and once again the only make-up she wore was lip gloss. Her top was conservative, and she wore a long maxi skirt, which brushed her ankles as she walked. Her feet were still bare as she answered the door.

"You're early," she told him with a smile.

"You look lovely, Lis," he replied, handing her some flowers, lilies, her favorite – which she had ingeniously dropped into conversation early on in their relationship.

Say thank you.

"Thank you. What's the occasion?" she eyed him innocently.

"Do I need a reason to bring you flowers?' he asked as she let him in. Seeing her unchanged facial expression, he continued, "I feel bad about last night. I just want tonight to be perfect." For a change, color rose in his cheeks, and she felt herself smile.

"Just give me a minute to get my shoes on and I'll be ready to go – will you put these in water for me, please?"

"Sure."

When she was ready, they headed to the car. Once again, he was walking by her side, until they reached doors and then he was somehow simultaneously beside her and a step ahead of her to open them for her.

Always with the chivalry.

She felt relaxed. She wasn't nervous, or apprehensive, and she thoroughly enjoyed his company. Before they'd reached the restaurant, her sides were aching from giggling. Until now, she'd felt like their conversations had often been rushed, clipped, and there was always something one of them had to either apologize for, or run off to. They'd made the best of what they had, but no matter how long they had together online, it just wasn't enough for either of them. They both always wanted more. This was different; she had him all to herself, and she was enjoying every second of it.

Dinner was delicious. They tried each other's food. She thought his was nicer than hers, and he thought the same of hers, so they swapped. She declined dessert, although when his came, she obviously asked for an extra spoon and helped herself. Dipping her finger into the whipped cream she smeared a little on to his cheek as she excused herself to go to the bathroom.

"You'll pay for that!" he exclaimed, smiling as he

wiped it off with a napkin.

"Bring it on, hockey boy," she retorted playfully.

When they'd finished dinner, they went for a walk. It wasn't cold, so she left her jacket in the car.

"Where to?" she asked him.

Shrugging, he answered, "Do we need a destination?"

"No," she replied, "I just assumed you had a destination in mind."

"I *am* capable of spontaneity you know," he smiled at her, nudging her gently with his elbow. "Not *everyone* needs a destination in mind at all times, Miss Planaholic!"

"I know that," she pushed him slightly harder.

"Hey!" he pouted, "that hurt!" He fake rubbed at the spot she'd pushed.

"Oh, give over!" she admonished. "Suck it up! You're a hockey player." She stuck her tongue out at him and they laughed. "We're *so* mature," she said to him, giggling.

"Speak for yourself," he told her stiffly, "I am the mature one." He puffed out his chest and his expression was like that of a teacher scolding his class.

Pretending to be offended she folded her arms and stuck out her bottom lip.

"See?" he scoffed. "That's hardly mature," he said giggling. Her face remained unchanged. She turned away from him, pouting. "Come on, babe!" he approached her from behind and slipped his arms around her waist. Resting his head on her shoulder, he whispered, "You're

really kinda cute when you sulk, you know that?"

No answer.

He tightened his arms around her middle and kissed the side of her neck lightly. "Ok, ok," he caved, "you're not immature." He sighed, "Will you talk to me now?"

Her face broke into a smile, and she turned to face him. She slipped her arms around his neck and licked his nose ever so slightly with the tip of her tongue.

"Hey!" he cried in mock protest. She turned to try and escape, but he had caught her by the wrist and was pulling her back towards him.

"I'm starting to think that maybe neither of us are very mature!" she managed to say through giggles as he tickled her. Regaining their composure, they continued walking. He slipped his hand into hers and pulled her close. Sliding his arm around her waist, he said, "You're walking awfully far away,"

"Well, Chelsea and Stephanie said hockey boys have cooties!" she told him in her sweetest, most childish voice. Taking one look at his face, she burst into fits of giggles. She tried to slip her arm around his waist, but he pulled away.

"Oh, no you don't! 'Cause hockey players have cooties!" he mocked her sticking out his tongue.

"Now who's cute when they're huffing?" she asked him smiling. As she moved closer, he backed away from her, they both quickened their pace causing him to bump into a lamppost. When he bumped into it, he looked at her, surprised.

"Gotcha," she smirked.

Holding his hands up in surrender, he started to laugh. "Ok, ok, you win!" He offered her his hand. She took it and let him pull her closer. "This time anyway."

They hadn't walked far, but she was enjoying herself, even if they were acting like kids.

It's kinda fun to act like a kid sometimes. I love that he brings out my carefree spirit.

Chapter 7

The sun set and the stars began to decorate the sky. It was still warm, and, as Lisa and AJ walked, she announced that she wanted ice cream. After twenty-minutes of searching, they found an ice cream parlor and they ate, sitting on a nearby bench. She sat at the opposite end of the bench to him and swung her feet up on his lap, ankles crossed.

She wanted more and suspected he did too. But it seemed as though neither of them quite knew how to crossover from seven months of being a vague, online “thing” into the “we’re finally standing in front of each other”, physical side of a relationship. She was happy to take it slowly, she didn’t want to rush, but she definitely felt a little torn. Part of her wanted to throw herself at him and tear his clothes off right there on the bench.

A big part.

I’m sure you’re delicious under that shirt.

Down, girl.

The other part of her had to constantly remind herself that they weren’t officially a couple *yet*, and they’d really only just met in person. Her self-confidence certainly wasn’t at the stage where she felt that she could take control, and she had a feeling that he was waiting and making sure that it was what she wanted. She'd traveled across the world to meet him, yes, but she got the impression that he didn't want her to feel pressured into sleeping with him, or as though after all those chats and emails, he only wanted her for one thing. It just didn't feel as though they were quite at the discussion stage of any of this yet. It hung between them heavily though. He was, after all, a red-blooded, athletic male who spent a lot of his time throwing his weight around on the ice. And *she* was, after all, a red-blooded woman who was sick of her "toy" box and more than ready to have the real thing.

She wanted *him* to make the first move.

How very progressive of you, Lis. She rolled her eyes at herself. *You're waiting for him and he's probably waiting for you. Quite the 'You're not getting laid' stand-off you've landed yourself in here. Good going.*

Score one for women's suffrage.

She definitely liked how their 'accidental' and 'innocent-ish' contact was increasing. Holding hands, how he put his arm around her, how he'd brush her hair from her face with his fingers and she knew that things would progress, or at least she hoped so. But in some moments, like sitting staring at him licking his ice cream, she certainly found it challenging to control her urges.

"Want to try mine?" she offered her cone.

"Sure,"

She sat up and leaned towards him, holding her cone

for him to try. She poised herself and, just at the right moment, she shoved her cone in his face, smothering him in ice cream and giggled hysterically. Before he'd recovered from his shock, she was on her feet and running away from him.

"That was for standing me up, AJ!" she called back to him.

"That's two I owe you!" he retorted. She didn't need to look back to know that he was on his feet. He was an athlete; he ran every day. He'd catch her in no time, and she knew it. She could barely run the length of herself. When he caught up to her, he picked her up and spun her 'round, "Ok, I deserved that," he told her.

"Yes, you did!"

I ran what? Ten feet? I'm already dying.

"Wanna watch a movie?" he asked as they started back towards the car.

"Only if I get to choose!" she replied grinning.

"Deal."

The trip to his house was spent bickering over who got to be DJ. He felt it should be him, because it was his car. She felt it should be her, because she was the guest. In the end, they listened to a bunch of half-lines of songs before they were quickly vetoed and turned over, even if they liked the other's selection. It was a matter of principle!

At home, he put on some music and poured drinks for them both. She kicked off her shoes and lay on the sofa. She lifted her head for him to sit down and rested it on his lap when he was settled. As she sipped her drink, he asked

"Picked a film yet?" running his fingers through her hair as it lay across his thigh. Shaking her head, she stifled a yawn.

"Nope," setting her glass down, "where's your room?" she asked suddenly.

"Over there," he pointed, looking confused.

And hopeful. He definitely looked hopeful. Thank GOD.

"I'm getting sleepy, and I'm not going to fall asleep in this if I have to wear it again tomorrow," she shrugged as she stood up.

"Help yourself," he answered.

"I was gonna, I just didn't know where to look," she added before starting towards his room.

"So, you're staying then?" he called to her, grinning.

"If I fall asleep? Then yes. Otherwise, maybe."

"Oh yeah? Isn't that a bit presumptuous?" he continued, still smiling.

"Well..." she started, "if you'd prefer, I could leave now!" She began to head for the door.

He started to laugh. "Don't go...please?" He gave her his best puppy-dog eyes.

"Damnit! If I only had a pillow to hand!" she retorted.

"Yeah, yeah," he smirked, "go change your clothes."

Throwing him her best "fine" look, she headed into his room and came out wearing a pair of his sweats and a matching UAH t-shirt. Her hair was pulled back into a loose ponytail and she was humming to herself.

"So," she started cautiously, "the chick's underwear on the radiator? Am I to assume that's Britt's?" She watched his face. "Actually – no, wait, do I even want to know? 'Cause if it's some kinda kinky stuff you and Jeremy got goin' on, I don't think I need to hear it!" she giggled nervously.

I'm actually not sure which answer I'm hoping for right now.

Returning her smile, he moved his legs and she sat facing him on the sofa. She drew her knees up under her chin and hugged them.

"They *are* Britt's," he told her. She'd heard about Britt, the best friend from childhood. Aside from his parents, his sister and Jeremy, the only other person she was nervous of meeting, was Britt.

"I've tried," he continued exasperated, "I can't get her to stop leaving her underwear lying around. I mean, I draw the line at her wandering around naked, or in her underwear." Seeing the look on her face, he quickly added, "Don't worry, she doesn't!"

"'Cause this isn't weird in the slightest!" she told him.

"It's not!" he protested, "We just live together. We're roomies!" he continued.

"Hey," she interrupted him, "You don't have to explain yourself to me, I trust you."

"Ok," he answered simply, but she could tell something was playing on his mind. She didn't push it. She'd learned by now when to push and when not to.

This was firmly a "when not to" instance.

At that moment, she heard a key turn in the lock. Her back was facing whomever was coming in.

"Hey you guys!" she exclaimed. *Bubbly.* Turning to look at her she realized just how pretty she was, too. She had seen a few pictures of Britt, and she was pretty gorgeous. But, in real life? She had that 'model' look going on. And there Lisa was, standing in her sweats and a college shirt.

She better not walk around naked. I don't care if she lives here. She BETTER not walk around naked!

Damnit! she thought, *She's bubbly and pretty? I bet she's nice too. Bollocks. Why couldn't she be nasty, bitchy and ugly?* It would make is so much easier to hate the woman living with her internet-maybe-boyfriend, if she wasn't so obviously *lovely*.

"Hi!" she chirped, returning her smile. *Give her a chance,* she told herself sternly. *Don't do the jealous, whack-job routine right off the bat,* she warned herself.

Standing, Lisa turned to face Britt, extending her hand, Britt shook it warmly, looking questioningly over her shoulder at AJ with her eyebrow raised. Lisa wasn't quite sure what the look was about, but when she turned to look at AJ, he quickly hid behind a smile a look she couldn't place.

Guilt? Was that a guilty look? Why is he looking guilty?

I swear to fuck if she walks around here naked I'm going to kill him with my bare hands.

"I didn't know you were coming to town! How do you like Alabama so far?" she questioned politely.

"It's nice," Lisa replied, "but I've only seen a bit of it,"

"I'm sure Age will be showing you round in no time,"

"Yeah, I'll bet!" she answered smiling.

Tension? Awkwardness? Hesitation? Yes, that's it, she's hesitating, she's thinking, she's being guarded. She's wary of me? No, that can't be it, can it?

Are you making things up in your head again, Lisa? Can't she just be as lovely as she seems?

No.

Lisa couldn't put her finger on it, but *something* was there. It was as if there was something she wanted to talk about, but couldn't, or wouldn't, or shouldn't.

Maybe she's just shocked that I'm here? Or thinks AJ kept this huge secret from her for some reason? Maybe I'm just overthinking it all and I'm paranoid and overly sensitive.

But there was definitely something in that look.

"Don't worry about me," she said, "I'll be outta here in no time. I'm just grabbing a bag, I'm going down to Roberto's for a week. That'll give you two some time together." Britt gave her a sly wink.

Feeling herself blush, yet again, she tried to think of an answer, something smart, funny – *hey, anything at all would be good at this point!* Instead, she picked up a cushion and hurled it at her. "Give over!" she drawled.

"Whoa! What a comeback, Irish girl!" she mimicked, "Got yourself a keeper there, Age!" she laughed as she headed to her room.

"Ignore her," he told her loudly. "She's just frustrated cause she hasn't gotten any, in, like, a month, or something!"

"Shut up, butt-head! Remember I could embarrass the crap outta you in front of your girlfriend!" she threatened, only half-jokingly.

"Ooooooh I wanna know now!" Lisa chimed in.

Is it bad that I'm enjoying this? she asked herself as she noticed the color rising in his cheeks.

Wait, she said girlfriend.

Am I his girlfriend?

Are we actually there yet?

"I'd love to stay and mortify him, but I gotta go! It was nice to finally meet you, Lisa," she said warmly and with that, they were alone again.

Despite the fact that Britt was leaving to visit with her boyfriend, Lisa couldn't shake the nagging feeling in the back of her mind that *something* was off, she just couldn't place what it was.

Lis, you're paranoid. And you REALLY need to get laid.

Chapter 8

"Well," Lisa began slowly, "that was..." she paused, searching for a word, "interesting!" She grinned.

"Wait till I visit you in Ireland," AJ told her. "I'm sure all your friends will wanna embarrass the crap outta you too!"

"Uh huh. But, for now, I'm on your turf – so deal with it!" She stuck her tongue out at him once again.

He threw a cushion at her, she caught it and hurled it back. He caught it again.

"Do you really want to start this with me?" she asked.

"Why? Whatcha gonna do? Hmm? Start *crying* or something?" he mocked.

"Oh, you're trying to rile me?" She threw another pillow at him, this time hitting him.

"Is it working?" he grinned mischievously. He sat up and moved closer to her.

"NO!" she huffed, shoving him gently. He shoved her back.

"You'd better be careful there, mister," she warned.

"Why's that?" he shoved her again. She knelt and shoved him with both hands.

"Don't you start on me, Pim!" she warned, still

smiling.

He poked her midsection.

Damnit, she thought as she flinched. *He knows I have tickles and I'm starting to think he knows I wanna tear his clothes off and do...THINGS to him.*

The second of hesitation was all it took. He was tickling her. She was giggling so hard she didn't realize they were slipping off the edge of the sofa, and, before she could stop herself, she was lying on her back with him on top of her, still tickling her.

She was forced to acknowledge that part of what was holding her back from jumping his bones was her overwhelming tendency to clumsiness. As well as his. She was quite terrified that she'd lean in to kiss him and he'd end up concussed, or with a bloody nose. She needed to find a way to feel comfortable around him before exposing just how much of a klutz she was.

Ok, come on! she told herself between giggles. *Get it together. You're going to let him win this?* Like everything else during the evening, it was like something out of a cheesy rom com. But she didn't care, it was fun. She hadn't laughed like this in a long time.

She tried to stop giggling and started to fight back.

"Realized I'm winning, did ya?" he asked, obviously amused.

"Shut up!" she said, wriggling and squirming to free herself.

"You're actually quite strong, really, aren't you?" he asked sarcastically.

"SHUT UP!" she repeated, struggling furiously now to escape.

She knew she had no chance; the guy was a defensive hockey player. He had her pinned, he had all the advantage. But she wasn't going to give up, it wasn't her style. He knew this and was enjoying it. She could tell. Truth be told, she was enjoying it too.

I mean, I'm pinned under a hot hockey player! she thought. *Who wouldn't be enjoying it? Now, where did I put my puck bunny ears?* She smiled to herself.

Maybe I should just stay right where I am.

Looking into his eyes she realized he was smiling at her; she returned the smile.

"Whatcha thinking?" he asked quietly.

She shook her head and closed her mouth tightly. He loosened his grip on her.

"Hey, it's the rules, babe. We gotta spill when asked. What's on your mind?"

Slipping her arms slowly around his neck, she smiled a half-smile.

"What if it's not appropriate to share, AJ?" she asked impishly.

"It's me, it's always appropriate to share,"

Realization dawned. *OHMIGOD. OHMIGOD.* she thought. *We're going to kiss. He's going to kiss me. I'm going to kiss him back! We're going to kiss!*

And then it happened. Their heads tilted; his face lowered towards hers. She closed her eyes in anticipation. Their lips met. It was soft, tender and filled with emotion. She tightened her grip around his neck, pulling him closer to her. The kiss lasted forever and only a few minutes all at once. It was good. Very good. She was very glad she was lying down, otherwise she might have needed to at least sit down.

Thank FUCK for that!

She felt herself smile, and he smiled back at her. "Now what are you thinking?" he quizzed her. Neither of them moved. She shrugged.

"You're a good kisser," she told him truthfully,

"Not so bad yourself," he replied, nonchalant.

"Hey!" she shoved him playfully, "Not bad?" she looked wounded. "I am a *great* kisser!" she exclaimed.

"Modest much?" he joked and kissed her again. "Yeah, ok, you are a pretty great kisser," he told her as he kissed her cheek gently. Helping her to her feet they lay down together on the sofa.

She was lying in the arms of the man she loved more than she cared to admit to anyone. Even herself. She felt happy and relaxed. She felt safe. "Not bad for a first date," she mumbled more to herself than to him, in a state of almost-asleep jetlag haze. He smiled, kissed her hair and tightened his arm around her, pulling her close. Somewhere between songs, kisses, conversation and satisfied sighs, she fell asleep in his arms.

"I've got better," he whispered, before he, too, closed his eyes and fell asleep.

Chapter 9

AJ had told Lisa he was an early riser and a light sleeper – up with the birds. But she woke up first, which she kind of liked. *He's probably just pretty tired,* she grinned to herself. She watched him sleep for a few minutes before she quietly got up. She pecked his cheek and headed for the kitchen. She poured some juice and turned on the news, *I don't even watch the news at home!* she thought, amused at herself. She needed a shower, and she wanted to wait for him to wake up before considering breakfast.

While the water heated up, she kicked off his sweats and dumped them into the laundry basket. Standing in her undies, she let her hair fall around her shoulders as she brushed her teeth. Someone was knocking at the door by the time she finished. *Damnit,* she thought, as she rinsed out her mouth, shut off the water and grabbed a towel and went to open the door. It was Jeremy.

"Morning!" she smiled, only half-opening the door, "what can I do for you?"

"He still asleep?" he asked as he let himself in, pushing past her.

She nodded.

"Late night?" he eyed her, suspiciously.

"It's not what you think, Jeremy," she said as she closed the door behind him.

"Uh huh, it's not like you're wearing just a towel or anything," he quipped.

"Shut up!" she blushed, "I was going to have a shower! Juice?" she offered as she took a seat in the kitchen.

"Sure, thanks,"

"So," she tried again, "what can I do for you?"

"HEY AGE, YOUR GIRLFRIEND'S TRYING TO KICK ME OUT!" he bellowed towards AJ's room.

"I'm not his girlfriend!" she hissed at him.

Except you kind of are.

"Yeah, right, you *so* are!"

"Not officially, not yet."

Except? You kind of are.

"Except you totally are. Stop fighting it, cupcake."

She handed him his juice, threw a tea towel at him and watched AJ stumble into the kitchen, yawning and half-awake. She wasn't quite prepared to assume the label unto herself as AJ's girlfriend yet. She wasn't completely sure that he wanted her to have the label yet either. She made a mental note to talk to him about it when they were next alone.

"Who the hell is yelling? Is the building on fire?"

"*He* is yelling," she said, pointing at Jeremy. "Juice?" she asked, smiling. He nodded in reply, and she offered him a glass.

"Thanks," he said smiling at her, "and good morning, gorgeous." He pecked her cheek.

"She's throwing stuff at me! She's *so* like you!" Jeremy said shaking his head.

She gave him a dirty look and said, "I'm going back to my shower."

"Have you eaten?" AJ asked, before she moved.

She shook her head, "I was going to wait 'til after my shower, make something and then wake you. But he—"

Jeremy cut her off, "Awwwww, how cuuuuuute!" He made fake gagging noises and pretended to throw up into the empty glass he was now nursing.

"Shut UP, Jeremy," they shouted together. She continued,

"But *he* wrecked that plan." She paused. "I'll be back soon."

"Take your time," Jeremy answered sarcastically.

"Shut up, man!" AJ countered, as he poked his elbow into Jeremy's ribs.

"Oh shit, dude! You have it *bad!*" Jeremy taunted.

That was it, they were on the floor wrestling, or at least doing some kind of flailing and rolling around in a vain attempt at displaying their manliness. Or, as the case turned out to be, lack thereof.

"Children, please don't break anything, or hurt yourselves! If you get blood on the carpet, I'm gonna be mad!" she cooed as she made her way to the bathroom.

"Yes *MOM*!" mocked Jeremy from underneath AJ.

"Ok. And AJ?" she turned, momentarily.

"Yes ma'am?"

"Kick his ass!"

"Yes ma'am!"

He grinned widely and returned to their play-fighting.

Her shower was great, long, hot, relaxing. *Everything a shower should be,* she thought.

When she emerged, twenty minutes later, she could smell eggs.

"Is he gone?" she asked as she took the towel off her head. She had thrown on another of his t-shirts and a pair of his boxers.

"Who, me?" she heard coming from the living room. "No, I'm still here. Age is cooking me breakfast!" he declared triumphantly.

"Actually, I'm cooking *us* breakfast. Lisa and me. But, since you're here and I can't ever say no to you..." he trailed off. His voice had taken on a mock-sultry tone.

"I seriously worry about you boys sometimes," Lisa remarked, shaking her head as she poured some water.

"Omelet ok for you?" AJ asked her as she moved to stand next to him. She slipped her arm around his waist, and he kissed her forehead. She nodded. "You sure? Cause I can make you something else if you'd prefer?"

"An omelet is fine, babe," she assured him.

"No mushrooms?"

She pulled a face.

"Just checking," he laughed at her making puking noises. "You sleep ok?"

"Mhmm," she confirmed, as she popped a slice of apple in her mouth, "just fine."

Turning to face her, he wrapped his arms around her waist and kissed her lightly on the lips. She returned his kiss, pulling him gently towards her. *Such a good kisser...*

"What the hell are you two doing in there?" Jeremy interrupted her thoughts. "I don't hear talking. It's not talking. Are you guys making out? Cause if you guys are making out, stop making out. If Jeremy isn't getting any, then AJ sure as hell can't get any!" He paused, "*Especially* if it isn't from me!" he finished.

"He has such a way with words!" she muttered, "Should I be concerned about your weird boy-relationship with him?"

"No, babe. I only have eyes for you."

She blushed. "I better go get dressed."

"Awwww. Really?" He pretended to be upset.

Giggling, she threw the same towel she'd thrown at Jeremy, at him. It landed on his head. "Yes, really!"

When she was dressed, she threw her hair up again. It was still wet, but she didn't care. Alabama was *HOT.* It would dry quickly.

"You forgot your shoes," Jeremy commented when she returned to the kitchen. He was already half-way through his omelet.

"I'm not leaving yet," she said through clenched teeth. He was pushing her, testing her patience. *I really don't like this douchebag,* she thought. She didn't like the fact that she was verging on detesting her not-yet-a-real-boyfriend's best friend. It would become problematic, she could tell.

"Tea?" AJ offered.

"Thanks, but I'll make it. You people can't make good tea!" she laughed.

"I would argue," he began, amused, "but I know you're right!"

"I'm always right," she announced confidently.

"Yeah, right!" Jeremy scoffed.

"Wasn't talking to you!" she replied.

"What does that matter?"

Pulling up a chair she sat next to AJ and started to eat her omelet in silence. Not a comfortable silence, a strained one. She felt out of place.

Talk about awkward. Is this Jeremy and me not gelling kind of awkward? Or is it Britt's knickers on the radiator and she's making weird eyes at my non-boyfriend-boyfriend kind of awkward?

Both?

"So, you guys coming out tonight?" Jeremy continued, ignoring the atmosphere that was creeping in between them. He seemed completely oblivious to the fact that she wasn't thrilled he was still there. She wasn't used to him; and she really didn't know how to take him. She couldn't tell if he was serious, or joking all of the time – even *some* of the time. Or maybe even *none* of the time. Maybe he really just didn't like her? She didn't like not knowing. Her go-to response to him seemed to be defensive and verging on confrontational. He was getting under her skin. She made a mental note to talk to AJ about how to better approach the Jeremy situation. She didn't want to make things awkward, and she certainly didn't want to be upset and annoyed every time he opened his mouth, but she couldn't stop herself from speaking before taking a breath when he was around.

"We have a game tonight," AJ told him. He wasn't having his usual pre-game breakfast. *He must have changed it*, she thought as she smiled to herself. Hockey players have very strict game-day rituals. They could be a terribly superstitious breed. They'd eat the same meals at the same times and often wear the same socks or undies on game-day.

"I *know* we have a game, Einstein," Jeremy jabbed, "I meant *after* the game. We're all going to the bar, you guys up for it?" he eyed her carefully.

AJ was watching her, too. She shrugged as she finished her food. "Sure," she flashed her best fake-smile, sat her dishes in the sink and was saved from any further questioning by another knock on the door.

"Popular this morning, eh Age?" said Jeremy.

"I'll get it," she said heading for the door.

"Morning, Irish,"

God bless you, Chelsea! she thought as she let her friend in.

"Morning Iowa!" she replied.

"You ready to go?" she asked as she rattled her keys in her hand.

"You're leaving already?" The disappointment in AJ's voice was obvious.

"Yeah, you guys have practice and then the game. We're going to head into town. I have to post a couple letters I wrote on the flight and pick up some stuff," she answered as she leaned over to kiss his cheek. "I'll see you later, skater!" This time, her smile was warm and genuine.

"Two minutes, Chels, I've got to get my shoes on!" Lisa called.

As she was leaving, AJ grabbed her wrist. Chelsea had already gone out to the car, and Jeremy was out of earshot.

"We don't have to go tonight if you don't want to," he began quietly.

"No, really," she insisted, "it's ok." She met his eyes, "Honest, AJ."

"Okay, well, if you're sure...I'll see you after the game?"

"Count on it! And Pim?" she said as she opened the door

"Yes ma'am?"

"Look after yourself."

"I will. Have fun today." He added as the door thudded softly behind her.

Chapter 10

That evening, against every instinct Lisa had, she was wearing AJ's Leafs jersey. She'd already worn her Giants one from home, and he didn't have any jerseys of teams she actually *liked*. He was wearing his Chargers one on the ice, which left either the Leafs, or, the alternative was to not wear one at all. Everyone else was, and it would have been too weird (and cold!) for her to go to a hockey game without a jersey on.

When in Rome! she thought as she slipped it on over her sweater. *Or, America – whatever!*

The Leafs were playing in the National league tonight, too. Had they been playing her NHL team, The Edmonton Oilers, she'd never have dared wear the jersey. But, as it happened, they were playing the team that had eliminated her precious Oilers from the Stanley cup the year before, so she was happy enough with the Leafs jersey.

When the final buzzer rang, the girls left the rink and made their way through the car park. The game was pretty good even though the Chargers lost.

"Jeremy said they'd meet us at the bar," Chelsea informed her.

"Oh, *did* he now?" Lisa groaned.

"Woah. Hold up a sec. What the heck is your deal with Jeremy?"

"He *HATES* me!" she wailed.

"He does *not* hate you; he just likes to wind you up."

"Well, it works, and I don't like it."

"Calm down, you take things way too personally! You're kinda easy meat, Lis."

When they arrived at the bar, they grabbed a table, ordered drinks. Nearly an hour passed and still no team. Finally, a couple of the guys came in and made their way to the bar. Mike, the netminder, and Marc, one of the team's top goal scorers stopped to say hi.

"Hey guys," she greeted them, "Where's the boy at?"

She didn't need to make introductions with most of AJ's teammates. They all knew who she was already, whether she'd met them or not. Most of them had been in the bar the night before. To her knowledge, there weren't any other Irish girls who'd come to visit one of the guys on the team. She couldn't be inconspicuous even if she'd wanted.

"He's on his way," Marc answered, sliding in beside her. Chelsea and Mike headed to the bar to order more drinks. Marc had a stupid grin on his face and he was giggling to himself.

"Marc, have you been drinking already?"

"A little," he admitted, "and, y'know? I think it's great!"

"What's great? Drinking?"

"No, you forgiving AJ after finding out about Britt. It's very big of you. We really weren't sure if you would or not!"

She glanced at the bar, there was a bit of a line, she had time.

I really do think something was off last night. Maybe Marc knows.

"What about Britt?" She was treading carefully; they were obviously hiding something from her and she needed to find out what that was. She let the silence hang having watched enough detective shows on TV to know that people being 'interviewed' had a tendency to need to fill the silence.

"At the wedding, he was wondering how he was going to tell you. He got pretty upset from what I hear. Jer said AJ cried and everything. I wasn't there, it was a tiny courthouse thing. But I guess he *was* pretty trashed. Who the hell cries on their own wedding night?" he started laughing until he saw the look on her face.

"Oh, shit. He hasn't told you? You didn't...SHIT," his voice trailed off, but she was already leaving. She was running for the door, tears streaming down her face. Jeremy was just arriving.

"Hey, *HEY*, don't worry," Jeremy grinned at her, "he's on his way, coach wanted to talk to him for a minute after the game-" He saw her tears as she pushed past him, not slowing down. Behind her, she heard him say, "Oh shit. You know..." before she slammed the door of the cab that luck for her happened to be waiting outside the bar with its available for hire light on.

"Where to?" the driver asked.

She looked in her bag to double check she had her passport on her and made a snap decision.

"Airport," she gasped between sobs.

If she took the time to go back to the hotel and collect her things, she'd run the risk he'd catch up with her and talk her out of it.

"Quickly, please."

"No problem," he replied. As the car pulled away from the bar, she saw Jeremy out the back window, he was talking animatedly on the phone. She knew who to. *Jackass*, she thought. *What an absolute prick.*

She'd invested seven months in this guy. If she had wanted a roll in the hay she could have just "swiped right". If she'd wanted a threesome with a married couple she could have turned to Fetlife. But she'd taken the time to get to know this guy online. They'd talked about everything. Or so she thought. She wanted to make sure that it wasn't going to end up being a one-night stand, hump him and dump him kinda thing. As it turned out, he wanted to make sure she was ok with the him-having-a-wife-thing before taking it any further.

Would he ever have told me if I'd never come here?

Why the hell did no one tell me before now?

I must have looked so damn stupid this whole time!

Pulling out her phone, she hesitated for a second, but within minutes, she'd finished her call to the airline and was booked on the next flight to Dublin.

Chapter 11

Lisa only had to wait an hour. *That's ok,* she reassured herself, *you can wait an hour. AJ and the others would never think you'd just up and leave Alabama.*

It's only an hour.

But as the minutes ticked by, she started to wonder if she was being melodramatic buying an expensive, last minute flight home. *He's married,* she reminded herself. The words reverberated angrily in her mind. He was married. *To Britt. Of course he's MARRIED to her.* It finally all made sense. The hesitation, the secrecy, her Spidey sense tingling when they'd met.

The underwear on the radiator.

I bet she DOES prance around the house naked, and looks absolutely friggin' fabulous as she does!

Lisa couldn't stop the tears; she didn't even try. She knew it was futile. People stared. She tried to ignore them. She got more embarrassed and cried even more. She boarded the plane, took her seat and watched forlornly out the window as the plane took off, leaving Alabama, and its cracked-open closet of skeletons, behind. She wondered why Ana hadn't told her, or even Jeremy. Someone. Anyone. Someone should have told her. Or hinted to her – so she could prod AJ for answers. Something.

You knew something was up though, you should have asked. You played dumb.

I did NOT! I wasn't sure.

Did Ana even know? She's his sister! Of COURSE she knew. What a bitch to have facilitated a trip knowing that he was married!

Oh my GOD, did CHELSEA know?

SOMEONE SHOULD HAVE TOLD ME!

Someone DID tell you, Lis.

Yeah, the WRONG person. In the wrong freakin' way!

She wanted someone who cared enough about her to have had the decency to tell her the truth. But, in the end, it was Marc, practically a stranger, who told her. Marc, who didn't give two hoots about her, had told her the truth. Accidentally, at that.

Eventually, she resigned herself to the fact that they were *his* people. As friendly as they were to her, she was new in their lives, and their loyalties lay with AJ. They had his back and probably wanted to stay the hell out of the middle of whatever this was. She couldn't *really* blame them, but it was proving hard not to.

Two hours into the flight, she finally managed to stop crying. As the tears abated, she realized no one knew where she was, so she picked up the in-flight phone, cringing at the thought of how much it would cost to make this call. She knew Chelsea would be going out of her mind, and no one was expecting her back at home.

First, she punched in her good friend Aoife's number, with no consideration for the time difference. It was the middle of the night back home, but she answered on the third ring.

"Hello?" Aoife sounded dazed and confused, and obviously she didn't recognize the strange number on her caller ID.

"Eef?" Lisa barely recognized her own voice. It was shaky and uneven.

"Lis?" The sound of her voice jolted her awake a bit.

"What is it? What's wrong?"

"I...I'm coming home, Eef," she started, fighting the tears as the panic rose again in her chest.

"What? Why?" Aoife was confused.

I don't blame her, I'm confused too, Lisa thought.

"I'm sorry to wake you. I just ... it's just ... He's ... He's ...He's MARRIED, Aoife!" she managed, before she lost it and the sobs returned.

"What?" Aoife's voice was filled with a mixture of shock, horror and fury. She was certainly wide awake now. "Oh pet, don't cry, it's ok..." she started.

Good ole glass-half-full Aoife, even when the glass is leaking out its arse, she thought, smiling through the tears despite herself.

"No, Eef, it's not. He's married. MARRIED!" she choked.

"Ok. Rewind. What? To who?"

"Yeah, that's about where I was until about thirty minutes ago. Right now, I just wanna kill the lyin' bastard," she vented. "He lied to me. He said he was single. He led me on!" Lisa couldn't stop the words spilling out.

"Wait," her friend stopped her, "you're coming home? You're on a plane?"

"Yeah," she sniffed

"Do they know where you are?"

Silence.

Aoife had met Chelsea when she'd visited Ireland. The two girls were similar in many ways, and Aoife was likely pretty sure Chelsea was not going to be happy that Lisa had disappeared across the Atlantic without a word.
"Lis...?" she started, "does anyone know where you are? AJ? Chelsea?" she repeated.

"Not...exactly." Her reply was muffled as she blew her nose.

"LIS! You didn't tell them you were leaving? Any of them? Chelsea knows though, right? Ohmigosh! Lis! She's probably going out of her mind! She's going to be *so* pissed! Where are you flying into and when do you arrive?"

She's not wrong.

"Five hours, Dublin."

"I'll meet you there. I may be a little late, but I'll be there. Go call Chelsea." The line went dead.

Shit, she thought. *I really should have thought this through. I have to phone her; she's going to be pissed.*

She was just about to dial Chelsea's number when the air hostess stopped by. "You ok, hun?"

Why yes, I always cry hysterically when I fly.

"Yes ma'am, thank you." *Liar, liar pants on fire.*

"He's not worth your tears, sweetie."

Call me one more pet-name and I'll – hey wait, how'd she know it was boy trouble?

She glanced up and met a sympathetic gaze. "I overheard you telling your friend. He's not worth your tears." She repeated holding out a couple miniatures and some tissues, giving Lisa's shoulder a reassuring pat with her free hand.

"Thank you," Lisa replied, choking back tears.

"Welcome. You let me know if you need anything, kay? I think I've got some ice cream knockin' 'round somewhere."

Lisa managed a small smile at her kindness. "No, thank you,"

"Wine?"

"No. Thank you though, I appreciate it."

"You just let me know, sugar."

Attempting to smile again in thanks, Lisa clenched her jaw and nodded, turning her attention back to the phone in the hopes she wouldn't get called another south-of-the-Mason-Dixon-line cutsie nickname.

Reluctantly, she punched in Chelsea's number. This was a conversation she did *not* want to have.

It didn't even ring once, before she picked up.

"Lisa? Is that you? Where are you?"

Silence.

How did she even know it was me?

She was crying again. *Damnit. Pull yourself together, woman!* She scolded herself. *Catch a grip!*

"Did you know?" Lisa managed to choke.

"Know what? Where the hell are you calling me from with this number?" She was confused and clearly worried about her friend. "What the hell is going on? Where are you and why are you crying?"

"You don't know?"

"Know *what,* Lisa?" she asked exasperated.

"He's married," she spat bitterly. "He's fucking married, Chels. He's nothing but a lying prick of a hockey player and he's bloody married!" Lisa was sobbing uncontrollably now, her shoulders shaking. People in the rows around her were looking at her with pity and sympathy in their eyes. She felt drained.

"Jeremy lied. And I'm sure Ana *has* to know! How could she not know her brother was married? She was probably a fucking bridesmaid."

"Holy shit," Chelsea began. "I'm so sorry Lis. I didn't know. I promise. I wouldn't have encouraged any of this if I'd known. Though that explains why Jeremy came in like a bull in a china shop and demanded to know *exactly* what Marc told you. He took one look at him and said, 'Does she know?', Marc nodded. Jeremy said something like, 'Shit. This is bad. Age is on his way. This is really bad, Marc,' and left. No one would tell me what the hell they were talking about. Marc had put his foot in it once already tonight by telling you, so he wasn't telling me anything, and I couldn't get hold of you."

Chelsea paused for breath.

"Dumb question: How are you?"

"I'm...uh. He's *married,* and half of the people on this plane are staring at me," was all Lisa could manage.

"It's ok, tell me where you are and I'll come get you," she asked expectantly, clearly not registering that Lisa had just said she was on an airplane...

"Wait, Lis? Where *are* you?" The penny dropped.

"Somewhere over the Atlantic," she stated as *nonchalantly* as she could muster.

3...2...1

"You *WHAT?"*

...aaaand, there it was.

"Don't shit your pants, Chels. I'm safe, I promise. I just couldn't be around him."

Then she heard *him* in the background.

"Chelsea? Where is she?"

"Chels? Why is he there? Where *are* you? Chelsea please don't tell him, PLEASE don't tell him," she pleaded. "I don't want him to know, or follow me. Assuming he even *has* a rational explanation and wants to give it to me." She paused and added, "I don't want to hear it."

"She's gone home, hasn't she?" he asked Chelsea somberly.

Damn you, knowing me so well, AJ.

"Chels, please?" she whispered, her voice barely audible.

"It's too late," her friend answered. "He's just left, Lis. I know I don't know him all that well, but I'd say it's a safe bet that he's going to follow you."

"No! Chels! You have to stop him! Make Jeremy stop him. They can tie him to some goalposts or something. I don't want to see him. I *can't* see him, Chels. He...I can't...Hold on, I...I'll be back..." A wave of hysteria hit and she cried so hard nausea wasn't too far behind. She dropped the phone on her seat and grabbed the barf-bag from the seat pocket.

This isn't going to be enough, she realized as she bolted from her chair, paper bag at the ready. Mercifully, the lavatory was empty and she barely had the door closed before she was sick.

After emptying her stomach, she returned to her seat and picked up the phone again. She felt awful. She'd caught her reflection in the bathroom mirror, her face was tear-streaked, her eyes bloodshot, and she'd just thrown-up, so she had that nasty vomit-taste in her mouth.

"You still there?" she asked.

"Damn straight. Where'd you go?"

"I was praying to the porcelain gods."

"You were talking to wh- oh, I got ya. Yuck. Feel better?"

"Not so much."

"Didn't think so, poor girl."

"Chelsea, what am I supposed to *do?*" Lisa was almost pleading, begging for answers from her friend. She knew, though, that Chelsea had nothing to offer her.

"I dunno girl, but if your crazy, impulsive ass had

waited half a fucking second before jumping a flight home, I'd have told you that running away wouldn't help. You need to talk to him."

"Chels? Now's *not* the time for a lecture, and I don't *want* to talk to him." She groaned. "That's not what I want to hear!" Her chest hurt from crying.

"How long have we been friends, Lis? When do I *ever* tell you what you *want* to hear?"

Lisa picked up her bag to get a Kleenex. Inside, she found an envelope that she hadn't previously noticed. She opened it and unfolded the page inside, forgetting Chelsea was still sitting on the line and how expensive the call would end up being.

Hey babe,

You're in the shower, Jeremy's flicking through TV channels and I felt a strange urge to write you a note. I guess with you being here, and using the phone more recently, we haven't written to each other in a little while. It feels weird when I've gotten so used to writing you multiple times a day. I guess I'll just leave it in your bag for you to find later, probably during the game tonight.

I don't even know why I'm writing. I'll see you in fifteen minutes, twenty-five if you wash your hair. Yup. Your boyfriend is a dork. Yup. I just wrote boyfriend. I think it's time we both started owning it, because I am. Your boyfriend, I mean. Unless you'd rather I wasn't. And

I know for damn sure that I want you to be my girlfriend. I know, I should probably say this out loud to you, and I will. I'm also aware I'm now talking to myself in a note. Your boyfriend really is a dork.
I guess I just wanted to say thank you. Thank you for coming to see me. I'm having a really great time and I just wish you could stay longer because I know, when the time comes, I don't think I'll be able to watch you leave.

You're everything I expected you to be when we met, and so much more. Anyway. Jeremy's now trying to read over my shoulder, and I need to go start breakfast – I don't know why I said I'd make breakfast. I can't even cook!

Love, your AJ.

P.S. – Have you smiled yet today?

She couldn't stop the tears. Not even to tell Chelsea that she'd found a random, rambling letter from her now *very* ex-boyfriend. She just said goodbye, told her she'd call when she landed, and struggled with waves of tears.

The air hostess popped by to check in with her occasionally – she'd added "darlin'" and "dumplin'" to the ever-growing list of folksy names. The woman in front of her turned around a couple times to make sure she was ok, too. Lisa was so embarrassed; she just wanted the ground to swallow her up.

Except there's no ground under me to swallow me up.

she thought glumly, *Though I'd happily go hide in the luggage hold if it were pressurized.* She spent the remainder of the flight, and her connection, trying her best to keep her emotional outbursts to a minimum. She'd already caused way more of a scene than she was comfortable with.

Keep it together. Keep it together. Keep it together.

Breathe. Breathe. Breathe.

Damnit, Lisa. Calm down.

More tears.

This is NOT breathing!

When they landed, she had no luggage to collect. Aoife was running late, so Lisa waited in the arrivals lounge and got herself a drink. She was cried out and exhausted, but she knew this was far from over. AJ was a fighter. And he loved her – she *knew* that he really and truly did love her. But he was married. *Hell, I've even met his fucking wife,* she thought bitterly as she sipped her water. *We talked about her lace panties over the radiator like I had asked him what the weather was doing outside*. She was convinced that no amount of drinking water today could rehydrate her after all that crying, but she knew she would feel better than if she stuck to her usual liquid diet of two liters of Diet Coke a day. Flying and crying was a bitch of a combo for dehydration.

I can't believe he's slept with her. I mean, they're married, they probably sleep together all the time. If I was his wife, I'd sleep with him all the time. I'd never leave the house 'cause I'd be too busy having sex all the freakin' time.

And HER! What kind of person? What kind of WOMAN would condone her still-in-the-honeymoon-phase-husband having a bit on the side? Even if it was only online. Not only that, but a long-term bit on the side? She'd even met the girlfriend. Me! She met me! We talked, we laughed, she even joked about my bedding her husband. Is THIS a cultural thing?

Wait. What?

No. Now you're just being stupid.

It's a fucked-up thing. That's what it is. It's an utterly fucked-up thing.

She sighed. She hated not understanding.

Don't you dare try to rationalize this, Lisa.

He was probably catching a flight right now and all she could do was wait. She hated waiting. She'd finished her water, bitten her nails to the quick and sussed out that no matter which way she sat, the CCTV cameras could see her crying and talking to herself like a crazy woman. She was certainly giving the guys in the security room something to talk about on their break.

I really hate waiting.

But she had no choice. She knew she'd have to face him; they'd have to have it out. It wasn't going to be pretty.

Chapter 12

The next few hours passed in a tired-blur. Aoife drove Lisa home to her parent's house in Newry, and Lisa had to force her to go to work and not call in "my bestie needs me" sick.

"I'm *fine,*" she insisted. "I really need some time alone, to think," she pressed.

Reluctantly, her friend acquiesced.

Lisa had been stewing the whole ride home. Things just didn't make sense.

You don't just go off and marry the love of your life while stringing along some long-distance, online-girl for no reason, right?

They didn't seem more than brother-sister, good friends - at most. But there was *something* going on, she'd felt it. He came across as so genuine with Lisa, so loving, and at no point did he ever mention a wife, a fiancée, a girlfriend, a friend with benefits - nothing.

It didn't make sense.

You don't talk about the possibility of marrying someone and then go and marry someone else. Ok, yes, he said that while he was incredibly drunk one night, and he didn't mean right away cause that's seven shades of crazy, but he did mean it, right?

It was why she was so convinced he was going to come after her. It didn't fit. While part of her burned with a deep rage, another part kept trying to pull her back to the facts. He was a good guy, kind and genuine. *Or so I thought.*

Despite her instinctive reaction to the situation being "What a cheating shithead," she couldn't help but feel like there was something else going on. What? She had no idea. But things just didn't sit right with her, at all. She knew AJ.

Or so I thought.

The AJ I know loves me, I'm sure of it – aren't I? He behaves like he does. Or did. I mean, people who love you don't run off and marry someone else, right? Damnit, AJ, you're making me question just about everything I've ever thought true about us. The AJ I know would realize I've gone home to Ireland and hop the next flight he could. He'd say, "Screw the expense."

What about the team? His games? They need him. Would he really abandon them to come after me?

Screw the fact I might not listen to what he has to say, or even give him the chance to explain. The AJ I know – or at least I think I know, would drop his life and fly across the world to win back the girl. Christ, Lisa. Listen to yourself. This isn't Disney.

Ugh.

But he would. Her inner voice persisted. She knew they'd never really defined their "relationship" out loud.

They were waiting until they stood face to face to make it "officially official," but something in her gut wouldn't quit. She was convinced beyond rational explanation that he'd hop two planes to cross the Atlantic to explain whatever the hell was going on. Assuming that was how things would go, she realistically had some time before his plane touched down – assuming he got the next flight out of Alabama – though she really needed to compose herself.

She needed to prepare what she was going to say, and run it over in her mind. In order to do that, she needed to figure out how she even *felt* first. And how she'd feel if she was wrong and he didn't show up.

Betrayed. Mainly, very, very betrayed.

She lay on her bed, for how long, she had no idea. She put on a Matt Nathanson CD and cried some more. The internet made her cry. Talking to people made her cry. Her phone made her cry. Thinking of him made her cry. Looking through the few pictures she had of them together made her cry. It seemed that no matter what she did, she cried. She didn't *want* to cry any more. She wanted to be mad. She *was* mad. She cried some more.

Jerk.

She sat in silence trying to sort through her feelings. She felt hurt, betrayed and confused. She was angry and embarrassed. She felt like his whole hockey team must have been laughing at her behind her back. Then she began to rationalize. *Maybe it's not as bad as it seems?* She just wanted to understand. *There has to be a reasonable explanation, right?*

Her head kicked at her heart; the voice of reason prevailed.

What are you thinking? You idiot! You're contemplating forgiving him, aren't you? Even if he says he loves her and he lied... Damn. You FOOL. You really love him, don't you?

Bollocks.

What do you think could happen here? Sister-wives? Polygamy is illegal, Lis. And you felt pangs of jealousy from seeing her underwear lying around her own house. You really think you could share your man?

Stupid, stupid, stupid girl. You should have paid more heed to Chelsea's hockey-boy history. Never fall for a hockey player – they're all jerks! I can't believe she was right. I so wanted to believe she was wrong, that she was just so hurt and bitter about her ex, that they couldn't possibly all be like him.

She knew her friend's warnings about falling for a hockey boy were, for the most part, in good humor. But with Chelsea, having been burned by a cheating hockey player she thought she was going to marry, there was always that unspoken glint of "don't do what I did, please be careful," in her friend's eyes. She'd thought that, despite hockey players' reputations for being "players", AJ was different. She knew that Chelsea thought he was different too, otherwise she wouldn't have introduced Lisa to him at all. That, or she didn't expect things to go as far as they did between Lisa and

AJ. *Maybe she thought he was a jerk but we'd just chat as friends and nothing more?*

He is a jerk. I thought he was different.

Sure, aren't they all different when it comes to the one you fall for?

Mad. Let's get back to mad, Lisa.

Incredibly mad.

She buried her face in her pillow. Her head and heart were trying to reconcile their views on this shitty situation.

It felt impossible.

She fell asleep in turmoil, jetlag really not helping her cloudy mind. She woke a few hours later, to *the* knock on the door. Glancing at the clock, her stomach dropped, as she suspected it was him.

Her dad answered the door, "Hello," he greeted the stranger.

"Hi," he paused. Suspicion confirmed. *He's probably waiting for dad to punch him in his pretty boy face,* she thought. "Is Lisa home?" he enquired politely.

Yes, I AM home, AJ, and I don't want to see you right now. I'm not ready. So, if you could just bugger the hell off until I sort out this avalanche of emotions, that'd be –

"Hold on and I'll get her for you."

DAD! You traitorous, traitorous man! I'm not ready!

She realized she hadn't *actually* told her parents she didn't want to talk to the ruggedly handsome, stubborn American stranger who could potentially appear at their front door sometime that day.

Shit. She cursed herself silently. *Note to self, next time I run away from the cheating, married, internet-boyfriend, at least tell the parents that I don't want visitors!*

"Lisa?" her dad called up the stairs.

"Yeah?" she struggled to keep her voice "normal".

"There's someone here to see you."

"Yeah."

She could hear confusion in her father's voice. She knew they hadn't expected her home so quickly; she'd barely said a word to either of her parents, feigning jetlag and needing sleep, and now a strange boy was at the door asking for her, mere hours after she'd hit the ground. Dads aren't stupid creatures; she knew he was doing wicked-fast mental math and adding two and two together to quickly come up with "This boy somehow hurt my girl."

She descended the stairs slowly, mainly because she was afraid she'd miss one and go on her arse. She looked like crap. Her hair needed washing and she was wearing sweats and a hoodie. When she got to the bottom of the stairs, she avoided both of their stares, tried to ignore her racing heart, and said, "Hi".

"Hi," he replied glumly. "Can we talk?"

No. No. No. No.

"Sure," she replied. Her mind was screaming "no", but her parents were watching, and, seeing him standing there in front of her, she couldn't find it within her to send him back to Alabama. She needed to know. Once and for all, she needed the truth.

Smiling weakly to her parents, she said, "I'll be back later. By the way, this is AJ. He's flown all the way from America because we had a fight, and I'm guessing he wants to apologize for being an arse."

Before they could answer, she slammed the door behind her, leaving them staring with dumbfounded curiosity at them, out the window. Taking a deep breath, she followed him down the steps. *This is it,* she told herself. *Make or break.*

Chapter 13

Break.

Break his bloody face for lying to me.

Calm down, Lis. Breathe.

When they got to the bottom of the steps, Lisa saw AJ's hire car sitting there. She had no idea how he'd managed to organize everything, she thought perhaps his lawyer-mom's PA had helped. Either way, it was just as well, as she didn't want to walk and talk, and it wasn't exactly warm, so a car came in handy. Especially with this kind of *stuff*. Stuff that would make her cry. In silence, they got into the car.

"Where to?" he asked quietly. She still wouldn't look at him directly.

"Just drive. I'll direct you when you get out of here."

"K."

She took him to a secluded area of land fairly close to home. The views were breathtaking, and there was no chance they'd be interrupted. It was quiet and serene. She, however, was not. At all. At least being here guaranteed that she could shout and scream should she need to. He'd tried a number of times to start a conversation, he'd tried to say he was sorry about twelve times between the house and here. Each time though, she'd just said, "Not yet," without looking at him.

He pulled the car into the lane and turned off the ignition. She sat staring out the window, as she still couldn't stand to look at him and she was struggling, once again, to hold back her tears.

Breathe, she reminded herself. She was heartbroken and really didn't want things to end with him. But she knew in her heart she couldn't be in a relationship with an already married man.

Society kinda frowns on that.

That's the only thing stopping you from being in a relationship with a married man? Society?

Reality check needed here, Lisa.

"I'm so sorry, Lis," he began.

She stayed silent, turned to look at him, glaring and let him talk.

"Britt and I have been best friends for life...you know I was born in the USA but spent most of my childhood in Canada. We were neighbors and I met her on my first day at my school. I spilled chocolate milk all over my shirt at lunch, and she happened to have a spare in her backpack. It had a sparkly pink frog on it, I think? I didn't care and she liked that about me. Anyway, we were immediate best friends. We've been side by side ever since. When I moved back home for high school, we were both devastated. We visited each other, turnabout, as often as we could. When I stayed for college at UAH, she was less than thrilled. She wanted to come to the US for college too, not just because of me – I saw that look, Lis – Really, there's never been anything romantic between us. Honestly, we're just really good friends."

He took a breath and continued his explanation. She remained silent, not meeting his gaze.

"She wanted to be closer to me, sure, but UAH wasn't the only college she applied to. And despite being so friendly, she's actually pretty quiet, and keeps to herself. Anyway, so now Britt's nearly out of school and she's not a U.S. resident. She can't live and work permanently in the U.S. where she really wants to be. She's also my mom's best friend's daughter. We get along well. Our personalities clicked from the get-go. We've had maybe one actual argument in our entire lives, even though we don't really have much in common either. We don't like the same food, the same hobbies, the same music. What is it you always say about you and your sister? Chalk and cheese. We are like chalk and cheese.

At the bar one night she got drunk and started crying about how she was staring down the barrel of deportation. One of the team jokingly suggested she and I get hitched to let her stay. She looked so hopeful. She knew I wasn't really even looking for a girlfriend, and it would obviously just be for a couple years. She never asked me outright, she didn't have to. She's my best friend. I'd do anything for her. And you and me? I wasn't really sure what we were. It never occurred to me I'd develop actual feelings for a girl on the internet.

Slap a ring in there and call it love and marriage.

Except it's not a *real* marriage. It's enough to pull her through until we're both out of grad school, and, hopefully, enough to convince the government to give her what she needs. Lis, I never set out with the intention of hurting you. I just wanted someone friendly to talk to and maybe even get a little flirty with. I cried on my wedding night because I was falling for you, and I knew that even if things didn't work out with you, I was going to be trapped in a marriage of convenience for years. It was a huge self-sacrifice, yes. But I also felt there was something potentially serious between you and me and I really wanted the freedom to pursue that.

I understand if you never want to talk to me again. Hell, I'd probably never want to talk to me again if I was you. But I needed to explain things to your face. You're probably sitting there thinking what bullshit I'm spouting, but it's the truth and it's all I got. I wasn't supposed to fall in love with you, Lisa, but I did. I really didn't think things would ever get so far that I'd need to tell you and then you came to visit and we really hit it off, and I just...I didn't know what to say."

His voice got quiet as he took a breath and looked at her, "I don't know what you're thinking..." He trailed off and she could tell he was struggling. So was she.

Tears were flowing freely now, and she didn't try to stop them. Her gaze fixed firmly out the window, she began softly,

"You should have told me, AJ."

"I know."

"No, AJ. You *don't* know. You have no idea how it felt to be told that you were married, by your teammate! How embarrassed and humiliated I feel. How stupid and naïve it made me feel. How deeply hurt and betrayed. You *lied* to me. Relationships are built on trust, none more so than an online relationship. I trusted you. I trusted you and you lied to me. You should have told me!" she repeated, her voice getting increasingly more shrill.

"I'm sorry," he repeated again, "I was afraid you wouldn't understand..."

"That wasn't your call to make, AJ. You should have given me *all* the information and let me decide how to deal with it. I *knew* something was off, and I couldn't put my finger on what. I thought I was crazy. We'd talked about so much that I was absolutely *sure* that you'd be honest with me no matter what. You thought I wouldn't understand? Well, I guess I kind of don't, she's Canadian – it's pretty friggin' easy for her to get a visa for the U.S. without marrying you. But AJ, I love you! I've spent every minute since I found out that the woman whose underwear was drying on your radiator is actually your WIFE and who probably even walks around in her damn underwear, trying to hate you, trying to resign myself to us never talking again. Don't you get it? I can't. You're a part of me now."

They sat talking it out for hours. She cried. She yelled. He cried. They cried together. They hugged. They talked some more. She yelled at him for lying. She told him she wasn't sure she could ever get over this, but she agreed to at least try. She offered him the opportunity to bare any more skeletons to her, here and now.

No more lies.

I really need to get better at trusting my gut. I knew there was something off when I met her and I thought I was just being paranoid.

Except you didn't really. You just ignored it.

It was getting late. Her tummy rumbled and she realized that neither of them had eaten for hours. Feeling a lot better having talked it out, she made a mental note to have a long chat with Britt, too. Just to make sure things were definitely ok – not that she didn't believe him, but just to cover all bases and be on the safe side.

It's not a real marriage, she thought trying to reassure her still-fluttery stomach. *It's a fake-marriage. A marriage of convenience. A sham marriage. That's totally a real thing. I've read about those kinds of marriages before. It's not a real marriage. You're not a home-wrecker. Breathe.*

She didn't really know what all of this meant for them. He was married, for the next few years at least. She understood that they had to convince the government that it was legit enough for Britt to get her citizenship and residency sorted out. Which meant that if she and AJ progressed in that direction, she couldn't marry him herself until it was all sorted. *Am I ok with that?* She wondered. *It's that, or lose him forever. But do I want to marry someone who lied to me about something so huge?* People marrying for a visa, a legal avenue to stay in the country so they didn't get deported, his story was plausible. Convincing. It *sounded* legitimate. Britt certainly didn't behave like a *normal* wife. And Lisa agreed that her having a boyfriend, was, in fact, bizarre, if they really *were* married, but also figured that sometimes people have open marriages and both parties can sleep with who they want. They agreed that she'd take some time to process everything. She could ask whatever questions she needed to, both he, and Britt would be completely forthcoming from here on in.

No more lies.

She felt a little better. She also felt hungry.

"Wanna grab dinner?" he asked, as though reading her thoughts.

"You read my mind!" she told him smiling.

"How does Olive Garden sound? I know you love their breadsticks."

"AJ, we don't have Olive Garden here." She turned to face him, "Oh. You mean, go back?"

He nodded.

"If you want to, that is. I don't mind staying here for a while. But if we stay, I need to go shopping, I didn't bring anything with me. If you come back to the states, you don't have to stay with me, you can go back to the hotel. Chelsea is worried about you, Ana feels terrible, even Jeremy feels bad. No one else knows you flew back here, but everyone is *pissed* at me, so it would totally be a fun trip for you!"

"You *deserve* to have everyone pissed at you, especially me," she began. "We'll stop for takeaway on the way home. I'll tell my parents not to cook, we'll eat with them so they can meet you properly, and then we can fly back, together, deal?"

"Sure, on one condition..."

"Whoa there, mister. You really think you're in a position to be making conditions?" she challenged as he started to back the car out of the lane.

"My condition is," he continued undeterred, "no more running away. No matter how much you hate me, or how angry you are. No matter how badly you wanna kick my ass. You stay put. We talk. You throw stuff at me. We scream, we shout, we cry – but we try to work it out *together*. Ok?"

She nodded, chewing her lip.

"Promise?" he asked her sadly, his eyes still glistening with tears.

"I promise," she answered firmly.

They ate dinner with her parents. She contemplated concocting some fabricated argument the two of them had that caused her to flee so quickly back to the comfort of the Emerald Isle – her parents likely wouldn't believe her, but they didn't really have to. She and AJ had cleared the air and that was all they really needed to know. Instead, however, she opted for telling them the truth, which went down better than it might have, probably because her parents had chosen not to marry, despite being together for thirty years. They saw the commitment as more important than a piece of paper.

They didn't exactly *approve* of AJ being even fake-married to another woman, and they were worried about Lisa getting involved in something so messy and complicated. But, for whatever the reason, they seemed to like him and they trusted her to make her own decisions in life, even if they didn't agree with them. She was an adult now and she knew they'd be there for her whatever she decided, though her dad did threaten to break AJ's legs if he ever hurt his daughter again. Despite being a joke, AJ lost all color in his face and stammered out a few "Yes sirs," which made her giggle and seemed to appease her authoritative father and comfort her mother, whom she suspected was doing a good job of hiding her worry.

Much to her parents' disappointment, she told them she was going back to the States in a couple days. So, knowing time was limited with their daughter's 'new' love interest, they quizzed AJ about anything and everything. He took it in his stride, not seeming phased at all. He actually seemed to enjoy it.

After dinner, they headed to the shops to grab some basic provisions for AJ. He didn't even have a toothbrush, or clean underwear. It was also *much* colder than the climate he'd left in sticky Alabama. The boy was wholly unprepared for the Irish elements. They went to Tesco first. It reminded him of a much smaller version of Target. Grabbing a trolley and a 'scan as you shop' machine, they started at the very first aisle and walked all the way around the shop, just to be together doing something normal. They needed normal after the day they'd had.

With the air cleared between them, she enjoyed the normality. It was nice doing something so humdrum as picking up things at the store. Clothes, toiletries, even some snacks and food items both for AJ to try while he was in town and to take back for Jeremy. It felt a bit ‘further down the line’, something a cohabiting couple would do. As they stood debating what color toothbrush AJ should have, and which of the somewhere in the region of twenty-three toothpaste options laid out in front of them they should pick, she couldn’t help but feel like she was getting a glimpse into their future.

Note to self, Google how to kill off the not-a-real-wife when you get home. KIDDING.

Kinda.

With a car-full of *stuff* they mostly didn’t need, they went for a drive.

It’s almost like being in Target with Chelsea!

Despite everything that had happened, it was still pretty early and they were still kind of coming down from their transatlantic flights and the emotional gauntlet they’d both run that day.

She directed him to Warrenpoint, a local seaside town she visited regularly throughout her childhood. The Aquarian in her loved everything about the water: the waves lapping the rocky shore, the smell of the sea air, the nostalgia of fish and chips, ice cream cones and skimming stones in the cold water. Here she felt calm, safe, and was reminded that feeling as completely out of control as the crashing waves often appeared, was not the end of the world. The tide would recede, the waves would calm and the water would still. It was just a matter of time. You just had to wait. Just as she'd pull herself together at some point, but being there reminded her that it was ok to feel like she was fighting the waves crashing inside of her every now and then.

The short drive was pretty quiet. They were still a little *off*. She figured it would be that way for a while. A lot had transpired in a short space of time, and she needed time to work through it all. She wasn't going to gloss over everything or pretend like things were fine. That would undoubtedly make things worse. Facing it head on was how they'd decided to move forward, but that wasn't an avenue without consequence.

"I used to come here all the time when I was younger," she told him. "The park down here is lovely. They have tennis courts, a gazebo, beautiful flowers. When we were kids, we'd sometimes get ice cream and sit on the wall watching the hubbub. If we hadn't already eaten, I'd take you for fish and chips, but if you feel like it, we could eat ice cream and sit on the wall. I mean, I know it's dark and you probably won't be able to see much, but it's still a nice place. People walking their dogs, ships coming and going. In summer you can't get moving with all the tourists."

He bought the two of them ice cream – thankfully the

shop took cards as he had no sterling on him – and they sat on the wall looking out over the Irish sea. It was cold, but not particularly windy. He had put on his new sweater – a proud Tesco purchase!

"A little cold there, babe?" she smiled.

"You could say that," he replied, shivering as he ate his ice cream. "I can see why you like it here," he mused, "it's quaint."

"It used to be the highlight of my week when I was little. The excitement of coming down that road to play on the beach and watch the windsurfers and jet skiers out there, or the crazy people swimming in the freezing cold water. I'd imagine that I was on some tropical island, with warm water instead of our near freezing waves, and golden sand under my toes instead of pebbles and rocks."

He pulled her close, and she sat with her back against his chest, relishing feeling it rise and fall. They sat for a long time, mostly quietly. Occasionally, he'd nuzzle into her hair or whisper in her ear that he loved her, or that he was sorry. She'd pull his arms tighter around herself and reply that she loved him too and that she knew he was sorry.

The more time she spent with him by herself, the surer she was that this hockey boy was *her* boy. The depth of emotion she felt for him scared her sometimes, but she was nonetheless convinced that this guy was sure to be *The One.* She just wasn't sure how to wrap her head around these new complexities in their relationship. He'd asked for her forgiveness and she wanted to give it to him, but wasn't sure how to go about forgiving him and rebuilding the trust that was broken between them. They were going to continue their long-distance relationship and she was scared she might become that neurotic girlfriend demanding to know every single thing about his life. There had to be a balance, and as long as they both worked on finding it, she had hope it could work.

When they got home later that night, they booked return flights together, via London, where they planned on spending a few days exploring, "just the two of them," as back to back transatlantic flights would be just pure insanity.

***

The following afternoon, they headed for the airport. She wondered how he had managed to convince his parents to pay for their flights back. *These last-minute flights aren't cheap,* she considered as she reminded herself that his mother was a big-shot lawyer. The fifty-five-minute flight was annoyingly over an hour late, but passed quickly enough once they were flying. With only their hand luggage on board, they didn't need to wait at baggage reclaim, and before long, they were on the Gatwick express, city-bound.

The Airbnb they stayed in was a short walk from Victoria underground station. It was pretty central and incredibly well priced for London, especially given how last minute they'd booked.

Exploring ignited a fire in her heart. He could see the excitement on her face from the minute they booked the layover. As soon as they arrived and dumped their bags in their room, Lisa pulled out the itinerary she'd quickly thrown together and thrust it in his face.

"Day One," he read aloud. "This is so *you*, you know that, right? Most people would take an impromptu trip to London in their stride and just find their way. You, on the other hand? You have practically no time to prepare, but manage to put together a *written* itinerary, with alternative suggestions to your main ones, places to eat along with highest rated dishes, opening times and prices for all of the tourist attractions. When did you even find the time?"

"Problem?" she asked eyeballing him from across the room.

"No ma'am, I love it when you get so freakishly organized. It's totally hot. I dig it. It's like weird Type-A foreplay or something. I'm just surprised you don't have day of the week underwear."

"Sarcasm?" she questioned. "I bring you an itinerary that every Trip Advisor user around the globe would be envious of, and you answer me with...sarcasm? And just 'cause you haven't *seen* my day of the week underwear doesn't mean that such underwear doesn't exist."

"Point taken."

He flashed a grin that was met with an eye roll and turned his attention back to the page in his hand.

"Okay," he read again, "Big Ben and the Houses of Parliament, The London Eye, Tower Bridge, Tea with Lizzy at B'ham Palace?" he looked up from reading.

"Only her besties get to call her Lizzy," she shrugged at his amusement.

"Westminster Abbey, feeding Lizzy's swans in Hyde Park, Piccadilly Circus, Covent Garden, Wicked at The Apollo Victoria Theatre..." His eyes scanned down the remaining attractions and *suggestions.*

"Jeez. Good thing you don't want to cram too much into this short trip to London, Lis. And, better still that neither of us is at all jetlagged to hell."

She laughed, "It's just a *guide,* AJ. We don't *have* to do it all."

"Uh huh. I know these lists. I've heard *all* about these lists from Chelsea and you when you went on your family vacation. Everything on this list will need a check mark next to it before we board the plane. Come on, get those shoes back on, we don't have a minute to lose!"

Considering it was early evening, they opted to grab dinner and go for a stroll around Westminster – stopping at anything that looked vaguely like a tourist attraction and taking selfies, or having strangers take their picture together. They laughed a lot and they kissed as the sun set over the Thames. Though Lisa was still wary after what had transpired, they bought matching "I love London" t-shirts and beanie hats from a street vendor 'cause their ears were cold and they wanted to be one of those sickeningly sweet, hopelessly in love, normal couples who wore matching tourist shirts around the city they were visiting.

They had crepes for dessert from street-food vendors after almost hitting up the London Eye but being deterred at the extortionate cost of tickets. Instead, they headed further down the river and took the cable car, not quite as fancy, but they still got an aerial view of the illuminated city.

On her way back to the hotel, Lisa remembered that there was only one bed in the room.

This is going to be awkward.

"There will be no sex for you this evening," she announced matter-of-factly as they rode the elevator to their floor.

"Uh. Ok? I had no expectation that there would be, but thanks for the forewarning, I guess?"

He sounded hurt that she felt the need to explicitly tell him as much. Her cheeks burned.

"I just don't want things to be particularly awkward, or for there to be any misunderstanding. I'm sorry, Pim, but I'm still processing everything and I just think we shouldn't get caught up in *things* and carried away."

"I get it, though I'm obviously disappointed. I'm definitely feeling *things* and think the make-up sex could be pretty epic," he answered as she swiped the key-card to open their door.

"It would be, but for one? I'm knackered – that was a jam-packed day. And for two, I really don't think I want make-up sex after the revelation that you're married to be our first sex." She saw him grimace and hurried to finish, "but, we can definitely make out and have make-up cuddles if you're interested?"

"Sold!" he announced pulling her into him for a hug. "I really am sorry, Lis."

"I know, I just need a little time," she chewed her lip.

"I understand."

He paused for a moment. "Hey wait – does this mean I gotta wear pants to bed?"

"It does. Be a good boyfriend and remove the temptation."

"That doesn't actually remove anything, it just covers it. Poorly."

Shaking her head, she laughed, as she walked into the bathroom to get ready for bed. AJ joined her, wearing only a pair of boxers and they stood brushing their teeth in silence.

So much sexual tension.

So much sexual tension.

Stop staring at his chest in the mirror. He can SEE you, Lisa...Damn he's fine.

She met his eyes and blushed.

This is going to be a long and hard night.

Ha! Hard may be the operative word there, Lis. But you've drawn your line in the sand and now you have to follow-through. Stick to your guns, even if you are drooling over his...

She took a little longer than AJ to get ready for bed. When she emerged and found him sitting upright in bed reading a book, her heart quickened.

I feel like he's deliberately trying to look more attractive than normal. I could absolutely jump his bones...

"You getting in? Or are you just going to stand there staring?" he grinned at her.

"You're enjoying this, aren't you?"

"Enjoying what?" he asked faux-innocently.

"You know what," she answered, climbing into bed next to him.

"Oh, you mean all this insane sexual tension and the fact you want to do way more than make out right now, but you've told me I'm not getting any and you know I'll respect it no matter how much you beg?"

"I don't beg," she answered. "And *you* want to do more, as well."

Why did I have to tell him he wasn't getting laid? I'm such a freakin' idiot. And he's stubborn enough now that even if I did beg, he wouldn't relent.

"Of *course* I want to do more, way more. But I'm not the one who announced in the elevator that you weren't getting any – if you need reminded of what you said, I'm sure the guy on the fourth floor - who probably was *actually* staying on the twelfth floor but just got out to avoid the awkward conversation we were having – remembers, very clearly, what you said."

Maybe I could tease him into doing way more...

"You've made your position very clear this evening, Miss Millar and, as a proper gentleman, I shall be respecting it," he paused, "though I'm not against doing everything but..."

"Everything but?" She looked at his cheeky grin and couldn't help but smile.

He can probably hear my heart thumping in my chest.

He dropped his book next to the bed. She swallowed, closed her eyes and took a deep breath as she felt his fingers trailing between her legs.

Breathe. You brought this on yourself. It's going to be the longest and probably the most torturous night of no-sex of your entire life and you deserve it. You absolute fucking idiot.

His lips were on her neck.

Her skin tingled.

Definitely the most torturous night of my life.

***

The following morning, they had a delicious breakfast in a French café. AJ had been smiling smugly to himself all morning.

"You're just so happy with yourself, aren't you?" she asked him.

"Well, you *did* say you 'don't beg'. Though, I vehemently disagree. It certainly sounded like you were begging last night."

She blushed and chewed the inside of her cheek.

Because you drove me fucking crazy.

"I still can't believe I couldn't convince you to just give in..." she answered, still in disbelief that his resolve had held so steady.

"What the lady wants, the lady gets. And the lady was *very* clear about what she wanted – that said, though, it was incredibly difficult, and for a moment, I thought I was going to die of frustration. Plus, I know you're worth the wait."

He kissed her forehead as they found the tube station to head to Piccadilly Circus. Try as he might, AJ couldn't wrap his head around the different lines, connections and directions of the underground right away.

"What is this? Some kind of railroad labyrinth? Do I get a prize if I get to where I want to go?"

At Leicester Square, they bought his and hers M&M mugs at the M&M store and filled a bag of the limited-edition extortionately priced flavors of M&M's to snack on during the flight.

I can't believe how much we just paid for sweets!

They also grabbed a couple of London red double-decker bus kits from the Lego store – she suspected one was for him to keep.

They enjoyed watching the street performers together. A girl in a brightly colored tutu with loud music was doing a routine on roller skates around a make-shift cone-track. There were Star Wars characters and a guitarist who sang Van Morrison and Billy Joel. They sang along as they stood watching parents sending their kids forward with change to drop into his guitar case.

Her favorite street artist was the guy drawing chalk-flags from various countries around a large *Welcome to London* sign. She dropped some coins on the Irish flag and AJ dropped some on both the American and Canadian flags.

The city was alive. Its pulse was almost tangible. They were surrounded by crowds of people, tourists and locals, shopping, taking in the sights, mostly sporting dark, heavy coats and wrapped up against the bitter chill.

Next, they headed to The Science Museum and later worked through the other attractions on their list.

Queen Lizzy wasn't home for tea the next day, but Lisa did convince AJ to try a posh afternoon tea at Claridge's, which resulted in an argument over whether it should be cream and then jam, or jam and then cream. They ended up sticky from both the cream and the jam.

Lisa loved exploring the city with AJ. He spied things that she didn't, and she remarked on things that he had missed.

"Can we travel together again in the future?" she asked him after a kind stranger had taken their picture at Tower Bridge.

"Of course we can, I've loved this trip," he answered sounding relaxed and happy.

"Me too," she grinned. "I've enjoyed spending honest-to-God quality time together. And I've enjoyed your best friend not bursting in the front door every time I try to tear your clothes off. It's been quite refreshing."

He laughed and agreed with her. It was nice to be able to be free with each other, holding hands, kissing whenever they wanted. They were much more comfortable than they had been in Alabama. London had been the perfect opportunity for them to recoup. They were on neutral ground; everything was out in the open, and there were no expectations or responsibilities. And, best of all, she didn't have to share him with a fake-wife. She felt regenerated, though *far* from ready to return to reality. Still, their London getaway had to come to an end sometime.

Chapter 14

It was the middle of the night when Lisa and AJ boarded the first of the two planes back to Alabama, an odd hour to travel, but the plane was busier than she expected. They had, as he'd predicted, ticked everything off her list, and while her feet hurt, she was happy. He lifted the arm rest separating their seats and tentatively slipped his arm around her. She obliged and rested her head on his shoulder.

He kissed her forehead and whispered, "I am really sorry, you know."

She nodded, "I know."

"And I really do love you."

She nodded again and breathed him in.

"I know you probably doubt that right now, but I do. Someday you'll believe me, and until that day comes, I'm going to make sure you have no other reasons to doubt it."

When she woke up, they were still flying.

"Are we there yet?" she whispered, smiling.

"About another hour to Chicago," he replied.

"Didn't you sleep?" she was concerned.

He shook his head. She could see the worry on his

face. The fear, panic, uncertainty. She could see the pain in his eyes, the pain from lying to her, the pain from her up and leaving him in the blink of an eye.

Good, she thought. *That's how it's supposed to be. He should feel guilty for lying to me,* she reassured herself. *You have no reason to feel guilty for how he's feeling, Lisa!*

She smiled slightly at him and leaned in to kiss him gently; he returned her smile and gave her a hug.

"Things will be ok, AJ," she told him, "I just need time to process it all, and to bitch to Chelsea about how shitty you are. Obviously." She squeezed his hand gently.

He laughed, "Obviously. Well, you're well within your rights to bitch. I deserve it."

"Yes. You do."

He knew he'd screwed up, and badly. She could see that at this very moment, he had no idea if it was even truly fixable even though she said it would be, much less how to go about trying to fix it. He was clearly convinced the trust she'd placed in him was now pretty much irreparably fractured. It pained her to know that he was in pain.

After they landed, they went straight to his place and promptly fell asleep. It had been a long night, a long week in fact, and emotional and physical exhaustion consumed them both.

Chapter 15

"Wake up, Irish!" Lisa felt the whack of a pillow thump her back.

"OI!" she grumbled loudly. "Go *away!"* She pulled the quilt up over her head.

Another pillow smacked her.

Count to ten, she told herself. *1...2...3*

Another pillow.

Screw counting.

"AGH! What do you WANT?" She glared as she sat up. Glancing at the bed beside her, she realized AJ was gone. There was a note on the pillow alongside a beautiful rose.

"Nice touch," she muttered wondering where the hell he'd gotten a rose from during the night as she turned her attention back to her friend, "well?"

"Read the damn note, grumpy smurf. Then get your ass outta that bed," Chelsea chastised, "and don't give me *that* look!"

"What time is it?" she grumbled.

"Noon – get your ass up!"

Another pillow.

"WHERE THE HELL DID ALL THESE PILLOWS COME

FROM?" she yelled at her friend, who was already in the kitchen. She could hear Chelsea laughing as she banged the cupboard doors.

She turned her attention back to the note.

Good morning, Babe,

Sorry to run off and leave you. You looked so beautifully peaceful lying there that I couldn't bring myself to wake you. I left that to Chelsea – I hope she was gentle with you.

My parents were meant to be in town for a fundraiser this weekend but now they can't make it. They've sent us their tickets instead. Mom's on the board of the charity, and she'd rather not leave empty seats at the table. Chelsea tells me you have nothing to wear, and since I have errands and a lot of groveling to do at hockey practice, I figured I'd leave you girls to go shopping. It's a gala ball or something, so it's all coats and ties. Should be fun.

I'll pick you up at seven, have fun shopping – treat yourself, you deserve it!

Love always,

Your AJ x

She stared at his credit card in her hands. He knew she wasn't one for splurging, especially on herself. He also knew that she was not likely to use his money to buy herself something either. They'd had this argument many times over the last seven months, usually when he'd sent her something for no reason, or offered to pay for something. He really was pretty traditional in a lot of ways.

She'd laughed at his frustrating double standard that it was ok for him to pay for her things, but not vice-versa. He never gave up, though. Despite her protests, he continued to offer, knowing perfectly well that she'd likely never be completely comfortable with it, but living in hope that she'd come around, at least a little. She was amused at his persistence. *He really can't help himself.*

All the same, she was touched by his obvious care for her. *Maybe 'cause it's a last-minute thing and he feels he should cover the unexpected cost?*

She couldn't remember a time when she had dressed so quickly in all her life. They were out the door in ten minutes and, as she climbed into the car, she started to eat her Panera Bread bagel. Chelsea knew her so well she'd arrived at AJ's with Lisa's favorite breakfast in her bag.

"You need a dress." Her friend told her simply.

"But I don't *do* dresses," she replied. "I guess I'm just not *that* much of a girl!"

"Don't gimme that crap. It's a ball, you're wearing a dress."

"But...I..." Realizing Chelsea was wearing her "don't fight with me" face, she finished her bagel and didn't argue.

Sure, Lisa was great at choosing a t-shirt for any occasion and she had about ten pairs of the same jeans in her closet. She had "College Girl" down to a fine art. But she acknowledged she was going to need her friend's help finding something to wear to a ball. Chelsea loved dressing up. She often coaxed Lisa into trying things she would never normally try on, let alone wear. Lisa knew that Chelsea's eye for fashion was far superior to her own and she *really* wanted to look good tonight.

It took them four hours to find a dress. Just as Lisa was about to give up, she spotted it. A beautiful, strapless dress, made from scarlet silk. Lisa couldn't help but feel a small surge of pride that it wasn't Chelsea who'd found it. She'd found it herself. Despite red not really being her color, it was love at first sight!

"That's it!" she exclaimed triumphantly.

"What is?" her friend asked, tired and burnt out by all the dresses. Lisa must have tried on three hundred different dresses over the course of the day, or at least it sure as hell felt like it. In Chelsea's opinion they'd found a good dress many, many times. But Lisa hated each and every one of them. Too short, too long, too tight, too loose, too "blah". What the heck even was "Too blah" anyway? Chelsea had demanded.

Picking the dress off the rail, Lisa hurried towards the changing room. The store was one of those trendy boutique types that only opened for a few hours every day, and only when Mercury was in retrograde or there was a supermoon. It was closing soon, and she still needed shoes and accessories. That would leave her just enough time to get ready.

"*This* is it!" she said as she emerged from the changing room. It was a bodice style dress: strapless, with a boned corset, detailed with delicate black stitching of a flower down the side. It pulled in slightly at her waist and then dropped to the floor. It didn't cling to her squidgy bits, and there was a thin layer of netting that made it sit out ever so slightly. It was simple but gorgeous. Just conservative enough, but still beautiful. She loved it. She spun around, the dress flaring as she did.

"Well?" she asked hopefully.

"It's...uh – wow!" Her friend was grinning, "That's gorgeous!"

"Go look for a pair of red ballet slippers, size seven," Lisa told her.

"Wait!" she exclaimed as her friend turned to leave. "That's a nine in American! I'll take this off and pay for it. I'll meet you at the door?"

"Ballet slippers?" her friend wore a puzzled expression.

"Not *actual* ballet slippers. What do you guys call them? Pumps? Flats? Flats. I don't do heels, and if I'm going to a princess ball, I want to be able to walk! I don't want to fall on my face, do I? Plus, no one will be able to see them under my dress. They won't know! GO!" she urged staring into her friend's *you really should wear heels* unconvinced face.

"Go!"

"Sheesh! I'm goin'! I'm goin'! But I'm sure as hell not getting you flats with that dress!"

En route to the counter, Lisa found a shawl to match

her dress. It was black with the same flower embroidered in red, and she found a clutch too. Grabbing them both she headed for the checkout to pay for her purchases. Lisa was feeling rather proud of herself, yet, at the same time, a little concerned and overwhelmed. It was a dress. She really didn't wear dresses. Ever. At all. Nor did she wear heels.

I'm wearing a dress, sure, but I'll only conform so far, she thought, smiling at the flats she'd picked up, despite Chelsea bringing her three pairs of heels to choose from.

Am I really going to a freakin' ball with AJ?

Well. This will certainly be an experience, she thought as her stomach did a nervous flip.

What the hell do I tell people? I'm his friend? I'm his friend. That's what I'll say. Note to self: ask AJ what the hell to say at the ball if people ask where his wife is and who the hell I am!

Standing at the checkout she had to decide whose card to use. In the end, she opted to pay for everything – except the shawl – herself. She knew that while it would be fine to let him pay for everything, she just wouldn't feel comfortable doing so. She also knew that he'd get pleasure out of buying her something, so she bought the shawl on his card, as it was the most "gift-like" purchase of the pile. She couldn't really imagine him going out and buying her a dress or shoes.

Minutes later they were standing at the exit of the boutique.

"Dress? Check. Shoes? Check. Shawl? Check. Shit! I

need a necklace!"

"No, you don't," Chelsea countered. "We don't have time!"

"You're right, I'll just wear something I have in my case, or something you have."

"I don't have anything to match that!" she exclaimed, adding, "I mean, you could check of course, but I don't think I do. Come on, quickly – we need to beat traffic!"

They raced back to their hotel. Lisa had a shower, turned on some music and carefully wrapped the large curlers that Chelsea had brought, into her hair. She stepped into her dress – time was starting to get away from her.

Popping on her shoes, she hummed along with the music and dried her hair with the curlers in. Glancing at the clock, she saw it was almost seven!

It's ok, she told herself, *you can do this. You have ten minutes, you just need to finish your hair, throw on some make-up and you'll be fine. Plenty of time. Don't panic. Plus, girls are supposed to be late!*

Tucking a towel around the top of her dress and spreading another across her lap, she dabbed the slightest bit of foundation on her face, with a little blush on her cheeks. She was pale by nature. People from Alabama could have a year-round tan if they wanted, but the Irish tend to be pale.

Or varying shades of lobster. I mean, it is Ireland, she thought, amused. *Our summer consists of a week of high twenties and we think it's amazing! What's that in*

American? Is it even seventy? Man, that's depressing.

Her makeup wasn't too dark, but gave her a little color and a slight glow. Using her finger, she smudged on some natural-toned eye shadow, painted on a smidge of lip gloss and smacked her lips together loudly.

I wish I'd learned how to apply make-up properly at some point. But time was almost up and she needed to be done. *Don't forget to ask AJ what the party-line is before you leave!*

Chapter 16

Pink was on the radio. Lisa stood singing as she teased the curlers out of her hair and let the loose curls hang lightly on her shoulders. Standing up, she took the towels away. She shook her head slightly to loosen the curls a bit, spritzed herself with her favorite perfume and looked herself over in the mirror one last time.

"Lookin' good, Irish," Chelsea grinned.

"Thanks Iowa," she said, her voice shaking ever so slightly. "Even with my bare neck?" She felt somewhat naked, but nothing she had with her, worked with what she was wearing.

"He's here," Chelsea replied, ignoring Lisa's question, "waiting downstairs."

"Ok," she said, pulling her shawl around her shoulders, grabbing her clutch and giving her friend a quick hug. She walked to the door of their hotel room, took a deep breath, patted down her dress and took the elevator to the lobby. A little girl loudly declared she looked like a princess as she walked to the main entrance. It made her smile despite her nerves. The concierge tipped his hat as he opened the door for her. Then she saw him. Her smile widened. He was about half-way down the steps, leaning on the handrail holding a corsage in his hand. *How very senior prom of you, AJ*, she thought, smiling as she started down the stairs. He was wearing a tux.

You are so freakin' delicious, she thought as she started chewing the inside of her cheek. Just when she was contemplating making a run for it back to the hotel room, he turned and saw her.

That smile could light up the Empire State Building. She sighed dreamily. *I constantly feel like a blethering teenager around this boy.*

He ran up the remaining steps to meet her, taking them two at a time – to take her hand and lead her to the car. *What a gent.* She almost expected him to fall flat on his face as he climbed the stairs – like her, the boy was pretty accident prone so it was hardly out of the realm of possibility. *As long as he doesn't take me out when he falls.* She struggled to suppress her giggle.

"Hey," he said kissing her cheek.

"Hey," she said returning his kiss.

It felt like a jolt of electricity through her body.

She'd expected a town car, but instead, he had a limo. It was gorgeous. The driver stood with the door open for her.

"You look...wow. You look beautiful, Lisa," he exclaimed.

"You don't scrub up too badly yourself, Pim." She grinned at him and started to get into the car.

"Hold up!" he stopped her, grabbing her arm gently.

"I have something for you." First, he put on her corsage, then he turned her to face away from him and he moved her hair gently to the side. She felt something cold against her skin.

A necklace? That's why Chelsea wouldn't let her go buy one! She knew! she thought. *What a sneak!*

He closed the clasp and she shook her hair back into place as she admired the necklace hanging around her neck. She smiled when she recognized what he had given to her. It was a hockey necklace, the logo of her home team, the Belfast Giants. She had never seen one before, did they even exist?

Well apparently, they do. She mused. *Either that, or he had it made for me and is using tonight as a reason to give it to me.* She wasn't going to question it. It was beautiful, delicate, and it was unusual. Thoughtful and creative.

"Read the inscription," he told her softly, breaking her thoughts.

Turning it over, she read,

Keep your stick on the ice.

<3 AJ.

Don't cry! she told herself, feeling a lump rise in her throat. *Don't cry.*

Keeping your stick on the ice was a pretty famous hockey expression, it's a fast game - and takes only a fraction of a second to score a goal, so it's important to always be ready. Where your stick is when the puck comes your way could easily make the difference between a win and a loss. They had bonded over their mutual love of hockey in the early days of their relationship, but in difficult moments throughout their time together, he'd told her to keep her stick on the ice. Reminding her to stay focused and prepared, in case of that lucky bounce or deflection that would help bring her out of whatever quicksand she felt that she was in and back on to solid ground. The necklace would serve as a daily reminder to keep herself grounded.

"It's beautiful," she managed, turning to face him. Their eyes met, "thank you!"

"You're welcome," he blushed.

"Hey, you two?"

Chelsea called them from the bottom of the steps. They turned to face her.

"Say cheeeeeese!" she called.

Slipping his arm around her waist, he pulled her close to him, and they turned to face the camera.

Snap. Snap. Snap.

"You're like the freakin' paparazzi!" she told her snap-happy friend.

"You kids go have fun," she told them. "And be good!" she added mischievously. "And if you can't be good? Be careful!"

"You really do look beautiful, Lis," he told her quietly as he took her hand and interlocked his fingers with hers.

Chapter 17

The gala was held in some fancy hotel downtown. Lisa's heart was pounding and she had goosebumps as she walked into the banquet hall. The only person she knew, in this room of three hundred people was AJ, but he seemed to know everyone. She was nervously excited.

With AJ and Britt being married, she didn't think she'd have the chance to experience much of his "outside" life for a very long time. She'd adjusted her expectations when he'd told her the truth. They couldn't behave like a regular couple; and they couldn't do regular couple things in public. Those new expectations had been up-ended, and she was now back to feeling confused. While the hockey team and his closest friends all knew the truth about his marriage, she was certain his parents' friends and the rest of the world shouldn't know that it was just a front. Not everyone would understand.

He'd told her that his parents also knew the truth, and while they admired his loyalty to his friend, they didn't think marrying for any other reason than love was a good idea. Despite Britt being the daughter of their friends, AJ's parents supposedly weren't thrilled that he'd married someone, anyone, he wasn't in love with and didn't want to spend the rest of his life with, especially for a visa she could have gotten herself with a bit of work. Lisa liked that about them, *though I coulda done without the raising him with such a strong chivalrous need to pay for every single little thing,* she mused, smiling as her fingers glided along the floral embroidery on her shawl.

This was a side to his life she was wholly unfamiliar with. She'd never met his parents and this fancy ball with a dress which made her feel like a princess was way out of the ordinary for her everyday life. She took her social cues from AJ. She didn't want to unwittingly land him in trouble, or reveal the truth about his marriage to the room. While they'd spoken about it briefly in the car, she was so nervous and so excited, she didn't want to mess up in a moment of emotional overwhelm. She was fairly sure having to keep any kind of distance from him – especially when he looked *this* good – could actually drive her to insanity.

It's probably best that I don't get too drunk tonight, she thought, whilst simultaneously mentally undressing him, afraid if she got too drunk, she'd attempt to *actually* undress him in a dark corner somewhere. She felt that it could go one of three ways. The first, she'd become giddy and happy drunk, confessing her love for AJ and being too "handsy" in public. The second, she'd become a tearful and upset drunk, confessing her love for AJ and being too "handsy" in public. The third? She had no idea, a combination of both, perhaps? Either way, she ventured a guess that she'd end up too "handsy" in public and opted to keep her wits about her.

Plus, if we do end up taking things further tonight, I really don't want to be drunk. I'm glad I started rationalizing all of this out before I went beyond this first glass of champagne, she thought. *Sober me is much more sensible.* She bit her lip.

Damn, he's hot.

Am I drooling?

Part of me wishes we'd been able to stay awake long enough in London to get down and dirty...stupid needing to tick everything off the damn list left us bloody knackered. Double damn him for being a stubborn gentleman. This prince and princess thing tonight definitely has that Disney-perfect kinda feel about it!

She expected distance, perhaps even an air of coldness between the two of them. She thought they'd leave their personal relationship at the door and be "just friends" in polite company. Maybe she imagined it, but listening to him make introductions to some of his parents' friends, some definitely felt much warmer than others. His parents had strong ties to Alabama. AJ's grandparents on his fathers' side were from there, and his dad had lived there until he met AJ's mom and she'd convinced him to try northern life. They still spent a lot of time there, and, while AJ never referred to her as anything other than a friend, she suspected that some of the people she was meeting might actually know the truth – and made a mental note to ask him later.

They sat at a table with four married couples, and the conversation was mostly pretty easy. His parents' friends complimented him on his hockey, talked about his future and, more often than was comfortable, his wife.

He was, after all, still married. So, when they asked where Britt was, or asked if Lisa was a friend, he casually explained that Britt was on holiday visiting family, and that Lisa was a family friend from Ireland. He tried to avoid the question if he could. It annoyed them both, as did the answer. She noticed that AJ hadn't drunk much either, despite the open bar. *Probably for the same reasons as me,* she pondered as she listened to his mother's oldest friend tell her a story about AJ as a child and how he often tormented his sister in that way only siblings can.

The couples at their table had such fascinating life stories to share. Lisa was sure AJ had heard them all before over the years, but he seemed as genuinely rapt as she was to hear them. In other moments she could feel his stare, watching her as she took in every word from the strangers 'round the table.

When the meal had finished and the tables were cleared and moved, the room became a dancefloor. Music began to play, and couples took the floor. AJ excused himself from her for a moment and left her with a few people from their table. She was enjoying herself. In her mind, her accent had never been particularly strong, but, nonetheless, on the advice of Chelsea and Ana, she attempted to speak more slowly and clearly.

She only had to repeat herself once or twice.

I could get used to this, she told herself.

He was back by her side before she knew it, although he didn't sit down. She looked up and saw he had his hand extended towards her. He looked relaxed and happy.

"Dance with me, princess?" he asked.

Nodding, she followed him onto the dance floor. The music was slow and she was ready. To her, there was no one else in the room. Just her, and just him. Though to the room they were "just friends," they knew they were together. He wrapped his arms around her to rest in the small of her back and pulled her closer to him. Her hands linked at the nape of his neck, their heads touching slightly, and they danced. For how long? She didn't know. But she was happy. She knew she was glowing. She wondered how anyone in the room could believe that they weren't in love. She felt like it was radiating from both of them, and, if she could have stopped time and immortalized one moment in her life thus far, it would have been this one, right here.

Pulling her head back slightly, she looked into his eyes, he looked as happy as she felt.

"You ok?" he asked her. She nodded. He slipped her arms down from his neck to his waist and rested her head on his chest. She sighed deeply, "Never better."

Chapter 18

The evening was perfect.

Sometime after midnight, the limo driver took Lisa and AJ home. They giggled together as they climbed the stairs to his apartment, talking about the evening; the people, the food, the dancing and what a wonderful night his parents had missed. In truth, she was really quite glad his parents couldn't go, as they had both truly enjoyed themselves.

She dropped her bag and shawl on the breakfast bar, flicked the switch on the kettle to make a cup of tea and then went to the bathroom. When she emerged, he was sitting on a chair, his back facing her, with his guitar propped on his knee. He was tuning it, and humming softly. Stopping, she leaned against the door frame.

"Sing for me?" her voice was almost a whisper. He didn't ask what. He didn't have to. He'd written her a song when they first met online and had sent her the lyrics by email. He had his band record it, with him singing alone. He sent her the audio, and she had fallen in love with it. The more she heard it, the more she loved it. No one had ever written a song for her before. It was so personal, intimate, and just for her. It made her glow inside, and she'd been waiting for the day when he'd sing it to her in person. She closed her eyes as he started to sing.

She walked up behind him and slipped her arms around his shoulders as he sang. When the song finished, he barely paused before he started to play a second song she recognized immediately. A duet, a song she had long wanted to sing with him. One of their favorites. She'd never sung with him before, and she was nervous. She closed her eyes again as he started to sing, and listened, waiting for her part to start.

His rich, mellow tones calmed her shaking nerves and she stood up behind him, not moving her arms from his shoulders, and sang. Her voice was a little shaky, but she tried to hide it. She usually didn't care what people thought of her voice. But him? She cared what he thought.

Calm down! she scolded herself. *He's heard you sing before!*

His voice took over once again as her confidence started to return,

Baby, I'm falling....

She could tell he enjoyed singing with her. He was smiling, she could tell that too. Her turn again, she breathed deeply and she relaxed into herself and sang again.

They were both enjoying this, and, truthfully, she was looking forward to the part where they sang together. Her voice joined his, she smiled with anticipation. *This could either go really well and work, or our harmonies will suck,* she thought. Luckily, she was used to harmonizing. She'd been in a choir for most of her life, but sometimes voices just didn't gel well, regardless of how good the singers were. She had almost no doubt in her mind that they'd be fine, but, for just a split second before she opened her mouth, she wondered.

They sang together.

She was in her element; her heart was soaring. She loved music, and singing was her release. She leaned forward and kissed his cheek as her singing faded and left him solo again. She kissed him again, soft, little kisses along his jaw line, and again slightly below at the top of his neck. His singing stopped, he tilted his head slightly towards her and she kissed him again. He sat down his guitar, and without moving he guided her in front of him and took her hands in his own. He pulled her towards him and turned slightly so he could kiss her on the lips. Deeply. She felt a flutter in her stomach and was suddenly glad she'd remembered to shave her legs.

"Hold that thought?" he asked when they finished kissing. She looked at him quizzically, "I really, really need to pee," he answered, blushing.

She burst out laughing, he laughed too. Things felt so easy and normal with this guy. In some moments, things felt like they'd jumped straight out of a Disney movie. In others, like right now, the every-day-ness of things made her feel like she'd known him for years and that they'd been a couple the whole time.

Standing up, he didn't let go of her hand. He kissed it and smiled. He went to the bathroom while she sat on his bed. She turned on the bedside lamp and hunted through his CDs.

"Mind if I put on some music?" she called to him.

"Go for it," he answered.

"Nathanson?" she called to him.

"Sure."

Pressing play, she kicked off her flats and sat cross-legged at the end of the bed, humming to the music. She played with the fabric of her dress. *Maybe I could be a dress kinda girl after all*, she thought. *It's such a pretty dress!*

As if he was reading her mind again, he said, "You really do look amazing tonight, you know?"

Looking up, he was in the doorway. He'd taken his jacket off before playing his guitar, but his shoes and tie were now both gone, and the top buttons of his shirt were open.

Damn this boy is epically hot...and the more he strips himself off, the less work I have to do! she thought.

He stood in front of her and took her hands. Getting back to her feet, she slipped her arms around his neck. As she stared into his eyes, she felt his strong arms slide around her waist, drawing her closer to him. She loved when he did that. She loved feeling like she was his. But, mostly, she just loved when he felt confident and comfortable enough to just take her in his arms, like she belonged there forever. She loved being close to him.

And we're about to get a whole lot closer, she told herself with a small smile.

"Did you have fun tonight?" he asked her.

"Yes, I did, actually. Did you?"

"I always have fun when I'm with you."

"How do you get away with calling me cheesy when you say stuff like that?" she giggled playfully and nudged his nose with hers.

"Well. Cheesy or not, it's true," he told her, nudging her back. "Have I mentioned how amazing you look tonight?" he finished.

She felt the color rising in her cheeks and smiled again. She couldn't stop smiling. Even if she didn't want to smile, he could make her smile anyway.

"You should wear a tux more often," she told him. "You look good, Pim," she said, "you look very, very good."

"I think I'm finally used to you calling me Pim," he said. "I kinda like it. It doesn't feel insulting like it does when Ana uses it. When you use it, it feels much more affectionate."

He smiled at her and kissed her. It was a soft kiss, the kind that leaves your lips tingling for a few seconds after you pull away – so you're not quite sure if you're still kissing, or not. Looking into his eyes she saw it all. The pain was still there, the pain of having hurt her, the frustration of having to live so far away from each other, the love he felt for her. As though he saw her searching his soul and reading his feelings, he blushed and kissed her again. This time it was a long, deep kiss, filled with a passion that made *her* cheeks blush. His palms spread across her back and he held her tightly. Her fingers played with the collar of his shirt at the back of his neck. She loved kissing him. She could kiss him forever, only to come up for air, *and chips and queso,* she thought, amused. As he unzipped her dress, anticipation fluttered in her stomach and she blushed as her dress landed on the floor.

Her fingers toyed with the buttons on his shirt, she kissed his neck as she opened each button slowly. She hesitated with the last button – but only for a moment. The fluttering in her tummy increased as his shirt, and then his pants joined her dress on the floor. She closed her eyes for a moment to try to steady herself. Standing in front of her was a beautifully sculpted athlete, who didn't have a spare ounce of fat on his body. Suddenly incredibly self-conscious, she looked away.

As if hearing her thoughts, he lifted her chin, forcing her to meet his gaze.

Could you stop knowing me so well for JUST a moment please?

I can't let him see me naked – I'm so squidgy compared to him!

She tried again to look away, but he cupped her face with both her hands and kissed her gently.

"You're beautiful," he breathed, as he tucked a stray curl behind her ear. "I can't believe you're mine."

Staring into his eyes, she realized that he truly meant

what he was saying. He wasn't poking fun at her. She knew he'd never do that. But her inner demons were so overpowering and so consuming some days. He didn't care that she had lumps and bumps that she, herself, hated. He didn't care that she had scars on her thighs from the darkest period in her life when she had cut herself. He didn't see what she saw. To him, she was as beautiful standing there in her underwear as he was to her.

She placed her palms against his chest, and slowly traced the lines of his muscles with her fingertips. He swept her hair off her shoulder and kissed her neck, stopping at her ear to tell her he loved her before leading her to the bed.

Finally! she thought as she lay down.

Lying under the covers, he was propped up on his elbow and leaning slightly over her. His free hand was tracing down her bare side. They kissed again. Her arm was under his elbow, playing with the hair at the nape of his neck.

"Penny for your thoughts?" she asked him, watching him intently. She could get lost in those blue eyes.

"You don't really want to know," he replied, grinning at her mischievously.

He rolled over on top of her as she slipped her arms around him. Her fingers danced along the contours of his back. She loved his broad shoulders, and, as a defensive player, his back was toned and strong. As her fingers moved up his back and over his shoulders, he shivered slightly. Realizing why, she reduced the pressure on his right shoulder. She could feel the scar tissue from a fairly recent hockey injury just beneath the skin.

He trusted her, so he let her hands explore his shoulders. She was gentle with him; she didn't want to hurt him and he knew she wouldn't. He ran his fingers through her hair and she smiled at him. She loved when he played with her hair.

Her fingers continued their journey along his shoulders, tracing little shapes on his smooth shoulder blades.

"Are you sure?" he asked her.

She nodded and bit her lip, "I'm sure."

He kissed her deeply and they moved together. Slowly at first, holding each other tightly. As their rhythm intensified their moist skin stuck together. It took a long time for their heavy breathing and racing pulses to return to anywhere near normal. As they lay still, she listened to the frantic thumping of his heart in his chest.

"You ok?" he asked as he pushed her damp hair off her face so he could see into her eyes.

She nodded and rested her head upon his chest listening to his heart slow down to resting. They fell asleep tangled in each other's arms.

Chapter 19

When Lisa woke, she wrapped herself in a sheet and went to the bathroom. She brushed her teeth and splashed cold water on her face.

Bang.

The front door slammed.

Moving the bathroom door slightly, she saw Jeremy appear.

“Goooood morning cats and kids, how is everyone this -”

He spied her standing in the bathroom doorway, wrapped in a bed-sheet. She was *sure* she had bed-hair, there’s no way her perfect curls would have survived not being tied up overnight. His jaw dropped. He glanced at AJ, who was propped up on his elbow in the bed with a boy-smirk on his face.

“Whoa! Wait!” Jeremy’s head turned quickly between AJ lying in bed and Lisa standing in the doorway, “YOU GUYS HAD SEX! Does this mean she forgives you for having a wife who isn’t her?” He bolted for the bed and tried to yank the quilt away from the very naked AJ, but AJ was too quick. He jumped to his feet and stood with his back against the wall gripping the quilt in front of him.

"Jeremy," Lisa's voice was soft, yet quietly commanding and she was struggling not to rise to the comment about AJ's wife, "back away from the hockey boy. We've both seen what's under that quilt. We also both know that he has absolutely no qualms about dropping it to kick your ass!"

He hesitated for a second or two, weighing up the pros and cons.

"Good point!" He realized she was right and backed off. "I think I'd better go," he laughed and turned to leave. "I'll let myself out," he called as AJ lay back in bed.

"Oh, Jeremy?" Lisa called. He paused and glanced back. "Next time, please don't just barge in unannounced. I realize that's how it's always been with you guys and I don't want to come between you both, but things are changing for all of us. Can we please maybe work on some 'AJ has a girlfriend now, to go with his wife on the side and she may be naked in his house' boundaries?"

"Yes ma'am," he replied with a military salute. "Age, your new *girlfriend* is a real ball-buster! Later, gators!"

With that, he was gone. She pulled a shirt and some shorts from his closet and headed back to the bathroom. When she emerged, she had the sheet neatly folded and placed it at the edge of his bed. Throwing him a quick smile, she headed for the kitchen.

"What do you want for breakfast?" she called to him as she took two glasses out of the cupboard and sat them on the counter.

"You." He answered as he slipped his arms around her waist from behind.

She hadn't heard him get up and follow her to the kitchen, but his touch made her tingle. Turning to face him, she kissed him deeply as he lifted her up to sit on the counter, carefully sliding the glasses out of the way. *Just how much does he bench-press,* she wondered. *He picked me up like I was as light as a feather.*

His hands slid up the back of her shirt as she wrapped her arms around his neck and linked her ankles behind his waist – pulling him closer to her. She loved being impulsive, *especially this kind of impulsive.*

***

"How about that orange juice?" she asked him with a grin once they'd recovered from round two on the floor. Getting to his feet, he offered her a hand-up.

"Sure," he replied, matching her grin, "and how about we make pancakes?" he added hopefully.

Laughing, she nodded, and before long the pan was heating up and a big bowl of thick pancake batter was sitting ready next to the stove. As she started to lay the table, he came up behind her, reached around and wiped a dollop on the tip of her nose.

"Oh, no. You did *not* just do that!" she exclaimed, removing the gloopy mixture from her face.

"Well, I clearly did," he matched her incredulous

tone, “I owed you.”

“You’re going to pay for that!” she warned, playfully.

“Oh yeah? What ya gonna do, babe?”

She walked, slowly towards him, slipped her arms around his waist and kissed him passionately. He didn’t notice that she was dipping her hand in the bowl behind his back.

“This!” she exclaimed as she drew a line of batter along his forehead.

He laughed as she ran to use the sofa as a shield.

“Brave move!” he challenged, as they circled the furniture in the living room. Her toes caught on the rug and she fell, landing with a thud on her side. Seizing the opportunity, he pounced. Pinning her hands above her head with one of his hands, he tickled her with the other, until she yelped and squealed so hard, she could barely breathe. Stopping for a second, she struggled to get free.

“Surrender?” he goaded her.

“*Never*!” she retorted hotly, he continued to tickle her. She put up quite a fight, but, once again, she was no match for his strength.

“Ok, ok!” she cried, eventually.

“Say you surrender!” he commanded.

“I surrender,” she mumbled grumpily as he let go of her hands. Not getting up from on top of her, he continued,

“Say, ‘AJ you are the champion’,”

Cutting him off with a shove, she pouted.

“So cute when you’re all sulky,” he jested and kissed

her pout. Sliding her hands down, she gave his bum a suggestive squeeze.

"Again?" he asked, his voice laced with both surprise, and excitement.

"Hey now!" she said, defensively, "*you're* the hockey player. Aren't you people supposed to have lots of stamina?"

"I have plenty of stamina," he grinned wickedly.

He kissed her again, and, as his hand travelled up her thigh, they heard a throat clearing behind them.

"Ahem," she said loudly. You could tell she was smiling.

Britt.

"Would you guys like to be alone?"

Roberto.

"You guys should *really* try locking the door!"

Jeremy.

"Not you, *again*!" Lisa groaned. "We talked about this, Jeremy!"

There were more noises than people she'd heard so far. She turned to see who else was there and groaned again. Roberto, Jeremy, Britt and Chelsea.

Perfect, she thought as color rose quickly to her cheeks.

"We came by to ask you guys to join us for lunch before you need to head to the rink, but," Chelsea paused and glanced over to the untouched bowl of pancake mix on the counter, "I see that you've not even made it to breakfast yet!"

They all exploded into giggles.

"Yeah, yeah, laugh it up!" she told them, her face hot. "What happened to pre-game? Did it go *wholly* out the window? Has coach gone soft in his old age?" She was clearly trying to re-direct attention from the embarrassing situation they'd just been busted in, but realizing it wouldn't work, she added, "We'll meet you guys there in ten."

No one moved, they all stood with amused looks on their faces.

"Leave!" she ordered, exasperated, rolling her eyes.

More laughing, but at least this time they moved.

"You're all just jealous that you're not getting any!" AJ hollered as the door slammed shut.

"Man, we gotta start locking that door!" she announced as they burst out laughing at their bad luck, just as the pan they left heating on the stove spontaneously combusted and set off the fire alarm.

Chapter 20

Lunch was fun, and Lisa was convinced she'd pulled a muscle or two from all the giggling they'd done.

That'll go well with the bruises from my fall this morning.

When it was time for the boys to leave for pre-game *stuff*, she kissed AJ goodbye.

"Go gettum champ!" she said with a wink. "Good luck, and I'll see you after the game. I told the guys we'd go with them for a drink after if that's ok?"

He nodded.

"Stay safe?"

He nodded again.

"Promise?"

"Promise."

He kissed her lightly and headed off to the rink.

***

The game was more physical than usual. There was a lot of on-ice tension. It was an important game, and both teams really needed to win. One player in particular on the visiting team, annoyed Lisa. He was a short and stocky guy, but clearly strong. In her opinion, he crossed the line from gritty into dirty too often – he was quick, so he often went unnoticed by the referee and linesmen. He appeared to have taken issue with AJ too, which was, of course, why Lisa didn't like him. She assumed he was going after AJ because he was one of the bigger guys on the ice and he played defense. The two seemed to butt horns more than necessary. They were always on the ice together, and she really didn't like it. There was way too much pushing and shoving for her liking.

I'm probably just being over protective!

If she had her way, he would be permanently on the bench, *sans* skates, and in a cocoon of bubble wrap.

He wouldn't like that so much though.

Good job I'm not the coach!

Maybe I could tempt him if I was wrapped up in the bubble wrap WITH him...

Tonight, he was certainly racking up the ice time. Watching things heat up on the ice, she grew increasingly concerned that it would all end in tears. Hers, most likely. The fans loved a good fight. It was often the best way to clear the air between teams – a well-established tradition in hockey. While it seems counter intuitive to non-hockey-fans, fighting in hockey arguably keeps the infractions in check. If you know you'll get your ass handed to you for a dirty hit, the theory is that you'll be less inclined to do those things. But now that one of the 'fighters' was *her* boy, she felt very conflicted.

The call was 'hooking', a two-minute, minor penalty for using your hockey stick as a kind of restraint. He had hooked AJ's right arm, hard. Hard enough that AJ fell to the ice. AJ was clearly on his last thread and snapped, dropping his gloves when he got to his feet – the customary invitation to fight. His buttons were pushed. The guy, wearing the number three, had seemingly started on him verbally, too. She could see his mouth moving and guessed he was trash-talking AJ. In fact, "Three" had thrown his weight around on the ice for the *entire* game thus far and had even messed with the netminder Mike. If you know anything about *anything*, you know you never mess with the netminder in a hockey game. That's just not a smart move. While AJ was not normally an instigator, "Three" certainly seemed to bring it out in him, and Lisa watched in horror as AJ dropped his gloves.

Three dropped his gloves in response and the circling started. The fight didn't last long. AJ was taller and stronger and he'd obviously thought this through, because after a few hits, the other guy was down. Despite AJ having won, they were both bleeding, but from where Lisa was sitting, it looked as if it was just superficial.

Probably another broken nose, she sighed as both boys skated off to the penalty box. A five-minute penalty each. The crowd had loved the action, but it seemed that Three was even more incensed. He tossed his gloves off in the box, and threw a tantrum like a little boy who wasn't getting his own way.

The Chargers won – barely, but it was still a win. When he joined her in the bar, she was still a little grumpy that he'd started the fight, despite knowing he'd been goaded into it.

"Hey," he leaned over to kiss her cheek. The bar wasn't too loud, yet, but it was a hometown win – the place would be packed within the hour.

"Hey," she replied.

"Sorry," he sounded kind of deflated.

"What for?"

"Dropping my gloves. But that guy, he just-"

She cut him off, "Pissed you off, I know." She sighed and turned to face him. "He pushed your buttons," she finished as she took him by the chin to get a better look at his face.

He had a bruise already darkening his left cheek bone and his bottom lip was swollen with a single stitch holding it together. She could tell his nose had been bleeding too.

"Oh Pim!" she sighed. "He got you good," she fawned over him. Tracing her finger around his bruise, she kissed him gently.

"Not as good as I got him," he winced as he put his arms around her to pull her in tight.

"How is it?" she asked, indicating his shoulder.

"Fine," he obviously lied.

"Urgent care in the morning?" she could tell he was putting on a brave face.

He nodded.

"Want to go now?"

He shook his head.

"You sure? They won't give you a shot in the morning if you've been drinking tonight, AJ."

She spoke to him like he was neither a grown man who could take care of himself, nor an athlete who went through this fairly regularly. Apparently, she was a mother hen, and she just couldn't help herself. Thankfully, he thought she was cute when she fussed over him.

"No, it's ok, honest. I'm not drinking. Plus, we're playing tonight. I gotta get on stage."

"When did this happen?" she asked, more than a little surprised.

"About ten minutes ago. The band cancelled, so we said we'd fill in."

"AJaaaaaaaaaay! But your shoul-"

"I'll catch you after, promise!" he said, kissing her quickly and disappearing into the growing crowd.

"I've been abandoned, by my bruised and stitched enforcer," she sighed as she plopped herself into the seat beside Chelsea. An enforcer's job on the team is to deter and respond to dirty play by the opposition, but tonight, she felt as though they were both at fault and she was less than thrilled that it was a double-header weekend, meaning they had another game to play before the weekend was over.

"He's playing?"

Lisa nodded. “Want a drink?”

“Sure! Want me to come with you?”

“No, it’s ok. It’s not too busy yet, I can handle it. I’ll be right back.”

The crowd at the bar was already starting to build, Lisa had to wait a little, but she didn’t mind. Her boy was singing, so she sang along softly until her turn came to order drinks. She placed her order with the barman and glanced up at the stage. AJ was smiling down to her as he sang, and she returned his smile, quickly glanced around to make sure no one was looking and blew him a kiss.

We are so friggin’ cheesy, she thought making inward gagging noises at this rom-com her life had become lately. She barely recognized herself.

Turning to pay for the drinks, she picked them up and started to walk back to the table. Out of nowhere, he was in front of her. The hooking guy, number Three. And he was blocking her path.

Chapter 21

Great. Just, great! Here stands before me one large asshole, Lisa thought. *Stay calm,* she instructed herself. She didn't want to cause any kind of scene, especially with AJ on stage. If this guy said anything to her, the quick game-plan she threw together in her head was to be polite and get the hell away from him as quickly as possible – even though what she really wanted to do was to tear his head off.

"Excuse me," she said politely as she tried to side-step him. He moved to block her path, cutting her off. She threw him her best confused-smile, "Could you let me past, please?" she inquired as she attempted, once again, to maneuver around him.

He intercepted her again. She was starting to get annoyed.

"You're not from these parts, are you?" He moved closer to her and she smelled alcohol on his breath.

This dude must have hit the bottle as soon as he stepped off the ice, she thought, grimly.

"No pulling the wool over your eyes, is there?" she replied dryly. Her patience was quickly wearing thin with this guy. He'd just hooked AJ's bad arm, busted his face and now he was kinda holding her hostage at the bar. She attempted to step around him once more, but he moved to cut her off. The old stereotype of hot-headed Irish came to mind as she stood deciding how to handle the situation.

I think I'm doing pretty well at keeping my Irish temper at bay right now, she mentally patted herself on the back.

"Excuse me!" she repeated. Louder this time. Before she could move, he was practically on top of her, her back pressed against the bar. The drinks she had thus far managed to keep intact, sloshed over the rim of their glasses, splashing over her hands and dripping down her arms. He reached around her, picked up a shot from the bar and downed it as she attempted to put her two glasses back down on the bar and somehow shake off the sweet and sticky drink from her hands. With her hands, now free, though sticky, she placed them firmly on his chest and pushed.

"Are you *crazy?*" she exclaimed hotly.

"For you," he replied with a lopsided grin. He slipped his hand around her waist and groped at her butt.

Is this guy for real? She wondered momentarily, trying, frantically, to come up with some rational explanation for the series of events that were unfolding around her.

"I'm only going to say this once," she started as calmly as she could muster, struggling to keep her voice steady. "Take your cheating, can't play hockey to save your life, hands off me!"

"I do *love* a girl with a fiery temper," he taunted, downing another shot from behind her.

Is there a never-ending supply of shots lined up behind me? she thought. *Cause I sure could use one right about now!*

She stole a look at the stage. AJ had noticed she was cornered by this imbecile. He was in the middle of a song though, and could hardly dive off the stage and ride up to her on a white horse and save her from this big bad troll. She almost imperceptibly shook her head at him. Concern furrowed his brow. Ignoring her, he waited for the next pause in lyrics and whistled in the direction of their table.

Probably to Jeremy, she guessed.

She tried to mouth, "I'm fine!" at him, but this delayed her in escaping the offending visitor – she still didn't know what to call him. *Asshole seems appropriate. Let's call him asshole* – had moved his hand and was trying to insert it between her thighs. Disbelief and anger flared like gasoline poured on an open flame.

"I TOLD YOU TO TAKE YOUR FUCKING HANDS OFF ME!" she yelled, as she lifted her knee, hard, and struck him squarely in the groin. As he doubled over, she grabbed him by the scruff of his neck and kneed him again in the face. "No means no, asshole. Consent is key. And you definitely don't fucking have it."

He slumped onto the floor, hissing in pain as he gripped his groin. Glancing to her now-open side she saw

Jeremy standing there, poised to intervene. She held out her hand to signal that she had things under control. She turned on her heel and headed for the door, not looking back. Once she opened the doors, she ran. She didn't stop until she couldn't run anymore. She bent over to catch her breath and throw up. *Christ, I'm so unfit*, she thought glumly, *Not the time to berate yourself for being unfit, Lisa.*

What about for running away from every overwhelming situation? Can we talk about that right now?

Nope.

Fine. Let's get to breathing, cause you sound like you're going to pass out any second.

She sat down on a nearby bench and hugged her legs to her body. She cried. This wasn't the first time someone had attempted to assault her, but it was the first time she had fought back. She sat, sobbing quietly and trying to steady her breathing as her tears fell.

Shit girl, you sure do cry a lot in America.

She quickly started to get chilly, but she didn't move. She just sat there, staring into the night. Hearing footsteps behind her, she still didn't move. She knew it was Jeremy. AJ was either reluctantly finishing the set, or beating the ever-living crap out of the guy she had left in a heap on the floor.

"Hey," he said. She could tell he felt uncomfortable.

"Hi," she answered softly.

"He's nearly done," he told her. He clearly had no

idea what to say to her and was looking more than a little uncomfortable. "Did he hurt you?"

She shook her head.

"I'm here!" AJ shouted from behind Jeremy.

"Talk to you later, yeah, Lis?" Jeremy gave her shoulder a little squeeze. "You done good."

"I'm sorry I wasn't there," he whispered through her hair as he pulled her to him and wrapped her tightly in his arms.

"It's ok," she choked, "I could handle it. He just pissed me off. You can't play tomorrow night, AJ," she warned. "You *need* to sit this one out. Please, AJ!" she shrieked, not realizing how close to hysteria she had been.

"Babe, I'll be fine," he assured her. "I can handle him."

"But he has it in for you, and now I embarrassed him in the bar. He probably knows I'm with you, and he's gonna be even more wound up!"

"I couldn't really see what was going on, but Jer said you *really* kicked his ass, babe," he smiled. "I was very proud of you," he kissed her forehead, "but please, try not to worry. I promise I'll be fine."

"You can't break promises, you know?" she asked weakly.

"I know," he kissed her again.

"Did you hit him?"

"No ma'am, you did a good enough job. I didn't need to."

"Liar! You mean you wanted to kick his ass some

more, but Chelsea or someone told you to forget about him and come find me?"

She could tell, even in the dark, that color was filling his cheeks. "You know me too well," he replied as he kissed her yet again. "Do you want to file a police report?" he asked her seriously.

She shook her head.

"You sure?"

She nodded.

"You can stop running, you know?" he spoke softly as he looked into her eyes.

"What do you mean?"

"I mean you're a part of my life here, Lis, you don't need to run."

Seems someone else has noticed I keep bolting away from awkward stuff.

"I was scared and embarrassed...I don't like causing a scene. I'm not supposed to be your girlfriend." She took a breath, realizing she was justifying herself and yet couldn't stop it. "I guess I haven't quite figured out how to behave in public with you yet. I knew you'd follow and I knew I couldn't fall apart in your arms in the bar. I didn't want your friends to see me upset. I didn't want any more trouble than had already been caused."

"Shhhh..." he soothed, stroking her cheek. "You don't need to explain yourself to me. I love you. I want to be with you. My friends know the truth about Britt, and about you. You don't need to bite your tongue or hold back. My friends are a welcoming bunch, they'll love you 'cause I love you. They'll protect you, because it's just what they do. You'll be part of the family. It's a tight-knit group to crack from the outside, but you're with me, and that's enough for them. If you want it, it's there. It's up to you, Lis. You can be as involved as you'd like in my life, the door is open. But, as far as everyone is concerned, you're here for the long-haul. I know you, you're a fighter. You're the strongest person I know. And you may feel like you *need* to run away, to hide who you really are from me, and from my friends, and it's ok if you do. But I need you to know that it's ok to run towards us, too. I'm not going anywhere. I am yours. My sister already likes you more than she likes me. The others likely will, too. But you need to be yourself. Speak up if you're hurt or angry, and don't shy away from them. I already know who you are and I'm ready for the rest of the people in my life to know the strong, spunky and outspoken Irish badass I fell in love with. Just be you."

Tears trickled down her face as she buried herself in the front of his shoulder. She was clinging to him tightly.

"I'm struggling, AJ. It's a lot to process. I feel like everyone's waiting for me to fall apart, but I already am falling apart inside. This isn't quite how I imagined our life to be once I stepped off the plane and met your sister."

"I know and I'm so sorry for that. It's ok to be overwhelmed and to feel like you don't know which way is up. You don't have to put on a brave face for the team, or my family, or even for me. I'm not ok with being fake-married right now, either. It's ok to feel the way you're feeling. You don't need to hide or run away."

"Thank you for always being there to dry my tears," she told him between sniffles.

"Well, since I'm largely the cause of them, it's the least I can do," he half-joked. "Plus, I'm kinda hoping you'll dry mine someday, when I need you to."

"Deal," she answered, and kissed him through her tears.

Chapter 22

The game was even more intense than the night before. Penalties were being called all across the ice, for both teams. The Chargers were lacking in power-play strength, but their penalty-kill was solid - so far, at least. It was the middle of the second period, and AJ and Jeremy were doing their thing. Jeremy sent the puck behind Mike's net where AJ was waiting. Lisa saw it first, a split second too late, and, before she realized, she was on her feet screaming – panic filling her voice.

"AJ! LOOK OUT!"

Three had gotten onto the ice without AJ noticing. She hadn't noticed either. He spotted AJ deep behind the net and skated straight towards him, his stick raised high. AJ had his back to him and didn't see it coming. She wasn't sure if anyone but her actually saw what she was seeing. AJ cleared the puck, but his skate got momentarily stuck between the boards and the ice somehow. Everyone's attention was on the puck, except AJ's as he was trying to get his skate free, and hers. Her attention was firmly on the asshole ploughing towards her boyfriend with his stick higher than it should be. It took only seconds.

Her scream came too late, people turned to look at her in shock as her worst nightmare unfolded before her eyes. She saw AJ flinch at the sound of her piercing scream, hesitated for just a second, and in that second everything changed. Three was skating towards him with a clear purpose and at a phenomenal pace. It all happened so fast. His stick met with AJ's shoulder and AJ crashed head-first into the plexi-glass, collapsing into a heap on the ice.

The whistle blew and there was silence.

"NOOO!" she screamed. She was already making her way through the crowd towards the ice. AJ wasn't moving. Nobody moved for what felt like minutes, then there was a blur of motion as players and officials swarmed around AJ's still body on the ice. She saw the in-house medical team crossing the ice and, in her periphery, noted a couple members of Three's team escorting him to the tunnel and away from the scene unfolding in front of her eyes.

She tried to climb over the barrier ,but one of the staff stopped her.

"You can't come on the ice, ma'am," he told her.

"But – he's...he's..." she replied hot tears burning at her eyes. Her voice cracked.

"You can't come on the ice, ma'am," he repeated; though his voice sounded compassionate, his eyes showed he wouldn't be letting her past.

"But-"

"No ma'am," he cut her off.

She saw Jeremy appear behind the steward. "Please?" she pleaded with him.

"You can't, Lis. I'm sorry."

She knew it wasn't really the *done thing,* not at all, but in that moment, she couldn't have cared less what accepted game etiquette was. AJ was lying still on the ice, and she needed to get to him. From where she stood, she saw what she guessed was blood speckling the ice. She felt nauseous and light-headed, but she could hardly throw-up on the ice in front of a rink-full of people, so she took a deep breath, looked at Jeremy and asked him what she should do.

"He'll be ok," Jeremy told her with a confidence she wasn't quite sure he felt.

She nodded, swallowing deeply and asked again what she could do. She wanted to touch him, but she knew until medical help came, no one should move him. Every part of her wanted to push past Jeremy and the stubborn steward and get to her boy on the ice.

"Did someone call an ambulance?" she asked.

"Yeah, it should be here any minute."

"Ok, it just feels like it's taking so long," she replied quietly, hugging herself tightly as the cold of the arena started to hit her despite her layers.

"I know, but they're coming," he assured her.

She nodded silently, her gaze returning to her unconscious boyfriend.

"Can I ride with him to the hospital?" she asked hopefully.

"I think so."

"Where did he go?"

"Who?" Jeremy queried.

"The asshole who did this," she replied curtly.

"Locker room, I'd guess. There's enough going on without a brawl breaking out," he answered bitterly.

Within minutes the ambulance crew was on the ice. They put on a neck-brace and rolled him carefully onto a stretcher. Jeremy told her where to go to meet the ambulance and the stubborn steward kindly offered to show her a short cut through the employees-only area. She was allowed to ride in the ambulance with him but only if she didn't get in their way and sat quietly. She called Ana to tell her what had happened and have her meet them at the hospital.

They've probably got a system in place for these kinds of situations, but I really just need to feel like I'm doing SOMETHING helpful right now.

She asked Chelsea to stop at AJ's for an overnight bag and meet them at the hospital so there was a car at the hospital to take them all home once AJ had been checked over.

Ever the optimist! she thought, as they got AJ settled in the back of the ambulance and took off at an alarming speed. The siren was louder than she'd expected it to be, but it was dulled by the panic ringing in her ears.

She sat quietly in the back of the ambulance, staying out of the EMTs' way and only talking to answer their questions as best she could.

When they got to hospital, they immediately whisked AJ away from her. The EMTs had called ahead and she knew the OR had been prepped – just in case. AJ had been hooked up to an IV and cut out of his pads and clothes in the back of the ambulance. They suspected pressure on his brain from knocking his head on the plexi; risks included a clot, seizure, brain damage. *Don't make an inappropriate joke about his brain already being damaged. Don't make an inappropriate joke about his brain already being damaged.* A hysterical half-giggle, half-wail escaped her as she stood holding his bloody jersey and staring at the double doors they wheeled him through, thinking that she didn't even get to give him a kiss, or tell him to keep his stick on the ice.

She heard the doors open behind her, and turned to find Ana. When Ana saw the cut shirt covered in her brothers' blood, she burst into tears. *Keep it together, Lis. Be strong,* she instructed herself as her sympathetic-crying reaction threatened to kick-in. Chelsea arrived soon after. As Ana stood crying, Lisa asked if she had called her parents to tell them what had happened.

"Can you do it? Please?" she asked through heaving sobs. "I can't".

"Of course," she replied. *I guess I could ask Jeremy after the game, but he would probably just say something awkwardly inappropriate and they need to know right away.*

A nurse appeared to tell them that AJ had been taken into surgery and Lisa excused herself to go and talk to

AJ's parents for the first time.

How does a person call their boyfriend's parents and tell them their son is in emergency surgery and may not survive? She'd both seen enough Grey's Anatomy and had enough warnings from her parents throughout her life to know that head injuries could be very dangerous.

AJ may not make it out of surgery, she thought as she pulled her phone out of her pocket. *I wonder if an Alabaman version of McDreamy from Grey's is in the OR working on him right now,* she wondered as she dialed from a piece of paper Ana had scribbled their number on.

What an odd thing for someone whose boyfriend is in critical condition to think. You're totally losing it, Lis.

Keep it together, she repeated to herself.

Sometimes in these kinds of situations she went to pieces, but, for the most part, she was the one everyone relied on and turned to for support. She was the one who kept a cool head. Right now, her head felt full of cotton wool, and anything but cool.

Stop stalling, call his parents. At least you're not a sobbing mess yet. Call them and tell them, before the sobbing. They need to know. If you don't tell them, some strange nurse will. When you're done, go ask for an update.

She took a deep breath and hit the call button. It rang once, twice, and half-way through the third ring,

"Hello?"

Shit. How do I tell this woman her son is in the

hospital with his head open? Ok, Ok, breathe. Suck it up she scolded herself. She sucked in a slow breath, realizing that his mom had repeated her "Hello?"

"Hello, is that Mrs. Williams?"

"Speaking."

"Hello Mrs. Williams, my name is Lisa, I'm-."

"Oh Lisa! How are you?"

"I'm fine, thank you, Mrs. Williams, but I'm calling about AJ, I have some bad news. There's been an accident." Her voice was shaking, laced with fear and uncertainty. She knew his mother could hear it, too.

She heard his mom take in a long, slow breath of her own before asking,

"What happened, Lisa?"

Knowing that it wasn't really the time to get into great detail about what happened, Lisa simply told her that her son had sustained a head injury from an accident during the game and that she and his father should come as soon as they could. She waited for his mom to respond; a heavy silence hung between them.

"Mrs. Williams?" Lisa prodded, thinking perhaps she'd lost the call somehow. She glanced at the screen and saw the call timer continue to tick. She heard his mom take a deep breath before she answered.

"We'll be there as soon as we can."

"Yes ma'am, I'll let Ana know." Lisa replied slowly, confused at his mother's lack of reaction. *Shock perhaps?* During their email exchanges, AJ had told her that his mother had never really been an "emotional" mother.

He said she was often seen as a little standoffish and seemingly unflappable. He'd only seen her cry a couple times during his life, though he had also recounted times where her love for him was more than evident. AJ had told Lisa that if his mother hadn't been a lawyer, he could have totally imagined her as a doctor; she cared for people, but had a knack for detaching herself from the severity of situations and remaining objective in order to get the job at hand done. Despite being aware of this, Lisa expected at least some form of initial reaction from the woman. But none came.

"Thank you for calling us, Lisa, it can't have been easy for you."

"Not really," she answered honestly, "but Ana's a bit of a mess and I thought you'd prefer to hear it from someone he knows rather than a complete stranger. I thought about having Jeremy call, but he'd probably have cracked a dumb joke. You know how he can be when he's uncomfortable."

"I do indeed. Thanks again, we'll see you soon."

"See you."

Just before she ended the call, she heard AJ's mom screaming for his dad to come to wherever she was in the house.

Poor woman.

Putting the phone back into her pocket, she rested her head against the wall beside her. Her mind was racing and her chest was tight with emotions. All of the "usual" ones were present: guilt, anger, denial, guilt...that one was persistent. She felt guilty. Guilty about the fight in the bar, guilty that she didn't recognize what was happening a moment sooner, guilty that she even considered for a moment that AJ may not survive surgery. *Why am I not a crying mess?* She questioned herself aloud.

You're in shock, her mind answered. *It'll come.*

Chapter 23

Feeling claustrophobic, Lisa stepped outside the hospital for a moment. She stood taking in a couple deep breaths and trying to center herself a bit. It was dark and cool. Looking up at the Alabama night sky, she hugged herself and said a silent prayer to whatever god was listening. *Please don't let him die. Please, please, please let him live.*

Walking back inside, not knowing how long she'd been gone, she headed to the nurses' station. Four nurses sat working. A couple had their heads buried in files and paperwork, one was on the phone and another was swearing under her breath at her computer. Lisa cleared her throat in an attempt to get someone's attention.

"May I help you?" one of them asked.

"Can you tell me how AJ Williams is doing in surgery, please?" She shuddered at the word surgery.

"Are you his immediate family?"

"No, but-"

"Well I'm afraid I cannot give out any information."

"But-"

"I'm sorry."

"But-"

"Those are the rules." The nurse's impatience with this foreigner was evident. She clearly wanted to return to whatever it was that she'd been doing. Perhaps she'd had a long and busy day. Perhaps she was just a generally unfriendly person – *though, if that were true, she's surely gone into the wrong career*, Lisa thought. *Plus, I've had a long and very bad day, too, and I'm still being polite.*

"Would you *please* let me finish *one* sentence?" she snapped. Her game-face was starting to show cracks and she was not in the mood for some ill-mannered nurse. Before she realized it, she was reading this nurse the riot-act.

"I am not some random person off the street. I'm his girlfriend. I'm not asking you for his social security number – I already know it. I know his home address, his birthday, and more than any of you will ever know about the man. And, if I were trying to steal his identity, I'm a penis short and two boobs extra. I came in the ambulance with him, clutching his blood-stained hockey jersey from a head injury. I'm not asking for you to go into the OR, interrupt the surgeon and ask him complicated medical questions. I'm simply asking for an update. Is my boyfriend still alive? For example. How long is the surgery expected to last? Maybe stretching to asking his chances of survival and recovery had you not been an insufferable mare and cut me off every time I opened my damn mouth. However, go back to your game of solitaire or whatever it is that's so much more important than common courtesy, and I'll go back to a room full of folks who have no fucking clue what you people are doing to their loved one."

Take that! she thought triumphantly. Then panic struck. *Girlfriend. I said girlfriend. Shit. He's married and not supposed to have a girlfriend. Shit. Shit. Shit.*

Never mind that. You called her an insufferable mare! I mean, you're not wrong or anything, but jeez, talk about crossing a line!

"Is there a problem here?"

Spinning to face the new addition to the conversation, Lisa snapped at him, too. *In for a penny, in for a pound, eh?*

"Actually, yes, there is. This incredibly rude nurse won't give me *any* information."

"Are you his immediate family?"

"No, bu-"

"Well then, I'm afraid we can't give out information about a patient to a person who is not direct family.

That did it.

"DOES ANYBODY IN THIS DAMN HOSPITAL LET YOU FINISH YOUR SENTENCES?"

They all watched her, mouths agape.

"He is lying on an operating table with his skull cracked open. His parents are on their way from Canada, his sister is a crying-mess if someone hasn't already sedated her. His team probably have to finish their game on the ice, and I'm keeping it together by a thread. One thread, which is unravelling pretty quickly due to you guys being a royal pain in my ass. And I *need* to keep my shit together."

She paused for a quick breath, but hurried ahead before anyone else cut her off. By this point, she didn't care *who* knew that she was his girlfriend. She wanted answers.

"I am not asking for missile codes to the White House, or trade secrets. I'm not asking you to describe, in painful detail the procedure they're doing on him right now. I'm asking if his heart is still pumping blood around his body and how long it will be before the people who love him can sit next to him, hold his hand, and give him an ear-bending for scaring the crap out of us. If none of you can answer any of those questions, then please find someone who can!"

Her face was hot and wet with tears. She didn't remember them starting, but now they wouldn't stop. She felt an arm around her shoulders. Jeremy was standing in front of her, still in his hockey gear – minus the skates. He wrapped his arms around her and let her cry.

"It's ok," he soothed, "let it out."

And then it all hit her; the events of the night caught up with her and she was completely overcome with emotion.

That didn't take long, she thought as she let herself shed tears into Jeremy's jersey. *What the hell? Is this the same guy you were pissed at for breathing the same air as you only a couple weeks ago?* She almost laughed at the thought of her and Jeremy potentially becoming friends. Who'd have thought? *Wait until AJ hears this!* she thought cracking a smile. She realized Jeremy was talking to the nursing staff, so she stepped back and wiped her face with her hands.

"Can you just tell us that he's still alive, please?" his voice was filled with emotion.

"And you are?"

"His best friend."

"We can't give either of you any information," the new guy to the party, who was apparently a doctor, repeated.

"Maybe not," a new voice entered the conversation. Ana.

"But you *can* give *me* the information."

"And *you* are?" he repeated.

"Ana Williams. The aforementioned *sister.* Is that family enough for you people? I'm also giving explicit permission for either of these two. If they have any questions needing answered, you have my family's permission to answer them. They are also allowed to see him as though they were immediate family," she paused, "because they are. Ok?"

The doctor nodded.

Lisa's eyes welled up again. She fought back tears as Britt burst through the door. She'd been crying and was out of breath. "Where?" she began between heavy breaths, "is he?" she doubled over to catch her breath.

"Doctor?" prodded Ana.

"He's still in surgery. He should be out within the next couple of hours. He'll be in recovery for a while. You can all see him there," he finished.

"Thank you," Ana snapped rudely and turned on her heel to return to the family room. She was clearly in no mood to "people". *Kinda glad I was the one who told his parents.*

Chelsea was in the family room waiting for them. "How you holding up, Irish?"

"Not great," Lisa replied, giving her friend a sad smile. "Just had a minor meltdown to Jeremy of all people, after a major blow-up at a doctor and a bunch of nurses. At this rate, I'll be in psych by sunrise!"

Chelsea walked over to her friend and hugged her. The tears came again. "I *know* he'll be fine," sobbed Lisa, "I do. I *feel* he'll be fine. But, what if I'm wrong?" Chelsea's shoulder was fast damp with Lisa's tears. "What if he doesn't wake up, Chels?" Her voice was filled with anguish and fear.

Chapter 24

Lisa and Chelsea stood hugging long after the others came in to join them in the family room. It felt like Lisa was waiting forever. Her tears had stopped. She knew AJ wouldn't want her crying, but she also knew he'd understand it. His parents would be there soon and despite what AJ had told her the night before, she felt as though she had to be strong, positive and confident, for AJ's sake and for his family and his friends. She couldn't lose hope. She *wouldn't* lose hope. They had been waiting for six hours. The doctor had told them it wouldn't take more than five.

I'd rather they do it right the first time, than mess up and need to go in again, she reassured herself for the hundred thousandth time. AJ's parents wouldn't be there for a few more hours, and she had resolved to take care of Ana at least until then. She was taking it pretty badly, which Lisa understood, but it also kind of confused her. This wasn't the first time he'd succumbed to injury. Lisa always assumed that it would get easier with time, watching AJ getting hurt on the ice. If she had a dollar for every time someone had said, "It's nothing," or "He'll be fine, it's just a scratch," she'd be rich by now, and she'd only known him seven months.

I guess they all just assumed it would always be "nothing" or a "scratch," but this time was a bit more than a scratch. She felt anger boiling in her stomach again – it was the one emotion she was struggling to control. It was also the strongest. She wanted to hurt the asshole who did this to the man she loved. She wanted to make him hurt like AJ was hurting. Like she was hurting. Like every other person in the room around her was hurting.

She was grinding her teeth. She walked to the window and stood sideways, still able to keep an eye on the room, but also buying herself the option of hiding her face and crying if she needed to. She stood in silence. Ana stretched out her legs and bent towards her ankles.

She obviously feels as stiff and tense as I do.

"We should have asked them to fix his shoulder while they were in there," Lisa joked.

"No kidding," giggled Ana. It was good to see her smile.

The door opened. It was Jared and Lindsay, friends of AJ's and Jeremy's. Despite not being able to do anything but sit together, Lisa understood the draw of coming to wait in the family room of the hospital. They said hi to her and sat next to Britt, who was pale, quiet and not at all the bubbly girl she'd met previously. Lisa wasn't quite sure how to behave. Everyone in the room knew the truth about Britt and AJ, they all knew Lisa was his girlfriend, but Britt had known him much, much longer and loved him too, in her own way. Lisa felt conflicted. *Do I take a back seat and let Britt, the best friend/wife "lead"? Or do I assert myself as his girlfriend? He told me last night to assert myself, but I'm really not sure he said that with something like this in mind.*

Her instinct was to lead, but she was open to following Britt's lead if she needed to.

Mike and a few of the other guys from the team had trickled in over the last few hours. At, first she was a little grumpy and wanted to kick "non-essential" people out with a promise that she'd update them all when he got out of surgery, until she realized that there was a deep comfort in all of these people who loved AJ sitting together, even when they all sat in worried silence. It was a powerful feeling. Each addition to the group brought with it a fresh breath of strength for everyone to draw from. Some of the boys still had their jerseys on, and a few, including Jeremy, hadn't taken the time to shower. They'd just come straight to the hospital, bringing with them their distinct "hockey boy funk," which was currently percolating in the small waiting room.

Ana sat up, looked at Lisa and stood. The two of them walked towards the surgeon who had arrived a couple steps behind Jared and Lindsay.

"Is he-" Ana started, her lip quivered, and Lisa could see tears brimming in her eyes. "Will he be ok?" she asked shakily. Lisa grabbed her hand and squeezed it gently.

“Would you like to step outside to discuss his condition?” he asked her, frustratingly respecting the confines of patient confidentiality.

“No, thank you. You can speak freely here. Please?”

“As you wish. He’s not out of the woods just yet, but the surgery went as expected. He may not wake up for a few days.”

“You mean,” she paused, confused, “he’s in a coma?”

The surgeon nodded slowly.

“How can he be in a coma, yet you say it’s looking good that he’ll wake up soon?” there was a distinct edge of hysteria to Ana’s voice.

“We have high hopes he’ll wake up,” he told her gently.

“But there’s a chance he won’t?” it was Lisa’s turn to ask a question.

He nodded.

“Ok,” Lisa said, more to Ana than anyone else. She squeezed her hand again, “Let’s think positive. He’s out of a successful surgery and the doctors think he’s going to wake up. It’s AJ, Ana. You know how much of a fighter he is.” She winced at her own poor choice of words. “You know what I mean. He won’t give up on himself, on life, and he needs us to not give up on him, either. You should totally give him shit for making you worry like this, ok?”

“Ok,” Ana replied, unsure.

“He’s in recovery. You can see him if you’d like,” the doctor told Ana.

"Ok," she answered again, and they followed the surgeon towards the recovery room.

"You go in first," Lisa told her. "I'll wait here. Take as long as you need to. Talk to him. I'm sure he'll hear you," she encouraged.

Nodding, Ana pushed through the swinging doors, reemerging fifteen minutes later tear-streaked and pale. The two hugged.

"That was quick. You can stay with him for as long as you want to, Ana. No one is rushing you," Lisa urged.

Ana shook her head.

"Sure?"

"Yeah, I'm going back to the others. I can't see him like that. It's just too hard. The bandages, the wires and tubes – I just can't," she wailed, hugging Lisa. As Ana made her way back to the family room, Lisa heard her sobs as she walked.

Waiting for Ana to walk out of sight, her breathing quickened. Her heart was sort of caught between her chest and her throat. Her palms were sticky as she walked forward and pushed open the door to his room.

Chapter 25

This is it, Lisa told herself. Stay strong. But, as she walked through those double doors, she felt anything but strong. Swallowing hard, she approached the bed. AJ was so still and looked so small, hooked up to a bunch of machines.

"You're so pale, AJ," she whispered aloud. She stood next to his bed and stroked his hair back from his forehead so she could kiss him. "You need a haircut, too. You're getting a little shaggy," she joked. She stood gazing at him, taking him in for a few minutes, before she dragged a chair close to the bed and sat, holding his hand.

Sitting in silence she watched him, letting the minutes tick by. She prayed silently. She wasn't overly religious, but having been raised an Irish Catholic, she believed there was a higher being pulling the strings. At this moment, she didn't like how the string was being pulled, and she gave a silent plea that it would stop.

The nuns from school would be proud. She rolled her eyes at herself.

Taking his hand up to her mouth, she kissed his knuckles. As tears fell, she spoke to him. Her voice wobbled and cracked, but she remembered reading somewhere that coma patients can respond to familiar voices, and she knew he was listening to her.

I'm pretty sure that was Grey's Anatomy again, Lis.

"You played so good tonight, Pim. I was proud of you. Even Jeremy was proud of you," she paused, pulled the blankets up a little on his chest.

"AJ-" she began, her voice wavering, "You have to wake up for me, you hear? You *have* to. Please?" She was pleading with him, in tears, "You promised me you would be ok. You *promised*! You don't break promises, Pim, you can't!" she gasped between sobs.

"I know you're a fighter. I know you're going to wake up, I do. I have faith in you babe. But I'm so scared you're going to leave me. You can't die on me, AJ, you just can't, ok? Because I say so. Now that I've finally met you, I don't want to let you go. I want to be with you, in every sense of the word. I want to wake up in the morning and have you run your hands through my hair. I want to make breakfast in the kitchen and rub pancake batter on your nose. I want to play chess with you, 'cause even though I suck at chess, I like it, and I like scrabble too. Let's play scrabble and make up words that don't exist, but get points for them anyway because it's sickeningly cute. I want to sing with you, and play Twister with you. I want to rub your shoulders after a game. I want to sit up all night talking to you about silly things, or where we're going to spend our retirement when the kids are all grown up, or what color we're going to decorate the living room. Then I want to decorate the living room and have a random paint fight where we'll end up covered in paint that won't come off and screwing on the floor!

I want to watch you play hockey, and scream at the ref when you're put in the box for being a butt-head, but I'll stand up for you anyway, because you're mine, and because he's a ref. I want to be waiting outside the locker room and walk past the puck bunnies, who'll be glaring at me because you're with me.

I want to watch the sun rise and set with you.

I want to lie at opposite ends of the sofa and watch random films, and throw pillows at you for checking out the girls. I want to meet your parents, in circumstances that don't involve you lying in a coma. I want to meet your extended family – I want to be your official, proper, exclusive girlfriend. And then I want to be more than that. And I want to argue about what color flowers we will have, or what kind of cake. And then what kids names we will pick, and no, Gretzky isn't an acceptable name for our children.

In the grand scheme of things, I've known you practically no time at all. A year? And I'm crazy about you, AJ. When I'm in Ireland, I wake up wondering how you're sleeping. When I'm eating, I wonder if you'd like it, or what you'll be eating when it's your meal time. When I'm watching hockey and I don't understand something, I want you to patronize me – with an S, not a zed, nor a zee, and repeat yourself six times over until I understand it. I want to know you better than you know yourself, know when you're sick and what you're thinking before you do. I want to look into your eyes and see your soul, AJ. I want to see the world with you and then go back over it and find stuff we missed. I want to talk about politics, and music, and films, and pretend to sulk at you for completely stupid reasons. I want to call you pet names and embarrass you in front of your friends, and surprise you on your birthday, and have you all to myself sometimes – without your friends barging in and finding us lying on the floor. But, most of all? Right now, I just want to be in your arms.

So, you have to wake up, AJ. You just *have* to! Please?"

She was exhausted from baring her soul, her voice was hoarse and heavy. The tears had stopped, her chest ached and, sensing she and AJ weren't alone in the room, she glanced at the door. Jeremy was standing propped against the doorframe, arms crossed and his face was filled with worry and concern.

"How long have you been standing there?" she asked him, suddenly embarrassed.

"Long enough," he smiled.

"How long?" she repeated, "I didn't hear the door open."

"I'm sorry," he said, "I heard most of it, I didn't mean to eavesdrop, but I didn't want to interrupt you." He looked terribly guilty. "It sounded like you needed to get it off your chest".

"It's ok," she told him, blushing. "It's not like you

didn't know it already," she said dismissively. "Apparently I have an I'M IN LOVE tattoo somewhere that everyone can see. Stupid thing. I wish I could find it and cover it up. I don't like being quite so transparent!

He laughed again, moved to the opposite side of the bed and pulled up a chair so he was facing her. "Well, I had my suspicions." He kicked off his shoes and put his feet up on the bed beside AJ, leaning back in his chair. "But I don't think I really needed to know that kind of detail!" He grinned at her.

"If you tell *anyone-*"she warned.

"Your secret's safe with me," he assured her, "Well, me and Pim of course."

"You think he knows how I feel?" she asked casually, staring at AJ on the bed.

"Well, yeah, it's pretty obvious Lisa. He knows."

"I hope so," she sighed.

"He does," he repeated firmly. "Trust me, he knows. He feels the same, you know that, right?"

She nodded, though she must have looked unsure.

"Dude! For reals? He never shuts *up* about you. It's always Lis this, and I gotta tell Lisa that. He's nuts about you. I swear, if he wasn't already fake-married, he'd real-marry you, like, tomorrow."

She nodded again, and glanced at Jeremy to check if he was joking. She could rarely tell.

They sat in silence for a while, her holding AJ's hand and him tilting his chair back on two legs with his ankles crossed at AJ's side.

"He'll wake up," she told him, definitively, after a while.

"I know," he agreed. "He's got a lot to wake up for!" He smiled.

"Yeah, I mean, who would want to miss you and me sitting in a room together having an actual, civilized conversation?" she joked.

Jeremy groaned and rolled his eyes.

"Does this mean, we're-" he swallowed hard, and whispered, "friends?" He said the word as though it tasted bitter in his mouth, then he giggled.

She looked stunned.

"Oh my gosh!" she exclaimed. "I'm friends with Jeremy? What kind of bizarre world is this?"

They laughed and a comfortable silence descended on the room again.

"You should go home and get some sleep, Lis," he told her.

"I'm fine," she replied.

"Lis-"

"I'm *fine,*" she replied through gritted teeth.

"But you need sleep!"

"We *all* need sleep. Everyone has been here the same length of time, Jer. I'm not leaving."

"You have to leave sometime."

"I'm not leaving until he wakes up," she repeated.

He looked at her skeptically.

"I'm serious," she continued. "I'll sleep here on this very chair if I have to. Or the floor, even. But I'm not leaving his side until he wakes up, and no one is going to move me!"

"But you need your rest, Lis. I have to look out for you while he's sleeping. Because when he wakes up, he'll be pissed if no one looked after you for him. And as his best friend, that job falls to me. Do you want me to get my ass kicked? Wait, don't answer that. Please, just consider it."

"Jeremy, you won't win on this one," she warned.

"Damn stubborn Irish," he grumbled.

"Did you really expect me to leave him?" she challenged.

"Not really, no, but I have to be able to say in good conscience that I tried! I'll probably be here a lot, too. And Ana," he added.

Nodding, she said, "And his parents."

"Yeah, that's not going to be fun."

"You're not such a hoser after all, you know?" she thought out loud.

"Ok, now that's just going too far! I have a reputation to protect! Take it back!" he joked, but then added, "You're not so bad yourself. Now, let's stop the mushy shit. I'm going to get a drink from the vending machine – you want anything?"

"Please. I'll take a diet and some crisps."

"You mean chips?" he queried.

"Yes, but you're Canadian – don't Canadians have crisps?"

He laughed as he opened the door. "Back in five," he said and left her alone once more with the patient.

Sitting there, Lisa didn't let go of AJ's hand. She talked to him softly until Jeremy came back. As they sat there, she firmly believed he'd wake up, but a shadow of doubt was lingering in the back of her mind trying to fight its way to the foreground. She knew she had to stay strong, to keep hoping. No matter what the doctors told her, he was going to wake up and get better, and she wasn't going to move from his side until he did.

Chapter 26

Lisa hadn't realized it had started raining outside. She loved the rain and its methodical, therapeutic pattering on the window. It calmed her. Jeremy had gone to get an 'overnight' bag with some stuff she'd listed for him to bring back to the hospital for both her and AJ. Chelsea had done a decent first pass, but there were a few things they still needed: The Elite League magazines she'd brought over from Ireland for him to read, some books, her laptop, laptop charger and some more clothes for them both. This hospital trip was apparently going to last longer than the original overnight bag was prepared for.

Britt and Ana had both left sometime after midnight to try and get some sleep. They'd both gone reluctantly, and after much debate. They'd left her strict instructions to call at any time, the moment there was any change – with the assurance they'd both be back the following morning. Lisa just sat and watched AJ and his machines, listening to the pitter patter of the rain.

"You even look good lying there in a coma," she whispered to him, smiling. She stroked his face. "Hospital gowns aren't exactly a look that many people can successfully pull off, AJ. You should be proud of yourself!" she joked.

Stay positive, she drilled over and over in her mind. *If he wakes up and finds you a crying mess, he'll be upset. Stay upbeat and keep up the not-being-funny-but-thinking-you-are-thing, and you'll be set.*

"What do you want to talk about?" she asked quietly, pausing for a minute as if listening to his response. She continued, "You want to sing? Ok, what do you want to sing?"

She thought for a few minutes before deciding. She knew it was likely she'd end up in tears, but if any song could help him wake up, this was likely it. After he'd written this one, his band put AJ's name forward for a local competition as a solo artist. It was his first solo gig, ever, in a local coffee shop, and he'd orchestrated for one of his friends to call Lisa in Ireland and let her listen to his set. While she was on the phone, he sang his song to her. She had no idea he'd written it, or that he was going to sing it, and it was probably at that point in time she suspected that he loved her, too.

It was a special song for both of them. Him, because he'd been having trouble articulating in conversation how he felt for her. And her, because she'd never had someone write a song for her before, not to mention she just thought it was a beautiful song.

"I don't have a guitar, Pim," she told him. "Even if I did, I couldn't play it! I'll have to slow it up a bit, and chances are it'll sound like utter crap, but here goes nothing." She paused momentarily, cleared her throat and started singing, softly.

The song, *All in Good Time,* was an upbeat, peppy number. She tried to keep her spirits up as she sang. It wasn't easy.

"You just call my name if you feel the same for me..."

She was right, by the end of the song, tears trickled down her cheeks. She kissed his hand, what must have been the thousandth kiss since she'd arrived. She could have sworn she felt the pressure change, or AJ twitch, or something. But she convinced herself it was just her being tired and *wanting* to see signs that weren't really there.

"Ah, the coffee shop song," Jeremy's voice startled her, "sorry, I didn't mean to scare you," he told her as he dropped the bag onto the floor next to her feet.

"Damn. You should wear a bell round your neck!" she said as her heart rate returned to normal. "You made me jump feet! Yeah, the coffee shop song, I thought it probably couldn't hurt. Although now I'm not so sure." She laughed, embarrassed that he'd heard her singing.

"You sounded good," he commented, "I know he appreciated it. He loves you singing with him, for him, at him, about him. He loves it all." He smiled.

"He's biased," she blushed.

"Eesh. You two are *so* alike. Can't you just take a compliment and let it lie without having some kind of smart answer to brush it off?"

She went quiet, her face now hot with color. "Sorry," she mumbled. "Thank you."

"Would you mind if I read to him?" she asked.

"Read what? Chick Lit?" he asked, eyebrows raised.

Shrugging, she picked up one of the hockey magazines from the open bag on the floor and showed it to him. He nodded and gave her a small smile. "Be my guest, I'm not up to date on my UK hockey." Jeremy got comfortable in his chair. "To be honest, most of the time I forget y'all have hockey over there."

Lisa gave him a look of faux-disgust. "The Giants are number one, that's all you need to know," she told him flatly.

"But-"

She cut him off. "No buts. Belfast giants, best in the league, the only important team. You dig?"

He nodded, and they laughed. She read the magazine from cover to cover, and, when she had finished, she lifted another one from the table. She never once let go of AJ's hand, and only left his side to use the bathroom. Jeremy fell asleep. She must have done, too, because before she realized, it was morning. She was losing all concept of time. How long had he been in recovery? Where were his parents?

Ana and Britt arrived with Starbucks, and Britt pulled Lisa aside for a chat about AJ's condition and the weirdness of the situation. She told Lisa that she felt strangely awkward and unsure of how to behave around her. Lisa confessed to feeling similarly uncomfortable and felt immediately better for having spoken to her. Britt had confided in her that as outgoing and confident as she seemed, she went to pieces in a crisis. "It's why I'm so quiet," she told her. "I don't really mean to be. I want to be encouraging and supportive, of course I do, I just can't stop thinking about what will happen if he dies," she choked. "He's like a brother to me."

I guess I can add comforting the wife of my unconscious boyfriend to the list of things I never thought I'd have to do, Lisa thought to herself. "You don't always have to be strong," she told Britt. "At least that's what AJ told me the other night. It's ok to fall to pieces. It's ok that we both love him – in different ways, of course – it's just not ok to give up hope altogether."

Drying her eyes, Britt gave Lisa a quick hug and thanked her for the chat. She suspected Britt felt better about things, just as she did, and while there was no real air to clear between the two of them, she felt like they were a more united front now. Lisa's heart hurt for Britt; she couldn't imagine what state she'd be in if it were Chelsea lying on that bed.

Probably in a similar state to right now.

When Lisa had finished her hot chocolate and shoved half a muffin in her mouth, the nurse showed her where she could have a shower. *This wouldn't happen in a hospital in Ireland,* she thought, feeling very fortunate to be allowed to stay with him as much as she had.

Feeling a little better, Lisa returned to the room and kissed AJ's forehead lightly. Turning to sit down, she realized there was a new person in the room. He looked vaguely familiar, but she couldn't quite place him. He took her hand, smiling warmly,

"You," he started as he shook her hand, "must be the Irish girl," he said grinning. Even his voice was familiar.

How do I know this guy? she thought to herself.

"That would be me," she said, returning his smile.

"I'm Brad." He added.

"Oh my GOSH! Why didn't you say so?" she exclaimed, catching him in a hug. "It's about bloody time we met!" she added. When she finally let him go, he laughed.

Brad and AJ were long-time friends, he didn't play hockey, but did play the guitar and was in AJ's first ever band. It didn't last long, according to AJ. Brad was too much of a free spirit to be pinned down by a band, yet he was always *there*. They didn't talk all the time, but when they dipped in and out, or hung out together, it was like old times. AJ often told her that he thought of Brad as a brother, that dependable person you could call at any hour of the day or night and he'd just be there. She'd talked to Brad a couple times online, but he was as inconsistent online as he was in real life. That said, she enjoyed talking to him and for some reason, despite being AJ's friend, she felt like she could still talk to him about AJ. The good and the bad. Standing in front of her, he felt more familiar to her than most of the others in the room. It was immediately comforting to her.

"Yeah, well, I'm a busy guy – y'know?" he grinned, "It took Age to fake a coma for me to clear my schedule and come meet you." Lisa shoved him playfully as his face turned more serious. He nodded towards his friend lying in the bed. “How’s our boy doing?”

Looking around the room she asked. “Has no one spoken to you about him yet?”

“They have,” he replied, nodding slightly. “But I want to hear from you. So, how is he?”

She sighed deeply. “He’s sleeping,” she started slowly, acutely aware that everyone in the room was hanging on her every word. “But he’ll wake up and he’ll be fine.” Her voice was strong and confident, and this time she really and truly believed he would be.

“You think?” he quizzed her.

“Yep,” she nodded emphatically. “I do.” She sat on the chair next to his bed. “If nothing else, he’ll want to pummel all kinds of crap out of the asshole that put him in here.” She grinned.

“True story,” Brad nodded in agreement.

“That’s kinda his job. I’d make a terrible enforcer, and I can’t really mess up this pretty face by fighting,” chimed in Jeremy.

“But seriously you guys,” she was now addressing the whole room. “He’ll be fine. He’ll wake up and go back to being regular Pim, or Age, or whatever you people are calling him this week.” Pausing for a moment she surveyed the group. They all looked tired. Some looked pale, frightened and unsure. “It’s AJ, guys. He’s a warrior. He’s a Williams. Plus, he’s got Irish blood in him from his granny. He’s made of tough stuff and will be back to himself in no time,” she told them all.

"You sound so *sure*," Britt said cautiously. "The doctors say it's possible that-"

Lisa cut her off. "Don't talk like that in here," she snapped. Her tone was soft, yet commanding. Seeing the look on their faces, she continued, "And no, I'm not in denial, or delirious from tiredness. Doctors are known to be wrong sometimes, you know? Plus, doctors don't know AJ like we know AJ. Like I know him. When has he ever just given up? He'll fight this, and he'll be fine. I can't explain how I know. But I do. I just, I *feel*. He will be fine. It doesn't stop me worrying about him, but I know he'll be ok. And anyone who doesn't needs to keep their opinions and negative juju outside of this room, ok?"

Everyone nodded in agreement. Brad looked at her and nodded. A look of understanding passed between them.

"I can see why you two get along so well," he told her, as he too found a place to sit. "You've got a fiery passion in you, or something." He saw her confused look and rushed to finish his sentence, "I mean, you're like, kindred spirits or something." He looked at Jeremy for help in what he was trying to say.

"He means you're brain twins," Jeremy added.

Shrugging and going a little pink from the attention being focused on her, Lisa sighed. "I love him," she paused and glanced at him lying there, so still and pale, "and you just don't give up on those you love. Plus, he'd never, ever give up on any of us if the tables were turned."

Chapter 27

Lisa had docked her phone into some speakers and turned on the playlist of all the recordings she had of AJ singing. Humming along gently, she wrote a letter home to Aoife. She was alone, it was lunchtime and, once again, she refused to leave when Jeremy and the others offered her a break.

"Have you been here this whole time?" a voice from the doorway asked. Startled, she turned to see who it was that had spoken. She recognized the couple from pictures AJ had sent her.

His parents had arrived at last. A mechanical issue had caused a long delay, then their flight had been cancelled and it had taken them a while to get to Alabama from Ontario.

Oh crap. Answer them!

"I have," she told them.

"It's nice to finally meet you, Lisa," his mom said warmly, extending her hand as she approached; Lisa was still holding AJ's hand.

"It's nice to finally meet you, too, Mrs. Williams," she replied politely as she let go of AJ, shook the woman's hand, and stood to create some space for his mother to sit with him. AJ's dad stayed standing next to the door, while AJ's mom sat carefully on the edge of the bed and angled herself towards AJ. With one hand she put his hand on her lap, and with the other, she gently stroked the side of his face. They sat in silence for a few minutes as she watched her son, lost in thought.

"Call me Cindy," she told Lisa smiling softly, absently wiping away a tear that had trickled down her cheek. "And this is my husband, Art. How's he doing?" she asked indicating to AJ. "We spoke with his nurse on the way in, she said he's stable, but that's not exactly specific. We've had a couple brief updates from Ana since you called and we managed to speak with the surgeon before we boarded the flight. He said the odds of AJ surviving are good, but he was non-committal as to whether he thought he'd wake up or not." Her face displayed concern, fear and tiredness.

"He's good," Lisa assured her. "He'll pull through this."

Cindy smiled knowingly at the Irish girl, who sat holding her son's hand.

Damnit, I hate that look. That's THE look. The 'I know exactly how you feel about my son' look. The 'I've been there and know how you feel' look. The sympathetic look.

"I hear you've been taking care of him," Cindy carried on, ignoring the color that was rising in Lisa's cheeks. Seeing the confused look on her face, Cindy continued, "I've heard you've been singing to him, reading to him, talking to him and just generally looking after him."

"Jeremy has a big mouth-" Lisa began, blushing again.

"Oh! It wasn't Jeremy!" Cindy was smiling, "The nurses said you refuse to leave his side. Thank you."

Lisa nodded. "He needs me," she spoke softly, not knowing why she was embarrassed to say this to his parents, "and I know if the tables were turned, he'd not leave my side. I don't mind sitting with him. Weirdly, I kind of enjoy it. I just wish he was awake to talk back to me," she added, smiling sadly at his parents.

"He knows I'm here though. Plus, it's early days, not even twenty-four hours. I think his body is probably protecting itself. He'll wake up in a day or two – or when he's heard enough of my babbling, he'll wake up just to tell me to shut up!" she smiled.

"Do you really think that?" his father asked. Eyes red and puffy, he looked as though he'd been crying.

I'm sure they've both had their moments since I called, she thought, remembering the hysteria in Cindy's voice when she thought the phone had disconnected after Lisa had first told her about the accident.

She felt like she was being tested. His mother, being a lawyer, was probably able to tell the difference between believing what she was saying and unsubstantiated hope from a mile off, so she stopped, thought about it for a few seconds as she watched AJ sleeping, and nodded slowly.

"I really do. He has too much he wants to accomplish. So much he hasn't done yet. He's not one to give up and walk away leaving doors half-open. He'll wake up." Her eyes stayed resting upon him, avoiding their questioning gaze. She felt a lump rise in her throat and her eyes began to glisten.

"Plus, he has you to wake up for," his father continued.

"Well, yeah. But even if he woke up never again knowing who I was, or never wanting to see me again – I'd just be happy to know he's awake, and that he's ok." Her voice was low, barely above a whisper and she felt a stray tear slip down her nose. "Even if he could never walk again, or skate, or even sing. I just want him awake. Anything else after that, and we'll face it as it comes. Right now, I really just want him to open his eyes."

Silence fell on the trio. Lisa stood up and kissed AJ's forehead gently. Tears were falling more freely. "I'm going to go outside for some air and leave you guys alone for a while," she told them, lifting her handbag and writing pad and heading towards the door.

"You don't have to go you know," his mother's face was filled with compassion.

"I do," she replied.

"We don't mind you being here," his father added.

"I know," she answered, smiling through her tears, "but, you two need your time with him and I need to go outside. He's been encouraging me to increase my vitamin D intake and add some color to my 'SPF-Irish' skin. Will you call me if he wakes up?" she added, letting the door close behind her.

Chapter 28

Time seemed to fly past as Lisa sat on the bench outside. She'd finished her letter to Aoife, written to another friend, Sarah, and had even written one to her family. Despite it being much more efficient to just pick up the phone and drop someone an email, she always enjoyed the more intimate nature of writing a letter. It was tactile. She enjoyed how the pen felt between her fingers and how the pages absorbed the words. Her cheeks were still wet from crying, and there was a deep ache in her chest. Now that she was alone for a while, she could allow the emotion of the previous twenty-four hours to wash over her. Although she truly believed AJ would wake up, she was struck by the sudden fear that she could be wrong.

Questions burned her tormented mind as she sat struggling to control her fear.

I'll cross that bridge if it's ever built, she thought, looking at her watch. She had been gone for just over two hours. Her head felt dizzy and her tummy grumbled. Just as she started to pack up, she saw someone appear next to her and turned to face Ana.

"Hey," her voice was rough.

"Hi," Ana looked at her with raised eyebrows, "you ok?"

Lisa nodded.

"You sure?"

"Yeah. I didn't realize you were here yet."

"Sorry, yeah. Everyone's here. Mom said you needed some alone time and only just let me come to check on you. You look like shit," she added, not unkindly.

"Thanks Ana!" Lisa giggled wiping her eyes. "I just had a bit of an emotional dump."

"Tell me about it," she replied, taking a seat on the bench next to her.

"I – uh-"

"I uh nothing, Lis, come on. Out with it!"

"It's ok. I cried, I panicked, I wrote, I vented, I cried some more, and now I'm ok. I'm back with the being all peppy and positive crap." She smiled.

"Lis...you can talk to me, you know?"

"I know."

"Jeremy said you *almost* started to talk to him, but then you clammed up. He said he heard you talking to Pim, but wouldn't say what he heard. Mom said you were starting to talk to her and dad and then you ran off. You've been avoiding Chelsea like the plague 'cause you know she'll make you talk to her, and now you're alone with me!"

Lisa looked simultaneously amused and confused.

"Am I that transparent? I'm ok, really. It's just hard. I'm in a foreign country. I'm out of my comfort zone and on someone else's turf. I don't know many people. All that's familiar is six hours ahead of me back home. I fly over to meet my internet non-boyfriend, meet his friends, and his sister. Turns out, he's every bit as wonderful as I thought he would be, and so much more. So, I let my defenses come down and think hey, it's totally ok to love this guy and imagine little musical, hockey-playing babies with him. Then BAM! I find out he's married. I fly home on the verge of a mental breakdown, with pieces of my heart on my lap and a *really* annoying yet simultaneously super-sweet air hostess. He flies after me, calms me down, explains some bizarre green-card marriage scenario. I believe him. We fly back. I go to a ball like Cinder-fricken-ella and had the most amazing time ever. I go to watch him do one of the things he loves most and now..." she took a breath, "now he's asleep and won't wake up. He may never wake up. I made an arse of myself in front of the nurses, the doctors, his friends, his sister and, worst of all, his parents – who, might I add, I was not supposed to meet without him being there to help me out and certainly not under *these* circumstances! What if he doesn't wake up, Ana? What if he wakes up and doesn't remember me? What if he can't ever skate again, or walk again, or talk again?"

She stopped, feeling exhausted and hoarse.

"Oh. Ok then. So, nothing much going on with you at all then? To be honest I'm glad to hear you're human after all. I was starting to wonder if you were Wonder Woman or something," Ana said quietly.

"I-"

"Found them!" Chelsea's voice rang out from a short distance away. Glancing around, Lisa spotted Britt, Brad and Jeremy headed towards them.

"You guys get lost?" asked Brad.

"Do we look lost?" Lisa snapped.

"No, but you look like crap," he fired back. She knew he was half-joking and half-concerned but she wasn't in the mood for funnies.

"Cause my married boyfriend is in a coma and I've been out here crying for two hours," she retorted.

Silence.

She was getting used to this silence thing. Her eyes met his, but she looked away quickly as she felt her jaw begin to quiver.

Damnit girl, get it together, she told herself sternly, as she fought the tears streaming down her face.

Brad walked up to where Lisa sat and held his arms out towards her. Getting to her feet, she let him hold her while she cried. She didn't hear the others leave, nor did she know how much time had passed, but when she finished crying, his shirt was pretty wet.

"Well, now I've made an arse out of myself to everyone that matters to him. He's gonna laugh his butt off when he wakes up and hears what a neurotic, crazy girlfriend he has gotten himself." She began to laugh off her embarrassment.

"You haven't made an *arse* of yourself, nor an *ass* of yourself. This is bound to be harder on you than on the rest of us. Though, really, you've only just met the guy, he's been bugging the rest of us for most of his life!" he joked.

She thumped him playfully. "Leave him alone, you. He's sleeping and can't defend himself."

"He doesn't need to," he replied. "You do a pretty good job on his behalf."

She stared at him blankly. "This is a weird experience for me," she told him. "I'm having a conversation with you that doesn't revolve solely around taking the piss out of each other. A similar thing happened with Jeremy, and it's incredibly strange. I'm not sure I'm prepared to cross over into serious conversation with both of you, let alone on the same day!"

He laughed. "I can be serious sometimes you know," he told her "when I have to be." He paused before adding, "Don't think I don't see how much you love him."

"But-" She was going to rush him with some bullshit, but he stopped her dead.

"Lis, I know you keep trying to brush it off. I know you don't want everyone to know just how head-over-heels you are for a boy you met on the internet. A boy who is married, even if it isn't for love, for an unknown period of time. But it really is as clear as day to everyone who simply looks at you both."

I should just paint my cheeks red twenty-four-seven, she thought as she flushed.

"I just hope he knows how much I love him," she replied.

"He does," he assured her. "You'll perhaps need to remind him when he wakes up, though."

She smiled. "I will, and I'll tell him just how mortifying this whole trip has been for me."

"You've no need to be mortified. We're all glad he's finally found someone who loves him as much as he deserves to be loved. He's number one on your list, even before yourself. You're perfect for him. Before you, he was with Angela, and that was a bad, bad experience for him. She treated him like crap, but he was blinded by love and stuck with her for all the wrong reasons. You and him? You work. And I *really* want an invitation to the wedding – seriously, what the hell am I saying? I hear what's coming out of my mouth and just can't stop myself. I'm making myself sick with this soppy crap."

She was giggling again.

"Dude, my point was, I think it's safe to say you've been accepted by everyone here. You just have to realize that, and let yourself find your place. If you keep thinking they all don't like you, or you have something to prove to them, or you're not his proper girlfriend because of his marriage to Britt, you'll drive yourself mad. You have nothing to prove. We all like you. I know you don't need our approval or whatever, but you have it. And, above all, he loves you. You're his number one, and that's all you need. That's all any of us need, and not just 'cause he can kick our asses."

"Wow, your head must hurt. You stayed serious there for a good few minutes and actually made sense!" she said getting to her feet. “I better get back to him. He’ll be wondering where I’ve gone,” she winked at him.

“One question?”

“Shoot. But I can’t guarantee an answer,” she warned.

“If he asked, would you marry him?”

Without thinking, she replied, “He’s already married, Brad. He’ll be that way for a few years at least.” She turned to leave.

“If he wasn’t?” he prodded.

“Why are you suddenly so concerned? You want an excuse for a piss-up and a new hat?” she joked.

“Well, no. Firstly, I have no idea what a piss-up is, and I doubt I’ll wear a hat – unless it’s a ball cap. Can I wear a ball cap to your wedding? Anyway. I figure if you’re willing to forgive him lying to you, and stick by him through something like being married to another woman, you must love him a lot. Maybe even enough to marry the man.”

“I do love him, though that really doesn’t explain why you asked,” she replied, chewing on her lip.

“Curiosity not enough of a reason?” he asked.

“Not really.”

“’Cause I think he’d marry you in a heartbeat.”

She smiled at him, “If you say so. I’m going back to sit beside him until he wakes up. I’ve been gone for too long as it is!”

Chapter 29

When she entered AJ's room with Brad, Lisa blushed almost instantly. She drew looks from everyone sitting around the bed. Jeremy stood to let her have "her" seat, but she shook her head.

"It's ok," she said as she walked behind him and sat on the edge of AJ's bed. She swung her legs up and sat stroking the side of his face as the conversation started up again. She was very careful not to move around too much and not to cause too much of a fuss. No one challenged her sitting there, so there she stayed.

"Brad?" she asked over the staggered conversation around the room.

"Irish?" he replied.

I guess that name is sticking around.

"I don't suppose you brought your guitar with you?" she asked. "Or AJ's?"

"As a matter of fact-" he got up and pulled the case out from under the bed. "Why? Are you gonna sing for everyone?"

"You gonna sing with me?"

"I will, if you will."

"I will, if you will," she mimicked.

"You're on!" He grinned as he slid the guitar out of its case.

I feel like I've been tricked, she smiled. *This must be how AJ ends up in strange situations with Brad. Definitely makes for great photos though. AJ's never going to live down just how poorly Drag-Queen AJ's make-up was at the Pride festival last year.*

They sang a variety of songs. Sometimes Brad, sometimes Lisa, sometimes both of them. Sometimes even some of the others joined in, too.

"I have one for you," he said abruptly, "Pim was learning this song. He said it was on a list you gave him ages ago. It seemed like a good tune, so I learned it too."

As soon as he started the intro, she felt a lump in her throat. It was one of her favorite songs, *Only Hope* from one of her favorite movies, *A Walk to Remember*. She thought he'd forgotten about the list as soon as she'd given it to him. It was a stupidly long list. One she'd really never expected him to look at, let alone learn songs from. It touched her that he'd remembered it and that Brad had learned it, too. She smiled, took a deep breath and started to sing.

When she'd finished, the room was quiet. She wasn't sure, but she thought she saw a few wet eyes as she scanned the room waiting for someone to heckle her.

"You guys sound great!" The doctor and a nurse were standing in the doorway. "How's the patient today?" the doctor enquired, addressing the squad in the room.

"I think he twitched, or flinched or something earlier.

But then I figured I was feeling what I wanted to and now I'm not so sure," Lisa said as she played with AJ's hair, avoiding the "don't listen to the crazy girlfriend, she's sleep-deprived" looks she could feel she was getting from around the room.

"It's possible," the doctor replied as he gave AJ a quick once over, "but probably just a reflex."

"Sure, I guess," she replied disheartened. "I still think he'll be awake in a couple days though, up and about a couple days after that, and be home within a week," she predicted.

"Well, staying positive is certainly the way to go," he told her smiling sadly, "but-"

"Please Doctor, no 'buts' in this room. At least not where he can hear. This, Doctor, is a but-free zone. The power of positive thinking and all that. So, if you're going to 'but', be a negative Nelly, or pessimistic Polly, you should go do it in a but-permitting zone."

They all giggled at her telling the doctor off like a school kid.

"You certainly have a way with words," Mrs. Williams said to her when the doctor finished his checks and quickly excused himself.

"Well, you know what they say about the Irish, right Mrs. Williams?" she grinned.

"Trust me, I do. But I still think you're a bit of a strange one. And I've told you already, it's Cindy," she replied with a laugh.

Ok. So, not quite the I-would-love-her-as-a-daughter-

in-law-path I was aiming for. But we can work with strange if strange is what we got. I could be worse than strange, right? I mean, I could be, uh... realizing she should probably come out of her own thoughts and back to the room.

Married. I could be married.

Not the time, Lis.

Despite the sterility of the hospital room and the potential severity of the situation they all faced, the atmosphere was warm and the conversation flowed. Lisa realized that sharing a hardship brought a closeness and comfort to everyone. They sat talking until the nurse came in to kick the group out for the evening – except Lisa. They had an understanding, the nurses and her. She got to stay. Shuffling down the bed, she tried not to move AJ too much as she rested her head lightly on his chest. She was intending to stay there for just a few minutes, listening to the sound of his heart beating and hold him a little.

When she woke, it was morning, and Jeremy was sitting on a chair next to the bed, reading one of the magazines she'd brought across the Atlantic. She noticed she had a blanket over her.

"G'mornin', sunshine," he grinned as she sat up and rubbed her eyes, yawning widely.

"Morning. What time is it?" she asked.

"It's after ten."

"How long have you been sitting there?"

"About an hour."

"And you didn't wake me because..."

"Because you're nearly as chatty while you're sleeping, as you are when you're awake. I wasn't sure if you were asleep or not!" He stuck his tongue out, and he saw the look of horror on her face.

"I'm *joking,* Lisa. I just figured you haven't been getting much sleep and you looked pretty peaceful, so I let you rest."

"Thank you," she replied, still embarrassed. "You're right. I slept better than I have in a while. I just meant to give him a cuddle goodnight, and I guess the rhythm of his heartbeat put me to sleep. I miss him, Jer."

"I know, sweet cheeks. I miss him too."

Chapter 30

Lisa spent the day by AJ's side. Visitors came and went, bringing get well soon cards and gifts. His team mates, kids from college, it felt as if everyone came at some point, and so many of them brought balloons. She was surrounded by helium balloons. She hated balloons. What did a guy in a coma want with so many balloons?

And why does this hospital allow people to torment me with friggin' balloons – aren't there rules here against this kinda stuff?

She talked to him a little, telling him about the hockey scores, the conversation she had with her parents earlier in the day, and anything else she could think of, just to keep talking.

Day blurred to dusk, and dusk faded to darkness. That night, she lay beside him again, falling asleep to the quiet thud-thud in his chest.

As the sun rose on day three post-accident, Lisa was still committed to the thought that AJ was going to wake up. If not today or tomorrow, someday. She was absolutely sure she'd hear his voice again.

I miss his voice.

She was starting to find a routine within the hospital

walls. It felt easier to keep an order to her actions because she was often finding it difficult to organize her thoughts. She suspected his friends and family probably disapproved of her spending so much time in the hospital, for her own sake more than anything else. The medical staff voiced concerns about her well-being, but no one objected too loudly, as long as she ate, slept, washed and went outside for a little bit every day. And, since she didn't interfere with AJ's medical treatment, they allowed her to stay for as long as she liked.

I'm so lucky the university was so understanding about my 'extenuating circumstances'. I can't imagine having to leave him here like this.

Lisa waited for someone to arrive and relieve her for a little while. It was, as she expected, Jeremy. He was an early riser. And peppy too. While part of her was surprised at how loyal and reliable "Joker Jeremy" could be, she was relieved to see, with her own eyes, that he was a good of a friend to AJ as she had heard he had been to him over the years.

She showered and went for a quick walk around the hallways, taking the stairs down to the cafeteria to pick up some breakfast for the two of them. She was adding an extra flight of stairs back up, every day. Today, being day three, that meant she walked three flights of stairs and took the elevator the rest of the way. AJ was on the ninth floor, so, if he'd still not woken up by day nine, she'd be carrying breakfast all the way from the cafeteria to the ninth floor. That didn't bare thinking about, on either count.

Breakfast choices varied. Today was croissants, fruit salad and orange juice. She could murder a decent cup of tea, but American tea tasted so strange to her. *Weird American milk*, she thought as she made her tea.

"Oh, what I wouldn't give for a *proper* Irish brew," she complained as she sat down, handing breakfast over to Jeremy.

"Ugh. Would you shut *up*!" he told her playfully. "That's literally all you've complained about since you got here. How weird our food tastes and how you want *real* tea!"

"Well, it's true! Your food *does* taste weird to me, and at home I'd be drinking ten cups of tea, good tea, *Irish* tea, every single day. Not stupid wannabe American tea with funny tasting milk. Do you know they put *ice* in their tea down here, Jer? ICE? Tea is not supposed to be cold like that. It's practically a crime against tea!" she ranted.

The days were starting to follow a pattern: visitors, check-ups, reading to him, doctors, nurses, physiotherapy – apparently so his muscles wouldn't go to hell in a handbasket while he was asleep, and so he wouldn't get bedsores. She had no idea how long it took for someone to get bedsores, but they insisted he needed to move.

The medical team took the time to show her a few exercises so she could help AJ between their visits. Today, she learned to work the smaller muscle groups. They asked her to help since he needed his muscles moved fairly regularly and she was there so much anyway. She knew when he woke up, he was going to be pissed that his muscles were deteriorating – he turned into quite the diva, when he missed even a couple days at the gym.

Jocks, she thought amused while they showed her how to work out his wrists, one at a time.

After a good session of moving AJ's limbs, Lisa's arms ached and she was tired.

When things quietened down in the afternoon, she sat with Ana, Britt and AJ's mom. She was reading; Britt and Ana were talking, and his mom was doing a crossword puzzle in the paper. Lisa was enjoying spending time with them, talking to them and getting to know them. Despite the awful circumstances, this was a good opportunity for them to get to know her, too. She was loving hearing stories about AJ and Ana's childhood, his teenage years, and even the more recent stories, filling in the gaps around what she knew from their constant conversations. They talked into the wee hours before Jeremy arrived to send everyone home and keep Lisa company.

Lisa and Jeremy sat chatting quietly. He was AJ's best friend, and Lisa was happy they had found some kind of peace between them. Not that she'd admit it to him, at least not yet, but she was even starting to like him. She wanted to get to know him, too. When he fell asleep, she sat next to the bed, whispering quietly to AJ, who still showed no sign of waking up. After about an hour, she was *convinced* she felt his hand twitch again. When she saw his toe move beneath the sheets, she was almost certain her mind was playing tricks on her.

"Jeremy?" she whispered, as she stroked AJ's forehead with her fingertips.

Nothing.

"JEREMY!" she hissed, "Wake up!"

Ok. Don't overreact. Don't panic. It's just his toe. Just a reflex. Not a conscious movement. The doctor said it was probably just a reflex so it's just a reflex.

Picking up her book, she chucked it at Jeremy.

You're panicking. Stay calm.

"OW!" he exclaimed as he rubbed the spot where the book had hit him. "What was *that* for?"

"Shhhhh." She snapped and then realized she'd just rudely, and probably painfully woken him from a deep sleep. "I'm sorry, but I couldn't wake you. He moved his toe, Jer."

"Lis-" he started cautiously.

"Jeremy. Seriously. I'm not seeing things. I'm not delirious from tiredness. I thought I was. But I'm sure of it. I'm sure he moved!"

He looked at her skeptically and lifted AJ's other hand. They sat like this for thirty-five minutes. Jeremy was ready to go back to sleep and give up on watching for signs of movement, when he saw it, too. The sheets moved ever so slightly. Jeremy alternated his look of shock frantically between her eyes and staring at AJ's feet.

She smiled at him – her best *I told you so* smile, tinged with relief. With one hand holding AJ's hand and with the other, stroking his cheek, she spoke to him, softly. Jeremy did, too. For the rest of the night they sat joking between themselves, trying to quietly coax AJ to wake up. There was a renewed sense of hope to their chat.

Every now and again, AJ's eyes would open and shut. The nurses had already told her this was common with people in comas but Lisa obviously couldn't help but hope that this was the beginning of AJ coming out of his coma.

The next morning, the neurologist listened as Lisa and Jeremy recounted the previous night's events. He repeated the test they'd conducted on AJ a couple days ago to determine the level of traumatic brain injury. The neurologist had explained that it was a scoring system called the *Glasgow Coma Scale* with three categories: eye opening, verbal response, and motor response. When AJ first came out of surgery, he had ranked a three, 'severe' on the scale, essentially non-responsive to any test.

I'm not sure anyone realized quite how bad he was on the scale. I don't think I even knew there was a scale. Before all this, there was awake and coma as far as I was concerned.

Lisa watched as the doctor conducted a series of tests to see if AJ was any more alert than he had been. He asked a series of questions and gave commands to see if AJ could open his eyes, move, speak, or understand what was happening around him.

"AJ, can you hear me? Do you know where you are?" He paused. "AJ if you can hear me could you open your eyes?"

Nothing.

"Ok, how about your toes? Can you wiggle your toes?" Lisa held her breath as she watched his feet under the sheet. There was movement. It might have been almost imperceptible, but it was there. Lisa clamped her hand over her mouth so she didn't squeal. She glanced at Jeremy to see if he'd noticed, he had and gave her an encouraging thumbs up.

"Good. AJ can you wiggle your toes again for me?" the doctor asked again as he scribbled something on the chart.

Nothing.

"Ok, AJ, you're going to feel a few pokes and prods now. It's just to test your reflexes and responses and it's nothing to worry about."

She watched as AJ's body flinched away from the doctor's tests. His eyes flickered open a couple of times when he was poked, but, again, she wasn't sure if it was a deliberate choice by AJ or a reflex. She couldn't believe what she was seeing, or hearing – she'd heard AJ make an indecipherable noise, twice.

"From these results, it would seem as though AJ is improving slightly." The doctor saw the excitement on Lisa's face and quickly continued. "Slightly" he repeated, "but even if this is the case, Lisa, there's a very long way to go. I'm going to order an MRI and an EEG to see if anything has changed in his brain over the last few days, and, not to give you false hope, but perhaps you should do some reading on what happens when coma patients *do* wake up. This is a good start. AJ seems to be moving in the right direction, but this is still considered a severe injury. Based on eye response, verbal response and motor response, he scores an eight now – this is obviously a marked improvement on his previous score. And I'm hopeful that over the coming days and weeks he'll continue to move forward."

Lisa's spirits wouldn't be dampened. She knew he was trying to wake up. She could feel it. She was researching how to handle it when it happened and, as the sun rose on day five of what was easily proving to be one of the most difficult times of her life, her resolve was stronger than ever. She was only leaving his side for a short while, a couple times each day. In the morning, just time for her shower, the breakfast run and to clear her head. She needed that time to gather her thoughts and psych herself up for the rest of the day. And, again in the evening, to decompress and wind down for the night.

As she stepped out of the elevator, she greeted the nurses. The same nurses, same greeting and the same, sympathetic, sad look on their faces, countered by the same cheery grin on hers.

"Hey, hockey boy!" she called to him as she entered the room, which, as usual, was pretty crowded. His parents, sister, Brad, Jeremy, Britt, Ana and a few of the players had stopped by early, before they took off for today's game.

Chelsea had gone home the previous day, she couldn't get any more time off work, but promised she'd be back down soon. Saying goodbye had been hard for both of them. Chelsea didn't want to leave her friend alone to deal with the situation. She had been there for Lisa through so much, not just on this trip, but throughout their entire transatlantic friendship. Chelsea had been her rock since AJ's accident, instinctively knowing when she needed to talk, or to be left alone. She was unimposing, yet always there.

Lisa knew she was being overly sensitive, but she felt like everyone thought she was a naive little kid for continuing to believe that AJ would be awake by now. When the doctor had mentioned it, she countered, "Maybe he's just being a stereotypical boy. He's loving being waited on hand and foot. Stop feeding him for a few hours, and he'll wake up brave and quick – mark my words."

"OHMYGOD!" exclaimed Ana, who had been holding his hand. Jolting Lisa out of her thoughts about her friend. "He *moved*! He moved his hand! It's the first time I've felt it."

Lisa was happy that his sister finally got to experience the moment for herself. She knew how excited she felt when she felt each small movement AJ made. It gave her hope, hope that he'd soon be awake again. She couldn't imagine how it made his mom feel, or his sister.

Obviously, they'd been completely derailed by his accident and were worried sick. If Lisa had completely neglected herself, Ana had been even worse.

"AJ? Can you hear me?" Lisa spoke.

"HE DID IT AGAIN!" she exclaimed animatedly.

Brad, sitting across the bed from them, lifted his friend's hand, and indicated Lisa should speak again.

"AJ, these crazy people are starting to make me feel sane. It's not the natural order of things so you gotta wake up and help me out here!" she told him.

Within seconds, the machines connected to him, started beeping, alarms ringing.

"GET THE NURSE!" Lisa screamed at Mike.

Or was that Marc? She wondered glancing at his back as he sprinted from the room. Hitting the call button on the remote, she tried to calm her panic. She instinctively shooed Brad out of the way and sat beside AJ on the bed, talking loudly enough to be heard over the various beeps and buzzing. She could see AJ's eyes moving rapidly under his eyelids.

"Hey, hey, mister, calm down." Her voice was level and calm. She spoke directly to him. She thought he was maybe having some kind of seizure, or maybe he'd heard her ask him to wake up and he was trying to do just that.

"Ok, you need to listen to me. I didn't mean wake up *right this second.*" She soothed. "Stop trying so hard, you're giving us all a headache! I'm sorry I called you lazy. I'm here with you, take a breath." Squeezing his hand, she felt tears threatening. "Your mom is here. Your dad, too. Ana, Britt, Brad, Jeremy, Marc, Lindsay and Jared are on their way up – you're freaking everyone out!" She paused, unable to stop her tears. "You're scaring me, AJ." Her free hand stroked the side of his face. "Don't push so hard. I know it's frustrating that you can't open your eyes. You can't move, or talk, or throw random objects at Jeremy and Brad. But it'll happen, don't force it. You're not ready, you see? And that's ok, babe. All these alarms ringing and machines beeping? That's them telling you to knock it off, you're just not ready. Quit trying so hard, Mr. over-achiever. You're going too fast and you need to slow down. I know that's difficult for you, Mr-fast-paced-do-everything-at-warp-speed-Williams, but do it for me? Please? You can wake up when you're ready. Just stop, AJ. Please, calm down, relax and listen to me. Listen to the sound of my voice. For crying out loud, work with me here!"

She spoke quickly as her tears fell heavily. She was filled with pain and grief seeing him shake before her on the bed. His mom had moved to sit opposite her and was holding AJ's other hand. She was talking to him, too, trying to calm him down and reassure him that he was going to be ok. Lisa sobbed as she waited, holding her breath for some kind of sign that he'd heard her, hoping that the nurse would arrive soon. It felt like they were taking forever. She pushed the button again as she started to hear a ringing in her ears. Her head felt dizzy and she could have sworn she was seeing tiny little stars appearing at the edges of her vision. She was hot. She tried to speak but nothing came.

Aw shit, was the last thing she remembered as she tried to stand and everything went black.

Chapter 31

When Lisa came to, she was in the recovery position, in her pjs on a hospital bed, and there was a nurse standing over her, taking her pulse and blood pressure.

"I'm fine," she grumbled, frantically trying to sit up. "How is *he*?" Someone was pushing against her to ensure she laid on the bed. Realizing it wasn't actually the nurse's hand, she turned to face its owner.

"Jeremy, I'm *fine*. Really, I'm ok. How is he? Did the machines stop beeping? Is he ok?" Panic filled her voice. He held up his free hand to silence her.

"He's ok. But I'm not sure the same can be said about you. Lie down," he ordered. She'd never heard him be quite so serious. "Don't fight. Just lie there and let the nurse do her job. When she's done, you're gonna lie there some more, ok?"

She lay quietly.

"Ok?" he repeated.

"Fine." She grumbled. "But-"

"No!" He was starting to get irritated. "No buts. Just lie there. You fainted. You need checked over, and rest."

He seemed emotional, angry and worried.

"Yes, doctor Jeremy," she replied trying to lighten the

mood.

"It's not funny, Lis. What good is trying to get AJ to wake up, when you're driving yourself into the ground?"

"I'm fi-"

"Do *not* tell me you're fine, Lisa." His voice was *definitely* raised now. He was so clearly fighting to keep himself together. "You're not eating properly. You're getting no sleep. You're stuck in the same room for twenty-three hours a day. You're worried sick. Literally. And that's not fine. That's so far from fine, fine isn't even in the same State as you right now." He rushed on so she couldn't interrupt him.

His voice was a little quieter now, "I *know* you love him. I *know* seeing him like this is breaking your heart. I know if it was my girlfriend lying there, it would take an act of God, or a crane, at least, to move me from her bedside. But he *needs* you in top form. Well," he paused to sit on the bed next to her, "as top form as can be expected in this situation. And," he took her hand, "I need you. We all do. Your positivity and your 'spit and fire' attitude, your blind faith that he's going to wake up no matter what. You buck everyone up. You keep us all positive. When we doubt, your faith is enough for all of us. When we question, you always have some kind of answer, even if it's sarcasm and sass. When we need a hug, or a flood-gate opening cry, you're there for that too." He smiled.

"You have to look after yourself. I have to look after you – you have to *let* me look after you. When he wakes up,

I'm already planning on borrowing Mike's pads to defend myself."

Seeing the look on Lisa's face Jeremy quickly added, "I know you don't need looked after, I don't mean that in a patronizing 'poor little woman' kind of way. It's just what family does, we take care of each other."

She giggled a little at the image of Jeremy standing at the foot of AJ's bed, fully kitted-out in goalie pads, having AJ hurl random objects at him.

He continued.

"Yeah, I bet that's a funny image for *you*. But it's damn sure gonna hurt me. Look, when you two first started talking, all of *this* wasn't supposed to happen. He was considering marrying Britt. I definitely didn't think that was a good plan, by the way – I mean, if he was going to marry anyone to give them a green card, it should have been me!"

She laughed again. "Aha! I always knew you wanted him for yourself!"

"I wanted to introduce him to a few girls, remind him that not every woman is like his ex and that he had other options open to him than signing years of his life away on a fake marriage. But he didn't want to hear it. Then Chelsea talked about you, and I figured you'd be a bit of fun for him."

Seeing the look on her face, he quickly backtracked again.

"Not *that* kind of fun! I just mean someone to talk to, let loose with, be himself with, someone to remind him that girls can be nice. Someone on the outside of the "group". When we started to email and chat a bit more, I was starting to see how good you were for him, how happy he was, how you pulled all-nighters to follow our games and to talk to him afterwards. When he had to cancel his trip to see you because of the playoffs, you didn't throw a fit like everyone expected you to. You even forgave him when you found out he was married – the one thing we all thought would break you.

The night of his wedding, he broke down, Lis. He didn't know how to tell you, or what to say. He was so scared of you walking away. And then you found out...like that...if you had walked, we all would have understood, because it's not an easy situation to understand. But you stayed. You surprised us all, and, ok, this is going on a little longer than I had planned, you definitely bring out the chatty-Patty in me, so I'll sum it up to where we are now. You've been at his bedside for five days straight – and your belief that he's going to wake up is stronger than ever, right?"

She nodded.

"Well, my belief that you are perfect for him is stronger than ever, too, and don't worry, my soppy soliloquy won't last much longer. But it's true. Everyone can see it. You bring out the best in each other. And you just, I dunno, you guys make sense. You're on the same level or something. I dunno. Lis, if – when – *when* he wakes up, and sees you've made yourself sick with worry about him, he'll feel like shit. He'll be pissed at you. He'll be pissed at *me* and everyone else who didn't try and help you. Just lie there, and sleep for a few hours, and tomorrow night – Doc permitting – you're going to dinner with the girls. Us guys will hold the fort down here for a while. If he wakes up, you'll be the first call. I promise. But you need a break, and if it takes me to force a break upon you, then so be it. We can do this the easy way, or the hard way. And for crying out loud, Lis, please let it be the easy way."

She smiled, crying *again*. She hugged him. That was a lot to take in.

"This is *so* weird for me, you're being-" she searched for the word,

"Nice?" he joked. They laughed, she nodded. "Sleep!" he ordered as he turned to leave her to sleep.

"Wait! What's wrong with me?" she asked him. "Aside from the fainting."

"They said you had low blood sugar and a couple other numbers that were off. Basically, listen to Doctor Jeremy here. You aren't looking after yourself. Dehydration. Exhaustion. They hooked you up to an IV, *obviously*. They're going to rehydrate you, give you a vitamin B12 shot, magnesium and told me to get your ass out for some vitamin D at some point. 'She's Irish' wasn't a good enough excuse for you being translucent."

"That's a big word for you, Jer," she said smiling again. "Jer?" she called sleepily as he moved to leave.

"Yeah?"

"I'm not American and I don't have insurance. I mean,

I have travel insurance, but I don't really know what that covers. I just got travel insurance cause it's what you do. But I'm guessing this fainting thing will cost me a fortune – did they tell you how much?"

"Don't worry about it," he told her.

"Jeremy?" she persisted.

"Don't worry about it, Lis." He repeated, "Art and Cindy have it covered. We'll talk about it later. Sleep."

He didn't need to tell her twice, because by the time he'd walked out of the room and the door had closed, she was already out for the count.

Chapter 32

Lisa woke up to Britt smiling at her.

“Hey sleepy head,” Britt said softly, “How do you feel?”

“My head hurts,” she answered honestly, “but I think I’m ok. How’s AJ?”

“He’s still asleep. But he’s definitely moving a little more. It doesn’t seem on purpose, and everyone keeps getting a fright when he does it. He’s making more noises, but not speaking any words and he keeps kinda opening and closing his eyes – it’s freaky. It’s like he’s there, but he’s not *there*. Most of the time he just opens them a little, I’m not sure its intentional or not, but the doctor checked on him again, said he’s ok and that it’s all part of the process.”

“He’s going in the right direction,” Lisa agreed, thinking back to her research and relieved at the continued though slow, progress.

Slow and steady. It’s supposed to be slow.

“What time is it?”

“It’s nearly seven.”

“PM? Wow. I guess I really did need some decent sleep after all. Have you been here the whole time?”

Lisa's eyes were wide with surprise.

"No, no, we've been taking it in turns. The others and me. Ana's next."

"Oh joy," she groaned. "Man, I'm such a pain in the arse!"

"Not at all!" she laughed. "It's given us something else to focus on," she told her. "I guess some of us needed a distraction from Pim. You still look tired. You should sleep more if you can – I promise we'll come get you if he wakes up when you're sleeping."

She nodded, turned over and went straight back to sleep. When she woke up at 3.30am she was feeling a *lot* better. Her head had cleared and the fuzziness had lifted. She felt well rested. Looking at her IV pole, she saw that a nurse had hung another rehydration bag but she wasn't hooked up to anything else. Checking her phone, she learned from Jeremy that AJ's room was only next door. The ward was quiet, and she guessed they figured that if they'd moved her to a different floor, she'd just become more of a pain, so they put her in the empty room next door. The nurse had told her that all being well, she could be discharged the following morning anyway. She got up and shuffled with her IV pole to the next room. Luckily the IV had wheels and she wasn't restricted to the bed. That would have driven her *insane*. She would have been very grumpy had she woken up unable to pee, or walk around.

Walking in, she saw Jeremy asleep in the chair. Not her chair though, he probably expected a visit from her at some point. Covering him in an extra blanket, she sat next to AJ on the bed. She took his hand, as usual, and she talked to him, keeping her voice to a whisper.

"Hey there, mister. How are you? I've had a bit of a day. I was starting to think I had completely embarrassed myself as much as I could in front of your tribe. And then, in true Lisa fashion, I managed to one-up myself, as always."

She made small talk at him for a while and then she moved to take up her usual position in her seat and fell asleep with her head on top of AJ's hand.

***

Fingers in her hair.

He knew it was something she enjoyed. She made a satisfied sound as the fingers traveled the length of her long, in dire need of a good brushing, hair.

Wait a minute, she thought confused. *Why is Jeremy stroking my hair? I know I'm lying on top of AJ's hand...*

She felt wildly for his hand. *No hand? What the hell? Where's his hand? Did someone move me?*

Her head snapped upright at the sound of him saying his ex-girlfriend's name.

"Ange?"

Chapter 33

"Oh my God," Lisa breathed, as yet more tears fell, "your eyes! They're open!" She gushed, "You're moving your hand!" She stuttered as his hand came to her face and stroked her cheek. "You're *awake!*" Realization struck, "Wait? Ange? AJ that's not funny..."

"Who are you?" AJ demanded, with no trace of recognition on his face. He looked at her like she was a stranger.

"AJ...it's me...Lisa, remember? I'm-" Her breath caught in her throat as she choked down a sob.

He was clearly confused. "Who are you?" he repeated, clearly confused. He spotted Jeremy asleep, "Jer?" he called.

Jeremy didn't stir.

Lisa hit the "Call nurse" button on AJ's remote control and crossed the room to shake Jeremy awake. Confused, Jeremy met her gaze and saw her tears, "What hap-" He glanced at AJ in the bed and realized he was awake. "Did you call someone?" he asked her. She nodded and chewed at her lip.

"The nurse. I pushed the button."

"Good. Why do you look so upset? This is good, right,

AJ? You're awake, man!"

"He-" she started at the same time AJ asked, "Who *is* she, Jer?"

Understanding registered on Jeremy's face as tears trickled down Lisa's face. "He thought I was Angela," she mumbled.

"This is Lisa, AJ. Your girlfriend. Don't panic, she loves you and you love her, and I'm sure whatever is up with your memory right now will be temporary and you'll be back to your old self in no time." He sounded way more confident than he looked. He'd turned as pale as the bed linen and kept looking at Lisa with sympathetic eyes, mouthing, "It'll be ok," at her repeatedly.

AJ looked visibly scared and was breathing faster.

He's starting to panic. She went to his side, pulling her IV pole behind her and tried to hold his hand, but he jerked it away from her in confusion. She backed away from the bed and let Jeremy take her place and hold his hand. He sat quietly reassuring his friend and attempting to keep him calm.

By the time the nurse reached the room, AJ had fallen back to sleep. The nurse took some readings from the machines and left the room to page the neurologist, who appeared quickly, made brief introductions and asked Jeremy a couple of questions before repeating the coma-scale test on AJ.

"AJ? I'm Doctor Murphy, I'm going to need you to open your eyes for me for a moment please."

AJ opened his eyes. She wrote something down.

"Good. Do you know where you are?"

"Hospital," he answered simply.

She wrote again.

"Good. Do you know why you're in the hospital?"

"No ma'am."

"You have no memory of what happened?"

"No ma'am."

"Do you know who these people are?"

"I know who he is," he answered, indicating to Jeremy, "but not her."

Her. Even the word sounded foreign and cold coming from him.

"Ok," she answered taking more notes, "What's the last thing you do remember, AJ?"

He thought for a moment, grimaced, as though thinking hurt. "Eh...I don't know." He was starting to get frustrated. "Why *am* I here?" he asked as he reached up tentatively and touched his bandages.

"It's ok, please try not to panic. You had an accident on the ice during a game a few days ago. You have had surgery and were in a coma. But you're awake now and we are working on getting you back fighting-fit." she assured him. "Let's try moving your toes."

He obliged, and she did a few more physical exercises with him. "We'll send you for a few tests in the morning, but for now, AJ, please rest and allow your body to heal. Don't force it. When you're awake, by all means try and talk to your friends in small doses – but don't push yourself. It's still early days and things are going to be very foggy for a while. It'll take time. You'll probably feel dazed and confused, and your body may not work the way you expect it to right away, ok? If you're in pain, the nurse can give you something. Do you have any questions?"

AJ shook his head slightly; he was barely awake and fighting sleep.

"Doctor?" Lisa asked quietly from her corner, not taking her eyes of AJ, "What was his score?"

"He's at a 13," she answered sympathetically, "much improved." AJ was starting to doze and Dr Murphy lowered her voice a little. "I know Doctor Davis recommended some literature for you to read about coma patients waking up, Lisa, and I know this can't be easy for you. Hang in there, ok? He's woken up and he can speak and move. He responded when I called his name to open his eyes. This is all huge. It's expected that things are a bit muddled in his mind for a while. He'll get there. Just be patient and don't rush him. If people are visiting, please make sure it's one or two at a time, and for quick visits. I'm sure the nurses will make sure he isn't overwhelmed. Stimulate his memory in short bursts, he's going to get frustrated and agitated that he can't remember things, or that his arms don't do what he wants them to do. He's going to pass in and out of consciousness a lot. His body will need sleep and he's likely to fall asleep mid-sentence for a few days, at least. It's going to be a long road, but he's taking the first strides and we are hopeful he will make a full recovery."

"Thank you, Doctor," Lisa managed through tears, "Do we have to call you each time he wakes up now?"

"No, the nurses will increase their checks accordingly. Have a good evening."

When she left, Jeremy took Lisa into his arms to comfort her. "I didn't expect him to not remember who I am," she sobbed into his shoulder. "I mean, I knew it could be an option, but I never really believed he would wake up and not know who I was!"

"I know," he answered rubbing her back. "He'll get there though. He loves you way too much to forget you."

I sure do hope so, she thought as she cried.

***

She jolted awake.

Disoriented. Her head had been resting on AJ's bed again, and she glanced across to Jeremy's empty chair trying not to move much for fear of waking AJ.

Where is he? she thought.

"You're awake," AJ stated.

She bolted upright. "Yes..." she started, panicked, "I'm sorry, I just... you were sleeping and..."

"It's ok, Lisa," he said softly. "Don't apologize."

"Do you remember me?" she asked hopefully.

"A little. Flashes of memories. Like someone dropped a thousand-piece jigsaw puzzle, only the puzzle is my memory."

She nodded slowly. "You should probably rest." She

encouraged.

"Please don't," he begged, "Please? I hate it when I'm sleeping. I keep having strange dreams, I can't tell what's real and what isn't. That doesn't happen when I'm awake. Please let me enjoy these few minutes before I'm dragged back into sleep?"

"Ok. How do you feel?" she asked, her voice filled with concern.

"I feel like I've slept for a week," he told her.

"Close enough," she replied. "We're just hitting day six, seven maybe? I dunno what time it is."

"Really? It's been that long?" he asked, surprised.

"Yeah."

"Why were you connected to an IV earlier?" he asked her with raised eyebrows.

"Shit," she groaned. "I forgot about the stupid IV. I fainted this morning. You had what looked like a seizure, but I have no idea if that's actually what it was because I freaked out. Then fainted. But I'm ok."

"Ok people don't faint," he answered matter-of-factly.

She smiled at him. "Touché. I guess I've been running a little on empty," she confessed. "Are you really ok? I've been so scared that you wouldn't wake up."

"I'm feeling a little better now that I've calmed down a bit and am more aware of being conscious. For the last while, I've been able to feel people holding my hand and the nurse washing me, but I haven't been able to do anything about it. I've heard voices, non-descript, kind of like I was under water, but I couldn't open my eyes. Having no control of my body, people doing whatever they wanted, whenever they wanted – even if it was medical staff. I didn't know that at first. I could hear everything, but I couldn't move, speak or stop them. I was helpless."

"It sounds so scary, AJ," her voice was almost a whisper.

"Terrifying," he replied as a tear slid down his cheek. Her instinct kicked in and she wiped away his tear, stroked his cheek and kissed his forehead before realizing what she'd done.

"I'm sorry," she began. "You've just gotten done telling me that you basically felt violated by everyone these last few days and-"

"Shhhhhhhh...." he soothed and held his arm out to give her an awkward hug. "I need you to help me remember," he told her quietly as he held her. "I've felt like I was sitting in a white room, waiting. There was no light at the end of the tunnel type-deal for me. Waiting for what? I have no idea, but I've been scared too, terrified. And I have a feeling that this isn't over, please don't give up on me, Lis."

They were both crying. The exchange had clearly taken it out of him so she stroked his cheek and shushed him, to sleep.

***

Lisa stepped outside for some fresh air. It was dusk, and she was starting to feel like the walls of the hospital were closing in on her.

What's that noise?

She stopped in her tracks.

Is someone crying?

She started to look around and quickly caught a glimpse of a woman sitting on a bench, clutching tissue to her face, her shoulders shaking with each sob. As Lisa approached, she realized that it was Cindy, AJ's mom. She froze.

Shit. Do I go up to her? Do I turn around and risk being caught?

What do I do? What do I do?

"Lisa?"

Double shit.

"Hi Mrs. Williams, are you ok?"

"Lisa, we've talked about this. Cindy, please." She answered through the tissue as she dabbed her eyes and blew her nose. "I'm not really sure how I am, Lisa. I think it's all just caught up with me. There's only so long you can be strong before reality kicks you in the behind." She went quiet, and her tears started to fall again.

Lisa sat next to her on the bench, hesitated for a moment, put her arm around her boyfriend's mom's shoulders and let her cry it out.

"I know he's awake now," Cindy said, trying to justify her tears, "but it's not really him, not yet. He may never remember anything. He didn't recognize his dad earlier. I feel so helpless. It's just..." she paused, searching for the word,

"Hard?" Lisa offered.

"Hard." Cindy agreed. "I've always been the strong one you know? Art has always been the fun parent, the emotional parent. I've always been the disciplinarian, the heartless lawyer-mom who doesn't feel. Kids can't have two fun parents, someone's got to make sure the chores and homework get done and the house doesn't burn down. But that doesn't mean I don't love my family. I do love them and right now I feel so helpless while my son is lying there in his own version of hell. I can't help him. I can't clean it up, or put a Band-Aid on it. I can't throw money at it, or find someone else to fix it, I just have to hope and pray that he'll come out the other side of this himself. I feel so helpless." She repeated as she cried again.

"I know you love them and *they* know you love them. You don't have to be strong all the time. It's ok to let the walls down sometimes – or at least, so Jeremy tells me."

Cindy laughed, nodded, wiped her face with a fresh tissue from her purse and gave a quick sniff. "Thank you, Lisa. I imagine this is quite an awkward situation for you to find yourself in, comforting your boyfriend's mother on a hospital bench, but I appreciate your kindness."

"That's ok, we're all in this together. Another Jeremy-ism. Just be glad I didn't sing *High School Musical* at you, like he did to me."

She laughed again.

"We all feel the same, you know? It kills me that I can't help AJ or ease his pain. But we're going through things too. It's ok to cry. It's ok to not be ok. Bottling things up isn't good Mrs. W."

"Cindy. *Please*? And I haven't been completely bottling them up. There's just usually no one around out here when I'm here."

"Cindy, ok, I'll try. If it's ok with you, I'm going to nip back in to see AJ for a few minutes and let you catch a breath. I'll see you inside, ok?"

"See you inside."

***

The door opened, and Cindy walked in with two steaming cups and offered one to Lisa. "Here you go," she said quietly.

"Thanks. He woke up for a few minutes. I think he's starting to remember more."

"I've spoken to the doctors and they say his scans are promising. We just have to keep prodding his memory and try not to overwhelm him. You know how frustrated he can get at himself."

They sat talking quietly for about an hour. A nurse came to take his blood pressure, and the cuff woke him up again.

"Mom?" he mumbled.

"I'm here, son." She brought his hand to her mouth and kissed his knuckles.

"Everything is so fuzzy," he told her.

"I know darling, I know. Just be patient with yourself," she advised.

"Where's Dad?" he asked.

"In the waiting room with Jeremy and a couple of the others. They didn't want to crowd you."

"I can step out and let him come in?" suggested Lisa.

"Don't leave," he instructed her, gripping her hand. "Please don't leave, either of you, please..." he pleaded as he fell back to sleep.

***

When AJ next woke up, Lisa was still sat at his side.

Day 8? I think? Or is it 9? How long have we been in this place?

The days were even more blended together now that he'd woken up than when he was asleep. He'd been out of his coma for two days so far. Though he'd still slept for most of that time, things were improving. She found herself even less inclined to leave the hospital, and he seemed to take comfort in her being there, despite his lack of memory when he first woke up.

He smiled at her, a kind of lopsided smile but it didn't quite reach his eyes.

"You ok?" he asked.

She giggled, "The coma patient is asking *me* if I'm ok! I'm fine, Pim. I'm so glad you woke up."

He chuckled. "You keep saying that, but...you knew

I'd wake up, right?"

"Of *course,*" she emphasized confidently. "You can't go for extended periods of time without causing some form of physical pain to Jeremy!" she jested.

"Where is he?" AJ asked.

"Most of your friends and family are only coming as far as the family room. The doctor said keep visitors to a minimum for a few days. We do keep rotating; you just happen to wake up more often when I'm sitting here. You just missed Erin and Ana. I was out doing laundry at your house."

He was still a bit groggy and his coordination, while improving, left something to be desired. She had to help him sit up in the bed, pour water, he even seemed to struggle with depth perception – when he stretched to scratch an itch on his leg, he was confused as to why it wasn't abating. As it turned out, it was because he hadn't reached it.

She checked the clock, 6am. The nurses would be there any minute. She grabbed a notebook.

"What are you writing?" he asked.

"Notes," she said, dropping the pen and moving to fix his pillows again as he was clearly still uncomfortable. She sat back down beside him on the bed, holding his hand.

"Any pain?"

"My head still hurts."

"How's your vision?"

"I can see you're pale as hell, could use a night's sleep

and probably a good meal, too. But it's less blurry"

"Any pins and needles, or numbness?"

"Have you been practicing this?" he asked her, grinning.

"AJ Williams, do you have any pins and needles? Or funny feelings?"

"Well, there's this one funny feeling I have..." Her eyes met his and she blushed.

"AJ. Be serious for a moment, please."

"I am serious! I've been out cold for days. I wake up to a beautiful Irish girl playing nurse. Do the math!"

She laughed and felt relief washing over her. His speech was markedly improved on when he'd first woken up. His awake times were getting longer, slowly. And his movements were getting stronger, too. She took his temperature with the thermometer the nurse had shown her in the drawer. Infection was a potential side effect of the wound on his head, so if she suspected he was warm, she could check his temp instead of waiting for the next nurse's check.

One of the doctors had happened upon her late one night reading on Google about AJ's condition like the neurologist had advised her to. She couldn't sleep, she was worried about AJ and thought educating herself on the ins and outs of what was happening, and what *could* happen, would help. Except it didn't help and he'd found her crying into her laptop. The doctor had been incredibly patient with her as he ran through the reality of the situation. She took notes, and he used every-day

English instead of incomprehensible medical language that would probably have terrified her and driven her back to Google. He told her which signs or changes would indicate improvement, or deterioration in AJ's condition. He and the nurse both explained what kinds of questions and things they'd ask when he woke up. The doctor had even said it wouldn't do any harm for Lisa to run through them while she waited for the medical team to arrive. If his answers differed between what he told her, and what he answered the medical staff, that could be an indication that something wasn't right after he woke up. When they left her in the room that night, she felt a lot more settled and slept much better than she had previously.

She hadn't had the chance to ask AJ anything when he woke up, because he was confused, irritable and speaking in broken sentences. Even if she *had* asked him the questions, she doubted he'd have been able to answer. But he could answer now.

"Any numbness?" she repeated.

"No, none," he answered, wiggling his extremities.

"You sure?" she eyed him.

"Yes ma'am."

Getting to her feet, she walked to the bottom of the bed. "Can you feel this?" she asked him, as she touched various parts of his feet and legs. He answered yes to all. Taking both his hands in hers, she asked him to squeeze her fingers. He did. She knew the doctors were repeating these tests every time they came to check on AJ, but it gave her some kind of comfort to feel his reactions herself.

Question time lasted a few minutes. Lisa just needed peace of mind before she could calm down. Every time AJ woke up, she was afraid he'd regress, instead of move forward. Fear cut through her when he started to talk, just in case he couldn't remember who she was again. While she wasn't sure he completely remembered everything between them, he remembered enough. But she was constantly terrified that he'd go back to how he was when he first woke up and didn't even recognize her.

"Would you stop poking the guy and kiss him already?" Jeremy told her from where he stood at the open door.

"I'm sorry," she started, "I just had to check."

"I know," AJ answered. "It was very cute." He smiled, wiping a stray tear from her cheek. "Please don't cry," he asked her gently, slipping his arm around her.

"You scared me, AJ," she said quietly.

"I'm sor-"

She stopped him with a kiss. A deep and passionate kiss as her tears fell freely and heavily. He tightened his grip around her waist and pulled her close to him. She rested her head on his shoulder and he let her cry, holding her. Soothing her. "It's ok, babe." He assured her. "I'm ok."

"Sorry to interrupt."

The nurse. The real one.

Damnit. Leave us alone! her mind screamed. *He's just starting to really remember me and I want him all to myself for a while!*

Instead of screaming, she wiped her tears and stood to face the nurse and the doctor behind her.

"Hi," she said.

"Good morning," the doctor replied.

"I took some notes earlier." Lisa extended the book towards the doctor as the nurse went to take readings from the machines. He took it from her and started to read, "Thank you. We obviously have to do all our own tests and checks on AJ, but it is always helpful to compare his answers."

"I just woke up and I gotta take a test? Can't I pretend I'm still sleeping?" AJ said, humorlessly. She glanced at him, concerned. His mood had shifted in a fraction of a second.

"Looks as though you still have your sense of humor AJ. That's a good sign. How do you feel?"

"I have a headache, and I'm sick of people asking me how I'm doing." AJ snapped.

"AJ?" Lisa questioned, "What's going on?"

AJ burst into a tirade of incoherent rage, before attempting to pull his IV out of his arm. The nurse had to call for a second nurse to help hold him while they sedated him, for fear he'd do himself harm.

"He was totally fine, and then...then he wasn't," Lisa said. "I don't know what happened."

"That's how he's going to be for a little while, Lisa.

Mood swings are very common for coma patients."

"Is there anything I can do to help him?" she asked before they left the room.

"You're doing everything you can. Just try to be patient."

Chapter 34

Lisa was on her way back from clearing her head when she heard what sounded like AJ screaming. She could hear a couple of sentences among grunts and incoherent noises.

"LET ME GO!"

"WHERE IS ANGELA? WHY ISN'T SHE HERE?"

"WHY WON'T YOU PEOPLE LET ME GO?"

"ANGELA? WHERE ARE YOU?"

Medical staff ran past her to his room. Lisa ran, too, and when she arrived, she hesitated and stopped outside. She didn't want to exacerbate the situation, so instead of going in, and instead of running away, she leaned against the wall and sunk to the floor, hugging her legs and crying into her knees.

When everything had calmed down, Jeremy came out of the room, cradling a bloody nose.

"How long have you been out here?" he asked cautiously.

"Long enough."

"He's been sedated again, only this time he's also been secured to the bed with wrist straps so he doesn't hurt himself."

"What happened to your face?"

"AJ happened to my face. He's hallucinating, apparently another common side effect for coma patients waking up – they say. I didn't move out of the way of his fist fast enough. I know he didn't mean it, he's not in his right mind right now, but it still freakin' hurt."

"But he's been better. He's seeming more coherent, stronger. I..." Lisa was clearly distressed, so Jeremy sat down next to her on the floor.

"I know. It's hard to understand. They say it'll take time. It's like a hurricane passed through his mind and left everything in the wrong order. Some pieces may have even been carried away forever. We just have to ride out the storm and hope for the best." He paused to rub at his face, "He can still throw a wicked punch, even with a broken brain."

"Is he in there alone?

"Nah, his folks are with him. Ana left; she couldn't handle the mood-swings. He didn't recognize her at first and then he did. And *then* he threw everything but the metaphorical kitchen sink at her. Years of sibling quarrels came out at her. He's messed up. Strangely enough he remembered Britt and the fact he wasn't actually in love with her, but was married to her."

"Should I leave him be for a while?"

"You already know the answer to that. You do what you need to do for your own well-being. But I really don't think there's ever a time where he has, or will need you to leave him be."

Lisa stood up, dusted off her butt and offered a hand to Jeremy to help him off the floor. "Go get some ice for your face, and maybe ask that nurse you have the hots for to help if it doesn't stop bleeding, ok?"

"Yes, Miss bossy pants. And which one? They *all* have the hots for me." He winked at her.

"Ugh," she rolled her eyes at him. "Wish me luck?" she added before he left.

"You don't need it. You may need patience, but you have plenty of that. You got this, Lisa."

"Thanks, Jer."

I got this.

***

Horrified at the sight of AJ lying tied to the bed, Lisa gasped as she entered the room.

"Not quite the kind of 'tied to a bed' I had in mind either," AJ joked.

"I...I thought you were sedated. How are you even awake?" she rushed to sit next to him on the bed and stroked his face.

"It's only a little sedation. It made me woozy, but I'm trying not to give in to sleep. It's worse there."

He started crying. Her heart ached. His mom sat in silence across the bed from Lisa, holding his hand, stroking it over and over, tears trickling down her face as well.

"Oh, AJ! It's all going to be ok. It really is, I just know it. Just don't give up on yourself, ok? We're all here for you." Lisa soothed as she rested her head against his and spoke softly to him. "I'm right here and I'm not going anywhere, you hear me?"

"Yes ma'am." His voice was barely above a whisper.

"I know it's not what you want to hear, but it's maybe even going to get worse and we need to prepare for that possibility. The doctor said it varies from person to person, but it will get better. It *will,* AJ. Please be patient with yourself."

He nodded again as she kissed his cheek softly. He turned his head to meet her lips with his as tears continued to trickle down his face.

"I got you," she told him when their lips parted. He turned his head away from her. She carefully turned it back to face hers and made him look into her eyes. "I got you," she repeated. He nodded through tears as she kissed his forehead again. "And you got this, Pim. Just keep your gloves up, ok?"

He nodded again, "Lis? Could you sing to me please? I'm scared to go to sleep, but I'm so tired. Maybe if you..." Her fingers silenced his lips.

"Sleep. I'll stay right here and sing for you, and I'll be here when you wake up," she told him as he closed his eyes and she started to sing.

He remembers I sing!

Hell, I'm just glad he remembers who I am at all, but he remembers the detail that I sing!

Progress! Maybe progress? Let's go with cautiously optimistic progress.

Cindy mouthed "Thank you" to her, and his dad closed his eyes to nap as well.

I got this.

***

The next day AJ had serious hallucinations. Each day seemed to bring some kind of new behavior. Despite being wide awake, he didn't seem to recognize anyone. The day after that, he somehow managed to pull out his

IV – despite being tied to the bed. Whilst he was thrashing around and trying to twist himself, he managed to get it caught on something, and when Lisa entered the room to bloodied sheets and floor, panic set in.

"It's worse than it looks," reassured the nurse who was cleaning up the mess. "He's all fixed up again now, and he's sleeping, not sedated," she told Lisa.

"Thank you, nurse."

"You're doing just fine," the nurse said as Lisa sat on her chair next to AJ's bed. "You all are, AJ included. It's tough and it's scary, but you really are doing everything you can and the doctors are hopeful he'll recover fully."

"Thank you," Lisa repeated, despite the lump in her throat, "and thank you for taking care of him."

The nurse smiled and left the room quietly.

"Is she gone?" AJ asked, eyes still closed.

"She is. Do you want her back?" Lisa stood as if to follow the nurse.

"NO! I want you alone. I miss you. There's always someone else here."

"I miss you too, Pim. How are you feeling?"

"A little clearer today, I think? Maybe? My headache isn't as bad. I'm awake more and more, though pretending not to be depending on the company. I'm slowly putting the jigsaw pieces back together in my brain. I definitely remember how much I love you."

Finally. He sounds so sure.

Lisa blushed as she stood to kiss him. "You have no idea how glad I am that you're coming back to me," she told him, staring into his eyes. "I miss you so much."

"Tell me what I've missed. Tell me what happened. What's happened since? I'll probably fall asleep at some point, but please just tell me."

She nodded and began to fill him in on everything he'd missed. He dipped in and out of sleep, but she was enjoying knowing he was inching closer to his old self.

"I forgot to ask how Jer's face is?" he mumbled to her. "Did I break his nose again?"

"Again?" Lisa repeated, horrified.

"Wouldn't be the first time," Jeremy answered grinning as he came into the room and took a seat next to the bed. "My face is as gorgeous as ever, man. See? A couple bruises can't hold this pretty-boy face back. Gained me some real sympathy with the lovely nurse, so of course I totally forgive you."

They laughed together. "I really am sorry, Jer. Can I play the brain damage card? How much mileage can I get out of that card? I mean, it's the truth, after all."

"Don't sweat it, and you've been playing that card for a while – though it has nothing to do with your accident!" he joked.

Chapter 35

They split the visits up between them: AJ's family, Britt, Lisa and Jeremy. The doctor had said to keep the circle close for the early days. Everyone took it in shifts, and they went in pairs so as not to overwhelm him. The pairings changed daily, based on everyone's schedules. By the time Lisa's turn came the next day, AJ's restraints had been removed, along with his catheter, and he'd even been allowed to get up and use the restroom.

"Well, well, well, look at you," she beamed when she walked in and leaned over to give him a kiss hello.

"I had an accident," he told her. "They had to change my bed again."

"Don't worry about that," she answered. "They told us it would be a while before everything worked how it's supposed to, remember?"

"I know," he sighed. "I feel like a friggin' baby though. It's so frustrating. I'd love to go for a run and clear the cobwebs."

"Not today, sunshine," she warned playfully.

"I know. If I can't even control when I pee right now, putting one foot in front of the other seems a stretch."

Jeremy burst in. He was running late, but he was also

holding a cooler bag. “Dude. Ice cream?”

“For real? I’m so sick of that crap they call food here. Hospital food really does suck. Hand it over!”

“I’m going to pretend I didn’t see this,” the doctor no one noticed coming in joked. “Though there’s really no reason you can’t have some ice cream. There are no restrictions on your diet. You’ve been eating well and you’ve clearly got an appetite. Welcome back, AJ. I’ve been out at meetings for a while, so I haven’t been around. We need to do some scans and draw some blood, but everything looks like it’s improving. I’m sure everyone is very relieved you have finally opened your eyes.”

Lisa recognized him from the night AJ was brought in. “Doctor? Now that he’s not catheterized, is he allowed out of bed more?”

“Not unsupervised, not yet. Physical therapy and occupational therapy will be a couple times a day for a few days, just until he’s strong enough to walk unaided. His body is still adjusting for now and we don’t want him taking any more falls.”

“So, he’s not allowed to go for a run?”

The doctor eyed her skeptically, “No ma’am. We’re definitely not there yet.”

“Thank you, just checking. He said he felt like a run – just making sure we get doctor’s orders on the record.”

The doctor laughed. “Any other questions?”

“I’m good. AJ?”

“Realized I’m still here, did ya?” AJ laughed “I don’t

have any questions, thanks, Doc."

***

It took about another week before AJ could handle more than two or three visitors at a time and the doctor finally signed off on allowing his friends and teammates to visit and spend time with him. During that time his coordination and memory both improved and the physio team was happy for him to go to the bathroom or to take a short walk to the nurses' station and back a couple times a day.

Progress. Definite, actual, tangible, measurable progress, Lisa thought as she walked next to him on their second trip of the day to visit the nurses.

"Penny for your thoughts?" AJ asked as they turned back toward his room. She could see a bead of sweat running down the side of his face.

"Are you pushing yourself too hard? Do you need to sit?"

"I'm fine, *mom*. I'll sit when I get back to my room. Really, I'm ok. Come on, tell me what you're thinking."

"I was just thinking at how you're progressing. It's been quite the rollercoaster couple weeks."

"I still don't remember a lot, but I'm definitely glad to be conscious and awake."

They'd already reached his bed and Lisa was helping him get comfy. At that moment, the door opened and people started to trickle in.

"Visiting time must have started," she smiled at AJ. "If it gets too much, let me know, ok?"

"Yes, mom," he joked again, though seeing her raised eyebrows, he quickly back-tracked, "Ma'am. I meant ma'am." He grinned at her and shrugged. "Brain damage!"

Lisa rolled her eyes. "That excuse is gonna get old quickly, AJ Williams, and certainly doesn't excuse even jokingly calling me your mom," she teased.

"But it's such a good excuse!"

"Man, I'm so glad your smart-ass was one of the first things to return!" she joked.

"You have always liked my ass."

She stepped aside while people came to see him, hug him, and to chat, welcoming him back. The emotion in the room was palpable and overwhelming. The relief and the sheer joy that he had woken up was a lot to take in for everyone. Lisa sat quietly beside the door, and let everyone have their time with AJ. She'd had plenty of time with him since he'd woken up, and for now she was happy to just sit and watch everyone else's excitement while still keeping an eye that he didn't get too overwhelmed. There were only four people there, plus her, but she was protective of him. Their eyes met from time to time and he'd smiled at her. A knowing smile, a smile that thanked her for understanding and being protective.

By eight o'clock, even she was tired.

"Hey, Irish? You wanna go get some food?" Jeremy

asked. Cindy had arrived to relieve her, and she knew he was keen to get her outside the hospital for a while. She looked at AJ. His visitors were largely gone, and he had fallen asleep. Mike was there as were Ana and their mom, she was sure he'd be fine.

"Sure, I'm starving," she replied quietly as she slipped out, quietly glad of a break from the hospital and some fresh air.

***

"Has anyone eaten breakfast?" Lisa asked the room the next morning, loudly enough to be heard, but hoping not to wake the patient.

Stupid question. She instantly regretted asking. Leaving with a shopping list, she made her way down to the cafeteria to buy everyone's breakfast. Standing facing the door marked "stairs" next to the elevators with her arms full of enough food to feed a whole hockey team, she opted for the "screw it" option of taking the elevator.

And I feel no shame at taking the lazy option right now.

By the time they'd all eaten, AJ had woken up and was nibbling on his own breakfast.

"What's your plan today, Lis?" he asked her over the chatter.

"I need to do laundry and go buy you some more suitable pajamas."

"What's wrong with my pajamas?" he asked, looking

down at himself.

"They're old-man pjs," Jeremy answered through a mouthful of food.

Wasn't the food all gone? How is he still hungry and where the hell is he putting all this food?

"What he said. You need cartoon character jammies. Or...something. Maybe unicorn jammies? But definitely not old-man jammies."

He smiled at her and patted the bed for her to sit next to him. "Unicorn jammies? Man! You're too good to me."

"Don't ever forget it," she said playfully, kissing him softly before taking her leave of the group. She packed up all her stuff and told them she was going back to AJ's for a shower and to do some laundry in case AJ forgot later and asked where she was. She kissed him on the forehead. She promised she'd be back again soon. Before she'd made it five feet outside of his room, she heard footsteps behind her.

"You ok?"

"Sure!" She answered cheerfully. Brad stood staring at her, not convinced.

"I am...ok...fine...Not really, Brad. I'm tired, overwhelmed. And I feel like I've been bathing in chlorine all week. I need a hot bubble bath, a change of clothes and a nap. I'll be ok. Please look after him while I'm gone."

"Sure thing."

She arrived back at his house and crammed all of the

dirty clothing into one load of laundry. She tidied up round the house a little while her steaming hot bubble bath was running. After an hour-long soak, she dried her hair, put on a pair of AJ's boxers and a t-shirt that was lying on his bed; it still smelled of him. Checking the clock, seeing it was midday, she set her alarm for 4pm and collapsed into bed.

Waking up a few minutes before her alarm was due to go off, she got up and dressed, brushed her hair, and called Jeremy at the hospital.

"Has he eaten?"

"No, he played with his delicious, Michelin-star hospital food for a while, but gave up on it. That's sarcasm in case you didn't get it. That crap looked like baby food."

"I'm getting pizza. You're in charge of distracting the nurses while I sneak it in." she told him.

"Sure, I'll get one of the guys to help."

"Who else is there? Just so I know how much food to bring."

"Everyone, for now, but who knows?"

"Ok, I'll grab a couple pizzas, some chips and juice."

"How about you get pizzas, some fries and sodas, Irish girl. And start speaking American!"

"Shut up and go come up with a plan to distract the nurses that doesn't involve getting arrested for taking your clothes off in public. I'll be there soon."

Hanging up, she giggled and called the pizza place AJ liked. After ordering seven large pizzas and some fries –

she was feeding hockey players, after all – she headed to the grocery shop next door to pick up some sodas. Before long, she was headed to the hospital. Mike met her in the parking lot and took the bag of heavy cans from her.

It was a flawless operation, mainly because no distraction was needed. The nurses' station was empty when the elevator stopped. As Lisa entered the room, she was practically attacked by a swarm of hungry guys.

She handed over the food and headed straight to her boy. Kissing him lightly on the head, she said, "You look tired, gorgeous."

"You look gorgeous, gorgeous," he answered, smiling and reaching his arms out to grab her and pull her down to his level. He kissed her lips softly, and she felt color rising in her face.

"You just proper kissed me in front of your parents," she hissed at him when they'd finished. "You must be feeling better!" She ruffled his hair a little and pulled up her chair. "But you do look tired," she finished as the room descended into a shoveling-food-in-their-faces-kind-of quiet.

AJ was sitting up, looking bright and happy, but he really did look tired. It had been a busy day for him.

The day probably drained him, she thought. *The number of people who came by must have been overwhelming – even though they didn't all come at once, and the doctors probably bugged him for blood and scans and tests. I'm sure he's feeling it.*

"He has definitely been cleared to eat this, right? The doctor said no restrictions?" she asked the room as she handed him a slice.

"Yes ma'am!" Jeremy answered through a full mouth of pizza.

"You been out of bed yet today?" she asked him as he took a bite of pizza.

He nodded. "I've done three trips to visit the lovely nurses – I think they've started timing me."

"You eating?" Jeremy asked her as he ate.

"I got something before I came over," she answered him, throwing him her best *don't start anything right now,* look.

"What's going on?" AJ asked, taking another bite. She'd never seen someone so happy to eat pizza before.

"I better get going," Britt chimed, unintentionally talking over him. "I gots me a boyfriend to go meet."

She made her goodbyes and said she'd be back in two weeks. Hugging Lisa, she added, "Take care of our boy?" with a wink.

"I better get going too," Ana added getting to her feet. "My flight leaves soon. I'll be back as soon as I can Pim," she told him, grabbing him into a bear hug and kissing his cheek.

"Good to get to know you, Lis," she said, hugging her tightly. "I would say look after him while I'm gone. But after everything, I have no doubts you will. You do, however, need reminded to look after *yourself*."

She made doubly sure Lisa had her number, said

goodbye to her parents, and left.

By this stage, the food had been devoured. Brad and Jeremy did a quick clean-up job. Lisa cracked the windows to clear some of the pizza-smell and grabbed a soda.

Glancing around the room to see who was left, she smiled slightly. Jeremy, Brad, Mike and Marc. Most of AJ's inner circle.

"So, you gonna tell me why you're checking to see if my girlfriend is eating?" AJ asked Jeremy. She turned her face to look out the window, as the room went quiet and everyone suddenly took interest in the hospital paint job.

"Dude. She fainted, remember? With you out of action, someone had to make sure she was eating!"

"Ok..."

Still looking out the window, Lisa avoided looking at AJ. He could read her like a book and she didn't want to get into it in front of his teammates.

"So," he continued, changing tactics, "who is gonna bring me up to date with what has happened in the last six days?" Before anyone could respond, the door opened. Three, the asshole that caused this whole mess, whose name she *still* didn't know, nor cared to know, stood staring back at everyone's dumbfounded faces.

Chapter 36

"Oh, hell no!"

Everyone turned to look at Lisa.

"You have some *nerve*!" she shrieked. "You are *not* welcome here! And you need to leave before I launch myself across this room. Do you understand me?" Her voice shook as she spoke. It wasn't exactly raised, but her tone was menacing enough to draw some raised eyebrows.

Jeremy knew who he was, as did the other players. They seemed to be too stunned to speak and were seemingly wondering what the heck she was going to do next. But Brad had no idea who the guy standing in the doorway was. AJ also seemed confused.

"Dude, what the hell did you do to her?" Brad asked, smiling.

"What did he do to me?" she asked, with visceral anger. "He sexually assaulted me in the bar," she snapped. Seeing the horror spread across Brad's face, she continued. "But that's not the worst of it, Brad. Oh, no. This is the dumb fuck who put AJ into a mother fucking coma," she fumed.

"Lis..." AJ's voice was quiet and steady.

"Don't...Please?"

"Don't what?" she spat, furiously. "Don't give him a hard time? Why not? He deserves it."

She could feel her cheeks getting hot. She wanted to launch herself across the room at this guy. *Why has no one else jumped this douche bag?*

She looked around the room. No one would meet her gaze and a couple of the guys shifted uncomfortably in their seats.

"I just came to-"

"You need to be quiet right now," she instructed Three, her voice low and shaking with anger.

"Lisa, please. Let him speak," AJ said.

She turned to look at AJ, stunned that he hadn't just told him to get the hell out of his room.

"Excuse me? Let him speak? Don't you think he's done enough AJ?"

"Lis, please?" he pleaded with her.

"Wait. So, one minute everyone wants to kill him for feeling me up against the bar. He almost kills you on the fucking ice. And now, what? It's all let's be friends? You're kidding me, right? Please tell me you're kidding me. Dirty, cheating asshole." She directed the last part at Three, but her voice was a mix of fury and sobs.

"Lisa!"

"Fine. If he's staying, I'm not." She picked up her bag and stormed out of the room pushing past him.

Clearly, AJ was letting the guy say his piece. She didn't understand why, but she knew she didn't want to be in the same room as him. She thought Jeremy should have thrown him out the minute he walked in the door. She was so filled with rage and confusion. AJ was clearly exhausted after a long day, but that didn't explain why his reaction to Three had been very different to hers. She wanted to beat the ever-living crap out of him. AJ wanted to talk to him. His parents had sat quietly. Waves of emotion hit her as she started down the stairs. She took them two at a time.

I can't be here. I need to get some air. I need to think.

Lisa hesitated when she got to the door of the hospital. Her comatose boyfriend had just woken up, his friends and family had grown to like her, and she *should* have been there, by his side.

What would Chelsea say?

She paused for a moment to think.

Don't do things because you think you should.

What else?

That it's ok to put yourself first, especially when you need to.

There was a cab waiting at the door when she got outside.

I'm two for two on serendipitously positioned taxis, she thought glumly as she got in and slammed the door. *Not to mention I'm running away from a messed-up situation yet again.* Guilt tugged at her. She directed the cab driver to take her to AJ's house to get a few of her things, and from there she took herself to a hotel. She didn't want to be found so she switched off her phone.

Once she had checked in, she fell on to the bed and cried and cried until the tears wouldn't come anymore and her throat hurt from the weight of her sobs. The last few weeks of pent-up emotions finally broke free. From not knowing if her fake-married boyfriend would ever wake up, to him waking up and not remembering her, albeit temporarily, to his mood swings and fractured memory, she'd been through a lot.

And then HE dared show his face? That douche bag who assaulted me, and almost KILLED AJ, and they all just sat so quiet and calm?

She was livid and completely overwhelmed by wave after wave of emotion. After all they'd been through, and he'd just let that asshole into his room? Just when things were starting to *really* improve? After what he did? To both of them.

"FUUUUUUCK!" she screamed loudly. *Why isn't he angry?* She wondered. *Why aren't ANY of them angry?!*

Am I being irrationally angry? Am I finally losing my mind? I don't think so, I mean, the asshole assaulted me and AJ did almost die.

Nope. Definitely justified anger.

She cried and punched the pillows a few dozen times, and when she had worn herself out, she ordered a movie on the in-room TV, called down for room-service, and curled up on the bed in her dressing gown. She was hurt, and angry and no amount of Ben & Jerry's would console her. She decided she should probably check her phone as she'd been gone for a couple hours.

Twenty-four missed calls.

Five voicemails and eight text messages.

She listened to the voicemails first. One each from AJ, Brad, Jeremy, Ana and Chelsea. Each one a variation of, "Lisa, everyone's worried sick about you. Where the hell are you? Let someone know you're ok." The texts were a similar shade of, "call me when you get this," and "Where the hell are you?????"

Sighing loudly, she pulled up Chelsea's number.

"Where the hell are you?"

"Why yes, Chels. I'm fine, thanks for asking."

"Lis, so help me God. Where are you?"

"I'm not telling you."

"Why not?"

"Because you'll send Jeremy over to babysit me and make sure I'm ok. And I don't want anyone over right now. I'm fine."

"No, you're not."

"Ok. You're right. I'm not ok. I'm seriously pissed off and need some space. I know part of me is reacting irrationally, but AJ sided with *him* over me. What the actual fuck?" she fumed.

"I already heard what happened. AJ didn't *side* with him, he just wasn't angry like you are. He wanted to let the guy say his piece. Remember, he has no real memory of what actually happened."

"You're siding with him now, too?" Lisa accused hotly.

"Lisa. Stop. That's not what this is. You gotta calm down. Your whole perspective is being blurred by anger."

"What the hell do you think I'm doing here?"

"Ok, Lis. Really. Sit the hell down and take some deep breaths. The last thing we need is for you to fall down again and no one have a clue where you are."

"Heard about that too, did you?" she asked quietly. She hadn't told her best friend about her fainting.

"I did. Only because they called me to try and find you – they assumed you'd told me. But yes, I heard. Jeez. Go sit down, your pacing is driving me nutty!"

"How do you know I'm pacing?"

"Lucky guess? I'm kidding. I'm not deaf, I can freakin' hear you!"

At that moment, someone knocked the door. Looking through the peephole, Lisa groaned loudly.

"Aw crap."

"What? What is it? What's wrong?"

"They found me," she groaned.

Chapter 37

"Who? Lis? Who found you?" Chelsea asked.

"Marc's at my door, with Mike."

"Open up. We'll start stripping in the corridor if you don't let us in."

"I've seen Marc naked, Lis," Mike added. "It's not a pretty picture."

With Chelsea giggling down the phone, Lisa banged her head on the back of the door.

"Can't you guys just leave me the hell alone? How did you even find me?"

"No. We can't." Marc replied.

Looking through the peep-hole, she saw he was on his phone.

"MARC! Who the hell are you telling?"

"The cavalry. Now let us in, Lis."

"The cavalry? Who the hell is the-" she paused as realization dawned and she repeated banging her head against the door. "You called Jeremy! Now he's going to come over and pep-talk at me. Damnit, Marc!"

"Seriously, Lis, if you don't let us in, we're going to climb up the balcony."

"As exciting as that sounds, I'd much rather be left

alone, guys."

"That's not an option," Mike added. "It's let us in through the front door, have us come up the balcony, or Marc is going to strip and cause a scene – your choice."

She said goodbye to Chelsea and unlocked the door, stepping back to let them in. She was still in her dressing gown and slippers, and had a towel wrapped around her damp hair like a turban. The empty tub of ice cream was sitting on the counter, along with a half-empty, huge bag of Doritos and a bag of popcorn. She was aware of the empty mini-bar bottles also sitting in view.

"Having a party, Lis?" Marc joked.

"Not exactly. How did you find me?" she replied, heading for the bathroom to get dressed.

"That creepy find my friend thing, when you turned your phone on. We were checking at the hotel across the street when you appeared on the map. Lis," he changed direction. "You need to understand, it's a hockey player thing." He spoke slowly, his voice deliberate.

"Oh, I *need* to understand, do I? Please continue to soften the ground for Jeremy to come lecture me," she called from the bathroom, slipping on a pair of jeans.

"Well, not exactly, I'm just trying to-"

"Marc?"

"Yeah?"

"Don't bother."

"Ok, but-"

"Marc?"

"Yeah?"

"No buts."

"Ok."

Mike grabbed Marc by the arm and tried to move him towards the door. "We should go," he mumbled avoiding looking directly at Lisa.

"But Jeremy isn't here yet," Marc replied.

Lisa sighed heavily and flopped onto the sofa, tucking her legs up underneath her. "Well, since you guys would only find me again, I'm not going to go anywhere. I'll wait here, listen to Jeremy's lecture and surgically implant it up his-"

"Well. That's not very nice." Jeremy grinned, appearing in the doorway.

"I'm not in a very nice mood," she grumped. "You *still* don't know how to knock? At least these two knocked!" she pointed at the others with her thumb.

"Did you two leave my door open for him? Or have you taken up magic as well, Jer? You got here awfully fast."

"Bye, Lis," Mike said, looking guilty and making a quick exit.

"Bye, Mike,"

"Bye, Lis,"

"Bye, Marc."

Feeling guilty at being so short-tempered with them, she tried to apologize.

"I'm sorry guys, I'm just-"

Mike interrupted her. "It's ok, Lis. You've been through a lot."

AGH! Why do you have to be so kind?
"That's no excuse for being a bitch. I really am sorry, guys," she mumbled on the verge of tears.

Jeremy closed the door behind them. "So, you wanna tell me what the hell that was all about?" he asked as he picked up the bag of Doritos and joined her on the sofa. She turned away from him.

The tears that had threatened were suddenly gone again, and Lisa was back to feeling angry, really angry. Angry that that jerk decided he was entitled to visit AJ. Angry that AJ had *let* that jerk into the room. Angry that he'd told her off in front of a room full of his friends, as well as that *jerk*. Angry that Jeremy hadn't flattened the guy as soon as he appeared. Angry that Jeremy didn't seem to understand what she was feeling and why she was feeling it. And angry that they wouldn't leave her the hell alone for a while. She was angry. So she sat in silence and fumed.

"Lis?" he prodded, munching on some chips.

"What?" she spat through gritted teeth.

"These chips need dip. Do you have dip? You can't eat Doritos without dip!"

She shook her head. "No dip."

"Strange, strange Irish girl," he said, half to himself, half aloud. "Well?" he continued. "You gonna talk to uncle Jer? I know you're angry Lisa, I get it, he could have killed AJ, Lis?"

She shook her head.

"Then at least come back and talk to AJ. He's pretty

upset."

"HE is upset?" she said with a look of mock disgust. "Makes two of us," she snapped bitterly.

"Ok. Whoa. We need to fix this. Lis, listen to me. It's a hock-"

"Jeremy. You sure as hell better not be about to tell me it's a hockey player thing."

He snapped his mouth closed.

"Because let me tell *you* something. It's not. Ok? It's a *crazy person thing*. The odd rough check into the boards? That's a hockey player thing. Having insanely odd and constant injuries? That's a hockey player thing. Screaming puck bunnies? Hockey player thing. Guys from other teams sexually assaulting your girlfriend? That's a breaking the law thing. Letting the guy who almost killed you, and there's probably an argument for it being deliberate too, the guy who put your friends and family through utter hell, into your room and pretty much taking his side over your girlfriend? That's a crazy person thing. And it's just plain wrong, Jeremy."

"Lis, it's hard to explain. There's, like, a player code, or something." He stopped, sighed, looked to be gathering his thoughts before trying again. "I really dunno if I can explain."

"Then don't bother. Just leave me alone," she said standing and turning away from him again.

"No can do, I'm afraid. Chelsea isn't here for you to talk to. You're pissed at our boy, and that leaves me. So, either you come back to the hospital and talk to AJ, or you sit your ass back down and talk to me. Those are your choices. Pick one."

His face reflected a steely resolve she'd become accustomed to seeing in him lately.

"Who's with him?" she asked.

"Mike and Marc are headed back there now and will sit with him until I get back."

She sighed heavily.

"Fine. Let's go," she grumbled, grabbing her coat and bag.

"I know this is hard for you," he told her quietly.

Seeing her obviously try to give her best, *are you kidding me right now?* look, he couldn't help but laugh.

"Ok, so I maybe I don't quite know *exactly* how you feel," he continued, "but I know you are finding it hard to understand, Lis. The guy came to apologize. He knows he was out of line and wanted to try and make things right. He could have been any of us. Many of us have been there. AJ could have died. *Asshole,* as you seem to have re-named him, could maybe even have been brought up on charges – he probably still could be if AJ were so inclined. I know that it was on purpose this time, or at least seemed like it. But many of us have been there by accident, and it's a horrible place to be. That feeling, knowing you've gravely injured someone, it's sickening. Waiting to hear if they wake up? Terrifying. It *absolutely* doesn't forgive him for laying hands on you, and you can pursue that further if you'd like – none of us would judge you for it, we'd support you one hundred percent.

However, when it comes to the game, we really are brothers in arms. They'll never be friends. They'll probably never speak to each other for as long as they live. They'll probably actively avoid each other on the ice at every game from now on, assuming AJ plays again. But they need to make peace. For both of them. I know this doesn't make things right. It doesn't. And nothing he could possibly say to you or to AJ, or hell, even to me for that matter – could make the last week and a half of your life any better, or hurt any less. But it's what players do when they're wrong. They suck it up, say sorry and try to put out the fire regardless of screaming hockey girlfriends, or best friends throwing them up against a wall – it's like, honor, or some crap I guess?" he finished, exasperated.

"Uh. I said fine. Let's go," she told him.

"Yeah. I know. But if I let you go back to the hospital like this," he gestured in her direction, "AJ might need some protection from his crazy Irish girlfriend – and that's not a fight I want to see. To be honest, you kinda scare me!"

She laughed and threw her jacket at him.

"Shut up, or I'll give you a reason to be scared!" she told him as they headed down to the car. "Can we stop and get me some food somewhere on the way?" she asked.

"You're hungry again? Sheesh, dude. You have the appetite of a hocke-" he paused and looked at her, "You didn't really eat earlier, did you? Just those snacks? Shit.

Lis, you gotta eat!"

"I don't eat much when I'm stressed out, Jer. That pizza earlier would have come back up if I'd tried. But I'm feeling a bit better now and I'm actually hungry. Turns out a deep and fiery rage makes me hungry."

"Your wish is my command," he joked as he did a deep bow.

They went to a local Tex-Mex, and Jeremy threatened to tattle on her if she didn't eat enough to appease him. He ate, too. Again. She shook her head and laughed.

"Hockey boys and their food," she said as she watched him shovel food into his mouth like he'd never been fed before.

Chapter 38

They took the elevator this time. Lisa was too full for the stairs. The nurses said hi as they stopped at the vending machine to get drinks. Jeremy entered the room first.

"Is she here?" Mike asked at the same time AJ asked, "Is she ok?" as she walked into the room.

"Later dudes," Mike said to AJ and Jeremy. "Bye again Lis."

"Bye, Mike, and thank you," she replied, noting that he couldn't get out the room fast enough.

"I really am sorry," she called to his back. *Man, I clearly have some making up to do with his hockey friends.*

Jeremy walked over to the bed and hugged his friend, "Dude, hands where I can see them," Lisa called jokingly.

"Yeah, yeah, I hear ya Irish. I'll get my lovin' when he gets outta this place! Peace out, peeps!"

"Later," AJ replied, "and thanks!"

"Sure," Jeremy answered as he came to hug the stressed-out Irish girl. "Go easy on him," he warned. "He's delicate." She raised an eyebrow at him. "He's been in a coma for a week and had his head cracked open!"

Lisa sighed, and laughingly dug his ribs with her fist.

"'Cause I've not been here for that?"

"I'm just saying!" Jeremy answered, rubbing the spot she'd hit him.

"Skedaddle," she instructed.

"Eeeeesh. Bossy! Ok, ok, I'm goin'!" Turning back to AJ he asked if Mike had left his pads.

Lisa chased him out and closed the door and hesitated for a moment or two before turning around to face AJ. He patted the bed beside him, indicating she should join him on the bed. She dropped her bag and coat on the chair and sat on the bed.

"I-" he began.

"Shhhhhhh," she placed her finger on his lips to quieten him, "it's ok."

"But, I-"

She shook her head, not lifting her finger. Their eyes met. "I'm sorry," he mumbled.

"Why are you sorry, Pim? I'm the one who lost her temper and stormed out of here. I just, I couldn't be here, not in the same room as him. I don't understand why he was allowed to come here, to see you, to *speak* to you, when all I wanted was to punch him repeatedly for what he did to you...and to me."

"I know, I get it. It didn't really occur to me when I woke up that he'd call by and we'd need a chat about it, but everything was so blurry. Even after the doctor said it was a hockey accident it didn't occur to me that I'd need to give it further thought, or that someone was to blame for it. I can't imagine how worried and upset you've been, and you've spent so much time in close quarters with my friends and family with no stress-release. I know you probably think I took his side, but that's not what it was. I know in the moment it probably felt like it though," he trailed off. "Lis, you're entirely justified to hate him. He assaulted you and he attacked me. The last few weeks wouldn't have happened if it weren't for him. If I were you, I'd absolutely hate him too, but I wanted to hear what he had to say, and try to understand what happened, why the hell he hated me so much, rather than kicking him out like you wanted."

"It's ok. I really am sorry for blowing up like that, it really wasn't the time or place. I just couldn't help it."

Understanding passed between them and she kissed him gently.

"Did Three have anything noteworthy to say?"

"Three?" AJ repeated, confused.

"Sorry, yeah, the guy who hit you. I don't actually know his name, nor do I care to really, so just call him by his number."

Smiling, AJ shook his head, "His name is Dwight, and he didn't really have a lot to say for himself, Lis. He's in his last year of college hockey. He wants a contract with one of the bigger leagues and it's not looking likely. He wanted to get his team to the playoffs and be a hero. The two of us getting into it with each other repeatedly pushed him over the edge. He swears he didn't mean for me to get so badly hurt, though, and apologized, a lot.

He feels pretty bad about it all. I don't think he wanted to bare his soul to me, but I got the impression there was maybe something else going on with him – not that that excuses anything."

She smiled at him and stroked his cheek, the wound on the side of his head was healing, but she could tell it still irked him. He kept trying to touch it and look at it sideways in the mirror. He was hurting elsewhere too; she could tell. His head hurt and movement down one side of his body was a little slower and more deliberate than the other. His grip was a little weaker, but she figured it would fix itself soon enough. She'd made a mental note to keep tabs on it but under his radar. Standing up, she kicked off her shoes so she could change into her pjs.

"AJ, close your eyes," she told him.

"Why?" he asked.

"I'm getting changed!"

"Babe, it's not like I've not seen you changing before," he answered as she slipped her jeans off.

He gave a low whistle. "Leave them off," he instructed.

"Like hell I will. Your medical team already probably think I'm a trouble maker. Last thing I need is for anyone to walk in and find my bare arse in the air."

He laughed. "You're paranoid, Lis, I'm sure they like you just fine."

As she lifted her leg to put her pj bottoms on, she heard movement behind her. Spinning around, she squealed. He was out of bed, which she knew was ok, but he had a look of mischief on his face. He was wearing some of his new pjs. *Harder to access than the open backed hospital gown, I grant you... Lisa! Get his ass back into bed! But...he looks so freakin' good...*

Shaking it off, she scolded him.

"What the HELL do you think are you doing?"

"Shhhhhhhh!" he said, moving towards her with clear intent. "What do you think I'm doing?"

"AJ the door doesn't lock! It's a hospital! You shouldn't be out of bed. You're tired, you've had a long and draining day. What if you collapse, Pim?" Her protests gave themselves over to her racing heart as he slipped his arms around her waist.

"Then put me back to bed," he winked at her.

"You must be feeling better," she said returning his smile and slipping her arms around his middle. *I've missed holding him so damn much.*

"I was out of bed for a while earlier, just after you ran off in a ball of fire. I'm allowed to be out of bed, nurse said so, doctor said so, physio said so," he insisted.

"Well. Nurse might say so, but girlfriend says your sexy butt needs to get back into bed, ok?"

"Only if your sexy butt comes with me," his hands slid down slightly below her waist and, squeezing gently, he bent his head and kissed her deeply.

"I guess at least Jeremy is gone and can't walk in on us this time," she giggled as she climbed into bed next to him.

"Well, I'm sure if he knew what we were up to, he'd try and walk through that door," he replied as he drew her close to him. "You two seem to be getting along better."

"He kept me sane."

"That's what he said about you."

She shrugged and kissed his cheek lightly. "I guess we kept each other sane. He had my back. I had his."

"Backs I can handle. As long as no one got any ass."

"Ooooooh. Are you jealous, AJ?"

"No. I'm just saying."

"Oh yeah? But it's *my* ass!" she argued.

"Yeah..." he thought for a moment, "but-"

"AJ?"

"Uh huh?"

"Shut up and kiss me."

She didn't need to tell him twice. She stopped in a moment of realization and moved herself to look squarely into his eyes, "Are you sure you're up to this, mister? Don't wanna drive you back into that coma of yours," she joked. "Actually, on second thought, don't answer that. I see you're more than up for it," she giggled and kissed him again.

Undressing her caused some technical difficulties for him, as did his injuries for her. But they managed eventually. With the door closed and the blinds closed they got gently reacquainted after their traumatic time apart.

During the time AJ was asleep – Lisa had taken to calling it that rather than being in a coma – she'd missed being able to hold him, to look into his eyes, to read him. She'd missed being able to kiss him whenever she wanted. She'd missed him more than she ever thought was possible to miss anybody. The fear of losing him forever had clutched at her and also overcome her hope of seeing him awake again.

That night, they more than made up for the time apart. And, when they eventually went to sleep, he held her close and so tightly that she couldn't help but smile. At random points throughout the night, she checked and double checked that he was still really 'just sleeping,' as opposed to the 'sleep', he'd just started to *really* wake up from.

Chapter 39

"Good morning, people!" Jeremy announced as he burst into the room. "Oh shit!" Lisa heard the door close again and people giggling.

Where am I?

She blinked awake and looked down.

Shit! I have no clothes on.

She blinked again and looked at the door.

Shit! People.

She shrieked, rolled out of bed, trying to grab the top sheet and fell onto the floor. On her way back up, she misjudged and smacked her head, hard, on the bed frame.

"Ow! Mother Fucker!"

The laughter continued. Glancing over her shoulder, she saw AJ was awake and propped up on his elbow, grinning at her widely.

"You two ok in there?" his mom asked.

Bollocks.

"Uh. Yeah, we're fine. I just hit my head."

More laughter as she scrambled to wrap a sheet around herself.

"On what?" Jeremy.

Of course he's here.

Looking to AJ for some kind of bailing out, she was met with giggling from him, too. She was flying solo.

Shit.

"The bed frame?" Her face was hot as coals. She ran a quick hand through her morning, post-sex hair, which she was pretty sure, looked wild as the jungle.

"Why were you under the bed in the first place?" Brad called innocently.

Oh joy! Can't a girl catch a break?

Opening the door, she stepped back to let them in, avoiding their accusing gazes and knowing smiles. She searched for some other witty retort – and her clothes – or swift change of subject to distract from the fact she was standing wrapped in a hospital sheet having had sex with the son of the woman who was standing in front of her. She failed to find that witty retort and instead opted for brazen.

"Because I was *naked*, Brad. Ok? A girl's gotta cover her bits when her boyfriend's mother shows up and hospital doors have no locks. Also, because I couldn't find my freakin' clothes and thought I'd be kind and not scare the crap out of you by opening the door without my sheet!"

She flashed a cheeky grin in the hopes that would be the end of that, still scanning the floor for her discarded clothes. *Where the fucking fuck are my clothes? Calm down. They have to be here somewhere. I came IN wearing clothes. Inanimate objects don't just grow legs and run away!*

They obviously weren't expecting her bluntness.

"Well, ok then. I don't think we need any more detail on that topic." Cindy swiftly put the lid on the conversation.

"I agree. AJ, where the hell are my clothes?" Lisa all but screeched at him as she carefully bent over to survey under the bed.

"You'll never know." He teased as her cheeks flushed red.

"You're lucky you're in a hospital bed right now, AND that your parents are here, or I'd... I'd... I really dunno what I'd do, but it wouldn't be very nice."

Unable to contain his laughter, he half spoke, half laughed, "Please don't make me laugh any more, everything kinda aches."

"Man, you coulda gone easy on him, Lis!" Jeremy spoke up again.

"Well. You brought this on yourself, Pim. You hid my clothes! I don't even know how. How DID you? Wait. When did you? I don't underst-" She had opened the cupboards and drawers in his bedside unit, but come up empty.

Still laughing, he patted the space next to him on the bed and motioned for her to sit down.

Lisa shuffled back to the bed and climbed in beside AJ. She felt less naked and more protected as she lay with her head on his chest, his arm around her tightly and listening to the soft thudding of his heart. He was still smiling as his dad came into the room. His eyes widened as he saw Lisa's bare shoulders over the top of the bed sheets.

"Please tell me you didn't interrupt," he said to his wife.

"No, they were finished by then," Jeremy answered.

"I think they were asleep to be fair," added Brad.

"ANYWAY!" Lisa attempted to steer the topic in the room away from her sex life, "What time is it?"

"It's only eight thirty a.m," his mom offered, "AJ, your father and I need to go back up north for a while, I have a trial. We have some things to take care of. We plan on calling multiple times a day. I need to see your face and know you're ok, ok? I know we're leaving you in very capable hands." She looked at Lisa, who blushed again. "And the doctor says you'll probably be out of here in the next couple of days. As long as you have someone to keep an eye on you at home, they'll let you go."

"I'm going with them, cause I gotta get back, too," Brad chimed in, "so we all came to say goodbye!"

After a rather embarrassing set of goodbye hugs, which involved her sitting up in the bed with AJ firmly gripping the sheet so it didn't reveal *too* much of his naked self – and hugging while simultaneously holding her own sheet, which wasn't as tightly wrapped as she wanted it to be, they all left. Jeremy was driving everyone to the airport, so they were alone again. When the door closed, she waited a few minutes for her heart to come back down to normal, and pretended to collapse on his chest.

"AJ! OhMyGOD! Thanks for the help there!" she exclaimed, jabbing him in the ribs. He rested his hands in the small of her back.

"You did pretty well on your own, babe." He grinned at her and pecked her nose.

"Well, I had no choice. They all knew what was going on and I'm hardly going to try and lie to your mother, am I?"

He laughed.

"Apparently not. I don't think *anyone* expected you to come out with what you did. Even Jeremy was kind of flabbergasted – and it's not easy to shock him!"

She kissed him. "Yeah. Well. It's hardly surprising really, and so very typical that we'd get caught again! Do you think we'll ever have uninterrupted sex?"

"You looked seriously hot standing there wrapped in that sheet," he told her grinning. "If my mom wasn't on the other side of the door I'd have-"

The door opened and the doctor came in.

"How's the patient this morning?"

She jumped out of her skin, rolled off AJ, but misjudged and went crashing off the side of the bed again, landing flat on her back on the floor, clutching her sheet for dear life, whilst AJ grabbed a quick hold of the only sheet keeping him decent.

"Don't you know how to knock?" she shrieked. "Don't you think about these things before you barge into the private room of a twenty-three-year-old guy who has been asleep for days? I mean, you're a guy. You get guy urges, right? Can't two grown-ass, consenting adults just *be* naked without being interrupted? Just *once*?"

Lisa was still on the floor, so she didn't see that a nurse had come into the room. She struggled to her feet; AJ was laughing again.

"I'm sorry, doctor," he began, through his laughing.

"I'm sorry, too," the doctor laughed somewhat embarrassed. "I didn't mean to interrupt, I just came to do some final checks for release later today. Certainly seems as though you're more than ready to go home."

"Well, trust me, he's fine. And if he's not fine, then let's just say, between friends since I'm sitting here mostly naked and all, that if he isn't fine, I'm not sure I could even handle him fine. Send him home. I'll look after him and keep an eye on him. I'll even spoon-feed him if you want."

He was properly laughing at her now. She didn't blame him. Had this been anyone else, she would have been laughing, too. She was sure when everyone else heard, they'd all find it hilarious. They'd probably end up as some mortifying viral twitter feed or Facebook post.

"I'd heard the Irish were brazen, but I thought it usually involved alcohol!" the nurse joked.

"Well, they aren't all like me. I'm just a frustrated girl who would just like some alone time with her boyfriend, without his best friend, or mother, or random physiotherapist, nurse or doctor walking in. Is that too much to ask?" she questioned desperately as she grabbed her shower bag.

"You," she said to the doctor, "*please* do whatever tests you gotta do. I'm going for a shower and to get out from under your feet because I'm afraid I may end up even more embarrassed and I'm honestly not sure what that might even look like. And you," she turned to AJ, "don't go jumping in to my defense or anything stupid." She kissed him lightly on the forehead, "and don't fail his damn tests, because we all need me the hell out of this place!" She shuffled over to the bathroom, still wrapped tightly in her sheet.

Chapter 40

AJ was released later that day, with strict instructions to remain in the house for a few weeks. He still needed plenty of rest and was only permitted light exercise alongside his physio appointments. Nothing too taxing the doctor had said, with a wry grin.

That evening, Lisa picked up take-out, a couple movies and a truck-load of junk food. They lay on the sofa chilling out. As they lay there, she watched him. His movement was slowly returning to "normal", and he said he was feeling pretty good – all things considered. Although she believed he was feeling better, she still needed to reassure herself fairly regularly.

They sat up all night, talking, laughing and eating *way* more than they should have, but they didn't care. When the movies were done, they stuck on some music and talked some more. The conversation topics were light, nothing too deep or emotional, until she came back from the bathroom and sat down next to him. She was staring at him again, her gaze rested on his wound for a few seconds, before she realized that he was staring back at her.

She laughed quietly as he held his arm out for her to

come closer to him. She did, resting her head on his shoulder. She let out an involuntary sigh.

"What's on your mind, babe?" he asked.

"It's the first week in April," she replied.

"I know. I didn't hit my head that hard."

She elbowed his ribs lightly and continued, "You kinda did though! I have to go home soon. I've already stayed longer than I intended. Playing hooky kinda took a turn. I know I got permission from the university and all, but I have stuff to deal with, like finishing up my degree, paying bills and finding a grown-up job." She sighed again. "But I don't want to go. I don't want to leave you. I'm afraid something else is going to happen and I'm going to lose you. I don't want to wake up and not be able to hear your voice, or see your face."

"That's understandable. The last couple weeks can't have been easy for you."

She laughed a humorless laugh. "Isn't *that* the understatement of the century?"

"Sorry," he started, "I know I don't really know what it was like for you. We can talk about it you know? Assuming you even *want* to talk about it." He paused again and kissed her forehead.

I do love it when you do that.

"My memory is still kinda blurry in parts, especially leading up to the accident," he continued. "But, I can guess it was far from pleasant. And I honestly don't know what I'd have been like if it had been you lying there on that bed. I don't know if I could have kept my shit together."

"You would have done just fine," she told him. "If someone had asked me how I'd deal with it before it happened, I would have said that I wouldn't have dealt with it at all. I'd have guessed complete and utter meltdown and inability to function and perform the simplest of tasks. In many ways, that's actually what happened. I mean, I managed, don't get me wrong. I had my moments, but I pushed through. I tried to stay positive as best I could. But man, it was so hard. The thought of never having you wake up again? Of never being able to talk to you, or see your smile, or hear your voice? Not knowing if you even know how I truly feel about you, or-" her voice broke and she was suddenly crying, "and now you're awake, and I have to go home soon, and it royally sucks."

"Hey, hey. It's ok," he soothed. But it really wasn't, they both knew it. Her trip, in its entirety, had been an emotional rollercoaster. Between finding out he was married, the guy in the bar, the coma, meeting his friends and family, it had been far from easy for her and a *lot* to take in.

I wonder if everyone's lives are this dramatic?

She had a week left and was determined to spend as much time as possible with him, taking care of him and making sure he was going to be ok when she left. Before the accident AJ had been planning to visit Ireland over the summer, but now it would have to be delayed due to his accident though at least they had something to look forward to when she left. She needed it. They both did.

***

Of course, the week flew past.

Before Lisa knew it, she was standing in the airport struggling to find the strength to say goodbye to Jeremy and AJ.

She'd sat pretty much in silence all the way to the airport. Struggling with her tears, she faced out the window so neither of them could see her cry.

AJ wasn't really supposed to be out of the house yet, but the doctor had given the all-clear for Jeremy to supervise his trip to see her off, on the condition he would go straight home afterwards. He was also going to be permitted a beer or two, to drown his sorrows.

Jeremy gave her a hug, said he'd see her soon and that he was thinking of going to Ireland with AJ when he'd recovered. She nodded silently as he gave her a second, slightly longer hug.

"I'd say it was good to finally meet you, but that's not really something you say after all we've been through together." He paused, "It's certainly been eventful – I'd love to see you and Chelsea try and scrapbook *this* trip."

She laughed. *Always the joker.*

"Take care of yourself, you hear?"

"You too," she managed, "and thanks for everything, Jer."

"Any time," he replied. "I'll leave you two to, uhm..."

he trailed off. Giving her a sad smile and AJ an affectionate thump on the back, he headed out to the car. “I’ll be outside.”

“Sure,” AJ replied.

“Ok, well, I better go,” Lisa said, trying to paste on her best ‘I’m fine’ face and willing herself not to cry.

“Yeah, let me know as soon as you land?”

“Sure.”

“Stay safe, and don’t worry. I’ll be there before you know it,” he told her.

She nodded and they kissed.

“I love you.”

“I love you, too,” she replied, and with that, she dragged herself away from him and headed through security.

She didn’t look back. She couldn’t. She didn’t want him to see her crying, and she didn’t want to see the pain he was feeling at watching her go.

It’ll get easier, she told herself. *As time passes, you’ll get used to this. You’ll be able to leave him at the airport and you won’t cry like a baby!*

Are you trying to convince yourself this is true, Lis? Cause you’re doing a shit job of it.

Why won’t he just divorce her and marry me?

Great. Now I’m talking to myself again. This has become way more of a habit than I’d like.

***

As she came out of the arrivals gate, Lisa looked for her family. She spotted her mum. They made a quick getaway and, as soon as Lisa collapsed into the car, she called AJ. It was the middle of the night for him, but she figured he'd have put his phone on silent and she'd just leave him a message when his voicemail picked up. He answered on the first ring.

"YOU should be asleep, mister. Doctor's orders," she said smiling.

"YOU should have landed, like, three hours ago or something. Something could have happened. I just wanted to make sure you're ok!"

"I'm fine. I landed safely. I'm in the car and heading home for a few days of sleep!"

"Ok, well say hey to your folks for me."

"Say hey yourself," she told him as she hit the speaker phone button. "Say hey to AJ everyone."

"How are you feeling AJ? Better I hope?" her dad asked loudly.

"Yes, and thanks for all your cards."

"No problem." He paused, "When are you coming to visit for real this time?"

"Uhm, a couple months."

"Ok guys, he really has to sleep. Say goodbye to AJ everyone."

Another chorus of goodbyes as she took him off speakerphone.

"Is Jeremy still awake?"

"Yup."

"Stick him on before I go."

"Dude, what's up?"

"Dude. I can't believe the words that are about to come out of my mouth, but put that boy to bed please. And I don't mean get *into* bed with him. Just make him go to bed. Change his Wi-Fi password or hide his laptop or something. Just make him sleep."

"Ok, bye." She could tell he was going to hang up without passing the phone back to AJ.

"Wait! Wait! WAIT!"

"Dude. What now?"

"Let me say goodbye to him first!"

"Ok. Peace out, princess."

"Stop calling me princess."

"JER? Lisa says stop calling her princess," AJ called.

"Sorry, I thought he was still on with me," she laughed a little. "Ok, go to sleep, rest and we'll talk tomorrow, ok?"

"Ok, sure. Hey?"

"Yeah?"

"Do you miss me yet?"

"Stupid question, AJ. I'm not even gonna dignify it with an answer. That's just how dumb it is. In fact, tell Jeremy to throw something at you."

"Uhm. I'm gonna go right ahead with a 'no' there," he laughed. "Well, I miss you," he told her. "I have no one here to look after me and play nurse." She could almost hear the pout.

"Aw. Poor baby. It's only what? A couple months 'til you get me again?"

"I'm counting the days,"

"Dork," she paused. "I am too. But really, you need sleep. Go!"

"Yes ma'am," he mumbled through a yawn.

"Talk to you tomorrow,"

"Love you."

"Love you too, babe. Sweet dreams."

Chapter 41

At first, Lisa really wasn't sure how she'd cope.

If I kept a diary, it'd read, "Day 2334543, I miss him. I miss him. I miss him. I miss him."

She'd officially turned into that pathetic, love-sick, puppy dog.

So much for that badass biatch who could run the world, she thought glumly. *Why aren't those Star Trek transporter things real?*

Dang girl. You gotta shake this off. You have exams to pass. Get it together.

She grabbed a notebook and a pen.

New rules for Lisa.

#1: ~~No pining~~. Less pining.

Let's go for less pining. It's got to be realistic, Lisa.

#2: Eat better, sleep better, exercise ~~more.~~

Ha! Let's not kid ourselves, shall we? Walking to the chippy and back does NOT constitute exercise, and chips are not a vegetable. Plus, you know he's back at the gym – you're going to need to up your game in preparation for ALL THE SEX.

#3: Buy workout gear.

#4: Buy vegetables.

#5: Screen detox. ~~One~~ ~~two~~ three phone-calls/week.

Do I really need this one?

LISA! Knock it off! Between revision, work, keeping up with his games, and your new exercise schedule of something other than walking to the end of the street, you'll be too busy to call him every day anyway. You can't afford to let the fact you're puke-inducingly in love factor into your plans to conquer the world. Plus, mum used to tell you all the time that you'd get square eyes if you stared at a screen for too long – what if she's RIGHT?

She'd been in love before, gotten engaged quicker than you can say, "Lisa I'm not sure this is a good idea." She'd changed the entire path of her life in an instant, for a boy she was barely with for a year. Her whole A-level year she'd told people she was going to Scotland, or England, for university. And then she met her boyfriend. When the time came to fill in her UCAS forms with university selections, she opted to stay on the Emerald Isle, because of a boy.

She'd resolved never again. Never again would she let a boy impede, or influence her decisions on her life. If the boy was the right boy, he'd be there when she'd figured herself out and done what she wanted and needed to do.

#6: Decide what you wanna be when you grow up.

#7: ~~STOP TALKING TO YOURSELF.~~

Never gonna happen.

She held her new rules out in front of her and studied them intently. This meant it was time to knuckle down, finish her degree once and for all, and then decide what to do when she stood, diploma in hand and ready to choose her next steps in life. She couldn't sit at the computer sobbing that AJ wasn't with her, she couldn't lose nights of sleep and let her work suffer for the sake of a boy – even if she believed him to be *the* boy – especially as he still had another year to finish once she was done. She'd already taken too much time off for her trip to go and meet him.

Never played hooky in your life and now this. It's like you saved up all potential hooky-days and had a massive blow-out!

For the most part, she'd kept up with her assignments while she was visiting AJ, though the university had agreed to cut her some slack after his accident and the weeks that followed, but she still felt like she was playing catch-up since her return.

She was proud of herself for managing to stay focused on the immediate task at hand and barely noticed the time speeding past her. And him? Well. He'd managed to stay out of trouble, and the ER, as well as keeping his own grades decent in school – despite his head injury and taking a bit longer than he should have to complete his assignments. She couldn't *wait* to see him.

AJ had finally booked flights, but he wasn't coming alone. Jeremy was coming over, too, and with four weeks to go, Lisa still hadn't figured out the details of their trip. She was starting to regret not having written up a minute by minute itinerary like the one she'd put together for their trip to London. They were arriving on a Friday morning and staying in Newry until Monday morning when they were going to drive to Carlow. AJ's mother's family ran a B&B down there, and they had offered to let them stay for a week.

Jeremy needs to find an Irish girlfriend so I can get some alone time with my boy, she thought to herself.

The few days in Newry would be spent in the Canal Court Hotel, a big, gaudy looking place. It overlooked the canal, and the bus depot, but on the inside it was beautiful.

Eesh! The Williamses' don't do things by half.

She had *no* idea what she was going to show them, where she was going to take them, or what they were going to do.

Lisa signed onto chat but AJ's status said busy. She knew from his schedule that he was in class. But class was nearly over. She was in a good mood and wanted to say hi.

`Lisa: Hey there gorgeous!`

It took him a few minutes to reply, she sat staring at the orange 'busy' icon next to his name, willing it to turn green.

`AJ: Hey babe, how are you?`

Her heart leapt.

I miss him. I miss him.

Lisa: I'm good, you?

AJ: Yeah, I'm good. Nearly time for lunch.

Lisa: Oh yeah? I'm sure I could help you work your appetite back up.

AJ: I really don't doubt that.

Lisa: Ha ha! Sorry, I shouldn't be distracting. I should be encouraging the studious AJ.

AJ: Yes, you should. But studious AJ is almost on vacation.

Lisa: Oh really? Anywhere nice?

AJ: Actually, it's kinda cold there, I think.

Lisa: Why would you want to vacation somewhere cold?

AJ: Because the company there will keep me warm.

Lisa: Oh reeeeally? Sounds like good company. So, where is this vacation to then?

AJ: 54.18 -6.35

Lisa: In English?

AJ: You need a hint? They're coordinates.

Lisa: You're a dork really, aren't you?

AJ: Yep.

Lisa: That looks an awful lot like where I live.

AJ: Hmmm. Perhaps. That might not be a coincidence.

Lisa: Oh? When's this vacation taking place then? Hmm?

AJ: Four weeks tomorrow actually.

Lisa: Oh AJ! I can't WAIT!

AJ: Me neither, babe. Me neither.

Lisa: I miss you, AJ. I really do. I don't mean to bring it up *again*. I mean, I've known from the beginning that it was going to be hard, but sometimes I just really want to hold you. Or hug you. Or throw random stuff at you - in a good way. And I guess I just feel incredibly stupid when I get like that.

AJ: Why? What's stupid about it? I don't think there's anything stupid about it. And it's not like you're the only one thinking that way.

Lisa: Ha! You have to say that now so I don't feel like a total loon.

AJ: I don't say things just to make you feel better. Well, I could. But that wouldn't make you better in the end. I do think of things like that all the time. Random things. I'll be walking around and wishing you were walking with me. I'll be watching a commercial and think about how I'd rather be lying on the couch playing with your hair, waiting for the movie to come back. Or the game. Or whatever. I'll be singing in the bar and thinking about how I wish you were there too, so I could focus on you and forget everyone else. I think about things like that a lot too, it's not just you. And therefore, you are not crazy. And, if you are… Shit, I am too. Maybe we can share a room in the loony bin?

Lisa started to cry. Falling for someone over the internet, despite having met him and then spending crazy intense time with him in person, made it very easy to convince herself that it was all one-sided, that he didn't love her the way she loved him, or understand how she felt. Or, as was the case here, that he was saying something just to make her feel better – despite her being pretty sure. Somehow, sitting in front of a computer made it incredibly easy to doubt herself. Not being able to see his face, his body language, or hear the inflections in his voice, all made it incredibly easy to take his tone the wrong way. They'd definitely had their share of stupid spats over misinterpretations or things coming across wrong in text.

Lisa: I ordered a Buffalo Sabres jersey.

AJ: What exactly do you think you're doing over there? I really don't know about you. We might have to cut this discussion short.

Lisa: Uh huh. Really?

AJ: No. But. Work with me for a bit. That's total blasphemy.

Lisa: Hey, now. I usually always work with you, except when it comes to hockey. They're really not that bad. I'm getting kicked out of bed, aren't I? So, like, even if I climbed into bed with nothing on, but my Sabres jersey, I'm still getting kicked out?

AJ: Yes. Yes, you are. You're getting kicked out until you come back with a better jersey.

Lisa: Or, you could just use your loaf and take it off, you big gobshite.

AJ: Nope, I'd have to touch it.

Lisa: You know I'll dance around wearing nothing but a Sabres jersey to wind you up, right?

AJ: Yes.

Lisa: You're a butthead. Would you really kick me out of bed?

AJ: Yes.

Lisa: I'd sulk.

AJ: We'd wrestle and you wouldn't sulk for long.

Lisa: I'm a good pretend sulker. I mean, you're kicking me out of bed wearing nothing but a jersey. I'll be cold.

AJ: It'd probably be more like this:

AJ's in bed reading a book waiting for Lisa to come to bed. Lis appears wearing a Sabres jersey and nothing else, knowing she's deliberately causing trouble. AJ sets down the book. Lisa crawls into bed. AJ wrestles Lisa out of bed. AJ keeps wrestling until Lis is managed out of the jersey. AJ brings Lisa back to bed for a few good rolls, and, when she's not looking, slides the jersey under the bed. He tickles Lisa and reminds her that that kind of paraphernalia isn't permitted in our bed.

She laughed. It seemed fairly accurate to her. Even before they'd met, they'd played this weird game of 'how would it go'. Turns out they were pretty spot on.

Lisa: Sigh. You gotta go, Pim. Not that I want rid of you or anything, but…

AJ: You're right, I better jet. I'll talk to you tomorrow. Sweet dreams babe, I love you.

Lisa: I love you too.

She powered down her computer and went to bed with her face sore from smiling.

Chapter 42

Lisa channeled all her frustrations into her studies and, as a result, she ended the school year much better than she'd anticipated. When she found herself flagging, AJ was there to support and encourage her, she'd surprised herself with how focused she could be when she wanted to.

With every day that passed, her plans changed for what she'd do with the guys when they got to town. When the day *finally* came, she was absolutely buzzing with excitement. They were due at midday, and as she stood tapping her foot on the platform, she silently urged the train to hurry up.

After what seemed like hours, the train arrived. The train from Dublin stopped on the far side of the platform, so she had to wait a few torturous minutes longer before she could see her boy. For half a second, she was afraid they weren't there. But then, there he was standing before her. Breaking into a smile he picked her up, spun her round in a huge hug and kissed her. It was a long, intense and passionate kiss that made her dizzy and her stomach flutter.

Jeremy cleared his throat.

"Uh, dude? You guys wanna get a room?"

"Uh, dude?" she said, pulling away from AJ. "Wanna give me a hug?" she said as she hugged him.

AJ's hand found hers, and the three of them headed off to re-meet the parents.

Except it wasn't only the parents. It was meet the parents, the sister, some cousins, and a couple of extended family members. AJ could have been forgiven for wondering if Lisa had set him up to meet everyone at once as pay-back. When they were done with the introductions, Lisa was only too happy to leave the family nut-house behind and take her guests to the hotel. AJ never left her side. They couldn't keep their hands off each other. They were either holding hands or had their arms around each other all the time. She loved it. *Sigh. He is much freer with his affection on Irish soil.*

As he unpacked his bag in the hotel room, she threw a pillow at him.

"Hey!" he protested when it slapped him squarely between his shoulders. "What was that for?" he asked, turning to face his grinning girlfriend, who shrugged.

"I felt like it." She stuck her tongue out.

"Oh really?" he said, returning the pillow to her the same way.

"Hey!" she said approaching him and smacking him, full thwap with the pillow.

"Oh no, you did *not*!" he exclaimed, grabbing a pillow of his own.

Pretty soon, they were play wrestling on the floor.

They somehow managed to knock over a coffee table and a lamp. Within minutes they heard knocking at the door. They had left the adjoining door unlocked while Jeremy unpacked next door as he kept coming in and out.

"What the hell are you two doing? Do I even want to know?" he asked as he entered the bedroom. When he saw them on the floor, he burst out laughing.

"I'm guessing you guys will need a few minutes before we go get some food?"

AJ had Lisa pinned to the floor; he was on top of her and had her arms pinned with one hand. With the other, he had somehow written "No. 1 Leafs fan" across her forehead. She was wriggling and protesting. Loudly.

"Um, Jer?" AJ said cautiously.

"Yeah?"

"Come here and hold her so I can run."

Jeremy laughed. "Oh hell no. You're on your own with this one, I'm not that stupid. Good luck!" And with that he left again, closing the door firmly behind him this time.

"If I let you go, are you going to play nice?"

"If you *don't* let me go, I'm going to kick your hockey playing ass," she said, struggling to get free of his grip.

"Lisa, are you going to play nice if I let you go?"

"LET ME GO!" she shouted.

He tickled her, and she giggled against her will.

"Arthur Justin Williams! Let me go before I get angry!"

He laughed, which made her angrier.

"Let me gooooo!" she demanded, realizing that she wasn't going to have an escape. He made her promise to behave herself and not retaliate.

"I promise," she hissed. As he let her go, she sulked with him. She scrubbed the pen off her head and grumped at him as they headed down to the lobby.

"Dude. You just got here and you're already in the dog house!" Jeremy said as he caught up to them.

"She's just pissy 'cause she couldn't beat me!" he retorted, tickling her sides.

"I may have promised no retaliation, but I can punish you in *other* ways if you're not careful!"

***

Is it really 9 o'clock?

"Thank you all for sufficiently embarrassing me in front of my boyfriend and our friend. I know you've got plenty more ammunition to use, but it really is time for us to go!" she announced to the table.

"It'll keep!" her father called as they got up to leave.

"I have no doubt!" she answered with a wave of her hand.

They headed to The Bank bar, which was bustling as always. They sat and had the *craic*, listening to a local band playing cover songs until closing, by which time they were all a little more than merry and the guys were well and truly suffering with jetlag.

***

As they climbed into bed, discussing the journey so far, Lisa realized that she didn't ever want to go to bed with anyone who wasn't this delicious hockey player lying next to her, ever again.

"I've missed you, Pim. I kinda like having you around," she told him as she cuddled into him sleepily.

"I kinda like being around. Maybe someday we'll make it permanent."

Once you get divorced, of course.

Chapter 43

"So," AJ asked expectantly after she'd had a stretch and a yawn, "do you have an itinerary for the next week? Or are we just going to," he paused, gasped for dramatic effect and whispered, "WING IT?"

She shoved him and giggled.

"Do you know me at all? Of *course* I have an itinerary prepared. What do you think this is? A vacation or something?" She laughed. "I was going to bring it to breakfast and see what you guys thought of it."

***

"Jeremy, reporting for duty, ma'am!" he said as he took a seat at the table. "Mornin' captain, where are we going today, then?"

Her eyes bulged at the pile of healthy food he'd put on his plate, next to his bowl of cereal. "Skipping the cooked breakfast in favor of the Continental, eh, Jer?"

"What? No. This is just the warm up. I've already ordered a 'full Irish', whatever the hell that is."

"Largely carbs," chimed AJ. "Many different kinds of carbs on a plate with some meat."

"Sounds delicious," answered Jeremy through a mouthful of cereal.

Rolling her eyes, Lisa started laying out her proposed travel plan for their visit. "I was thinking we could stay local for at least today. For two reasons. First, jetlag – it will hit again, and it will hit hard. I don't want to give you boys long car trips to nap through when you're trying to adjust to living in the correct time-zone. You *will* stay awake 'til at least nine o'clock tonight, despite feeling like you may die of exhaustion."

"Got it. What's the second reason?"

"My friends will kick my ass if I don't bring you up to the Ring of Gullion for a walk. It's so beautiful and one of our bigger tourist attractions here."

***

They compromised on The Poets Trail, a 'medium', six-mile circular trail which followed a public path to a graveyard, through Glendesha Forest, and around the mountains of Croslieve and Sliebrack.

The boys wanted to do one of the longer hikes, but she'd been adamant that was not going to happen.

"If you're not letting me get away with doing the *magnificent ten-mile scenic forest DRIVE,"* she read loudly from the leaflet, "nor the one-mile walking trail," she paused to make her point, "you *better* believe I'm not doing a ten-mile hike. You guys would have to bury me somewhere along the path. The only option is for us to do the six-mile. SLOWLY. You know, for the brain-damaged among us. He's got to take it easy."

They laughed and started up the hill.

Of course it starts with a hill.

I'm so bloody unfit. Why did I have to tell them that there were walking trails? Couldn't I have told them there were bears in the forest and we had to do the drive?

I hate exercise. I should have paid more attention to rule number two on my "be a badass" list. He's going to kill me with his stamina, isn't he? I can see it in the local paper now:

"Newry girl dies in bed with hockey player. Cause of death was ruled as being severely unfit and eating too many chips."

What a boring headline. Don't give up the day job, Lis.

"Newry Girl Completely Pucked!"

Better, but non-hockey fans wouldn't get the pun.

At various points throughout the "Don't worry, it'll be a slow and easy walk," which, in reality was more like the boys dragging her unhappy and unfit ass around the six-mile trail, she complained. They laughed at her and promised her chips when they'd finished.

I don't think the chips are worth it anymore.

I hate exercise.

Despite the beautiful surroundings, Lisa was happy when it was eventually over. While she knew her energetic and athletic visitors enjoyed exercise and would think the climb was worth the reward of such a breathtaking view at the top, she had been overly optimistic about her own fitness levels and was more than ready to be done.

"I thought Americans were against 'cruel and unusual' punishment?" she grumped.

"Canadian," called Jeremy from ten feet ahead, "We're fine with it," he joked, "though we probably apologize about it."

The boys decided they'd have to come back again in the morning. They'd agreed that they at least needed to do some form of daily exercise to contend with the plates of carbohydrates they'd been putting away since their plane touched down.

Maybe it's not so bad Jeremy came. If he wasn't here, AJ would drag ME out to exercise at Satan o'clock, and that sure as hell isn't going to happen.

"I'm hungry."

Jeremy.

He's always hungry.

"Let's go grab lunch."

She took her visitors to McCooey's, a café in her hometown. When they'd finished with the food and the banter with *the* one and only McCooey herself, they kept the afternoon low-key, went bowling with her brother and watched a movie before collapsing into bed. The boys *barely* made it to nine o'clock before conking out, but slept well and were up bright and early the next morning and ready for adventure.

Day three was spent up in Belfast City. They grabbed

themselves tickets for a hop-on-hop-off bus tour and off they went, beginning at the Titanic museum as it was overcast and raining.

"Didn't it sink?" questioned Jeremy. "Don't you want to show us the best of what Northern Ireland has to offer rather than some sinking ship?"

"She was fine when she left here," was all Lisa would reply. It was the standard Northern Irish response to digs about the sunken passenger liner.

"Wasn't she on fire when she left here?" Jeremy asked.

"That's not a commonly known fact. You read about it on Google before you came to wind me up, didn't you?" Lisa glared at him.

"Lil bit," he answered laughing.

From there, they visited the HMS Caroline and took some pictures with Samson and Goliath, the bright yellow twin shipping gantry cranes in the Harland and Wolff ship yard.

"The cranes are inherently Northern Ireland," she beamed, proudly. "If I ever fly in to Belfast City airport, seeing the cranes out the window means I'm home."

Having predicted they would be exhausted after a full day roaming around the "Big Smoke" and planning to head further north for the following day or two, the three of them stayed with a friend of Lisa's in Belfast to avoid extra driving.

Over the coming days, they saw quite a lot of Northern Ireland. They took a black taxi mural tour of

Belfast and saw the still-active peace walls. The boys couldn't quite believe that gates in interface areas were still locked at night, separating the Catholic areas from the Protestant ones.

They drove up the North Coast, stopping at in the old capital of Ireland, Carrickfergus, to check out the castle and had lunch overlooking the marina. They drove further north still and visited the Carrick-a-rede rope bridge and the Giant's Causeway, stopping also in Ballintoy harbor for Jeremy to snap a selfie at another of the Game of Thrones sites.

She'd done more walking since they'd arrived in Ireland than she'd probably done for over a year.

I REALLY hate exercise.

When they got back to Newry, she took them to the cathedral for a visit. They went up to the Flagstaff for the breathtaking views, down to Carlingford and Omeath for a walk around other sea-side towns and, on their last night, they spent some time on Cranfield Beach and watched the sun set over the water. Lisa loved being able to share her childhood stomping ground with the boys and was already dreading their departure.

Chapter 44

"How'd it happen?" Jeremy asked as he threw the last of his things into his suitcase for the third time. No matter how much he sat on it, wiggled things about, folded, or refolded, the amount of stuff he owned couldn't physically fit into the amount of space he had to work with. But, of course, he was convinced he could squash it all in. He'd done a lot of shopping on their trip to Carlow.

"How'd what happen? How did someone manage to explode their suitcase while staying at a B&B in Carlow?" Lisa queried. "I honestly have no idea. It's not like Carlow is the shopping capital of Ireland. What did you even buy?"

"How did three weeks go by so quickly?" he grumbled. "I'm not ready to leave. And bread, chips, cookies and chocolate...basically food. And my case hasn't exploded...yet."

They'd extended their trip by a week, because she and AJ had had the very same conversation a week previously.

***

They left Lisa crying at the airport. She couldn't help it. She wanted them to stay, or for her to go with them. But, hating the Atlantic more than ever, she realized that she and AJ hadn't actually discussed the next time they'd see each other. By the time she got the "I'm home," phone call, she was feeling quite low and upset. She missed him already, and he hadn't even been gone a day. And, aside from his birthday, or Christmas... *wait a minute* she thought, frantically as she reached for her phone, *his birthday!*

"Jer?" she said excitedly as her call connected. "I need you to help me plan AJ's birthday!"

"Lisa, you do realize it's months away, right? You have plenty of time!" came his muffled reply. Glancing at the clock she realized she'd woken him, and, as her laptop buzzed to life, she answered impatiently.

"Yes, but this plan will take a lot of time to get organized!"

"Ok, ok, I'm up. What do you need?" he asked yawning.

"Top secret?"

"Sure."

"*Jeremy!* I'm serious. Top secret from everyone, even Chelsea, ok?"

"Ok, ok. Sheesh. I said ok!"

She laughed. Now she had the foundations of a plan. She just had to start the ball rolling and wait for December to arrive.

Chapter 45

As Lisa flew back to Alabama, she was secretly very impressed with herself. Jeremy had arranged for a "get together" for AJ's birthday. The team, his sister, Britt, Roberto, Jared, Lindsay, Stephanie, the players' girlfriends, even Chelsea had been persuaded to go down – because Lisa couldn't be there, Chelsea had to be there in her place.

When AJ found out there was a "fuss" being made, he enquired what the heck was going on.

"Dude, your girlfriend said, 'Jeremy, I can't be there to give my boy a great birthday. Make it special for him.' And I ain't sleeping with you, she'd kill me dead if I took you to a strip club, so you have to make do with the guys, burgers, beer and the band – 'cause I know you like alliteration."

"Fine," he sighed irritably.

Jeremy raised his eyebrow. "Dude! Rude. I know you miss her, but come on, the gang's almost all gonna be here. At least *pretend* not to hate every minute?"

"Sorry, man. I do appreciate the effort."

Jeremy had left AJ's house unlocked, and, as Lisa got ready, she listened to his playlist on his computer. AJ was planning on jamming with the band at his party. She guessed the songs he'd planned on singing from the number of times he'd listened to them.

He's certainly thorough.

The band had, at one time, sung a version of Warren G's Regulate, which, for some obscure reason, Lisa loved. It should have been so wrong, but instead it was oh-so-right. She was glad to see it had made the setlist.

***

As the band set up on the stage. Jeremy snuck in the cake and her bag of boxes.

There were five boxes, all the same size, and numbered one to five. He carried them, hidden as best he could, to the table AJ had been sitting at and placed them in a row. Ignoring AJ's look of confused amusement from the stage, he indicated they should start, and so they did. Towards the end of the song, she came out of her hiding spot and walked over to the table. She stood and waited for him to notice.

She didn't need to wait long.

"Holy crap, it's Lisa!"

Chelsea.

Worse still, drunk Chelsea. As she turned to look in the direction of the exclamation, she saw that everyone was gobsmacked. *Mission accomplished.*

Spinning back around to face AJ Lisa realized that the band had stopped playing and she was suddenly incredibly self-conscious. She was wearing a skirt; she didn't do skirts. *Just like you didn't do dresses before the ball.* And the new boots she was wearing felt weird too. Right now, pretty much everyone in the room was staring at her, shocked.

"Um. Surprise?" she laughed a little.

"You're here." AJ said, half to himself, half probably an unintentional out-loud reaction.

"No shit, Sherlock!"

She couldn't tell who said it, but it made her smile.

"Happy birthday?" she tried again.

"Uh. Thanks?" he said, putting his guitar down and jumping down from the stage. He picked her up and spun her around. *I love when you do that.*

"How did you? What did you? Uhm. Huh?

She giggled.

"Surprised?"

He nodded.

"Good, that's only the first one!"

"The first one?" he managed. "What's the other one?"

"Well, I have a few," she started. "You might want to get a drink," she told him grinning.

"Ok." He kissed her. "You look good," he said, smiling.

"You ready to go, Irish?" Jeremy asked.

"Go? Go where? She just got here!" AJ protested, slipping his arms around her. "Where does she have to go?"

Producing a microphone, Jeremy handed it to her,

and she said, "Up there," pointing to the stage.

"What? You? Why? I'm so confused."

"Get a drink and sit down," she told him smiling, "and don't worry. I'm not leaving. Also? Don't touch your presents until I say so, ok?"

"You got me presents, too?"

"Yeah, the boxes."

"They're from you?" His confusion seemed to only be growing, not abating, which made her laugh. She nodded.

"One surprise at a time," she told him with a wink as she made her way to the stage.

Now it was time. She was dreading this bit. Singing to him in the hospital in front of his friends and family was one thing, but now she was an emotional wreck. That was allowed to be piss-poor and pitchy. But this was in public. With his band. In front of his people, his friends, family and a bunch of strangers. It was, after all, a bar and she wasn't a performer. Usually, she hated singing in front of people. This was an exception and she had to do it. So, standing on the stage she cleared her throat and started,

"Hey everyone. So, at least this bunch of people over here know who I am. And, if you don't, well, my name is Lisa, and I know you're expecting to hear AJ and the guys, but I have something I'd like to sing for AJ because it's his birthday and I flew the whole way from Ireland to sing this one song to him on his special day – would that be ok?"

The room clapped and cheered.

Shit.

Ok, calm down. Some of them are for sure drunk already. Just ignore them. Focus on AJ, she told herself. *No one else is here. Well they are here, but they don't matter. It's for him, for his birthday, so suck it up and sing already!*

Giving a nod to Brad, who had agreed to play with her, the music started up and she sang. It was a song he had sent to her at the very beginning of their relationship. When they barely knew each other. The song immediately reminded her of them.

I hope he likes it, she started to panic.

Her eyes met his, and she held his gaze. He probably knew how terrified she was. So, he smiled encouragingly, and returning his smile, she didn't alter her stare. *It's only AJ.*

Keep your eyes on him, she told herself focusing as she began to sing *Riot*.

When she had finished, she half shrugged as people clapped, and he grabbed her in a HUGE hug as she tried to get off stage.

"Thank you," he whispered through her hair.

"Any time," she told him, blushing.

"Again?" he asked, hopefully.

"Any time, but now. Plus, you owe me a dance, and then have presents to open," she told him, in an attempt to distract him.

"Oh! I forgot I had presents!" He turned to face the

table and the five boxes. As he did, Jeremy slipped her an envelope which she handed straight to Chelsea to hold for a few moments – indicating not to open it, or tell anyone, or show anyone. Brad hurried back to the DJ station and put some Jason Mraz on while Jeremy set up the cake.

Taking AJ's hand, Lisa led him to the dance floor. The song made them smile. The night she first heard it was the night after their first phone call. He'd said, "I sent you a song. It makes me smile and think of you." She had opened her inbox where she had found what had quickly become one of her favorite songs. *I'm yours.*

The lyrics had made her cry. The fact that he had thought of her when he had heard it. She didn't tell him at the time that she'd cried. She was way too embarrassed. She was an emotional girl. She had warned him that things like this had a huge effect on her.

When the song was over, they found their way back to the table. She gave Brad the thumbs up from across the room. The lights went dark. Everyone sang "Happy Birthday," and she made him make a wish as he blew out the candles on the cake she'd picked out for him.

The cake was designed like a hockey rink, and said, "Happy birthday, Hockey Boy! All my love." There was a little sweetie bunny stuck next to it. AJ smiled and kissed her. Then started to cut the cake. Before he'd gotten too far, Jeremy hollered, "Time for presents, Pim!"

Chapter 46

"Number one?" AJ asked, turning to Lisa for confirmation that it was ok to open them. She nodded. This was embarrassing. She hadn't planned on doing this in the bar, and she hadn't run it past anyone. It was impulsive. Her original plan had been to just give him the envelope, but she figured this would be more fun. She was now sort-of regretting it. It was *supposed* to be a guessing game. Something to spice things up a bit for his birthday. As he turned to face the boxes, she quickly reclaimed the envelope from Chelsea who was still closely guarding it.

He shook the box, then paused.

"Is it ok to shake?" he asked her with a concerned look.

"Yup," she answered grinning. "They all are."

He opened the lid and inside she had shredded tons of tissue paper, so he'd have to look for what was inside. It was a little model plane.

"You're going back to Ireland, dude!" Jeremy shouted. "I bet she got you a ticket to Ireland, man." He was drunk. This amused her. She giggled and told him to shut up.

Looking bemused, AJ closed the lid on the box. He sat

it on the table with the model airplane on top of it.

"Can I go on?" he asked tentatively.

"Sure, work away," she told him as the confusion returned to his face, and color to hers.

Box number two. He shook it and opened the lid. More tissue paper. This box held a tree, a maple tree to be precise. She knew not many people would be able to easily identify a maple tree, but she was sure AJ would know what it was.

"It's a tree. Ireland has trees. It's pretty green. I think you're going to Ireland," Mike chimed in. "Jeremy's right."

More confusion, as he placed the tree on top of the box and regarded the airplane, and then the tree, and then the airplane again – as if searching for a connection.

Crap. He hasn't figured it's a maple tree, she thought worriedly.

He opened box number three to find a puck. Realization began to dawn on him, as he smiled a half smile, though still looking a little confused.

Box four contained a tin of oil.

As he stared at the four objects sitting on top of their respective boxes, he turned to her and grinned.

"You know what it is?" she asked him.

"I have an idea," he replied.

Realizing her hands had remained behind her back the whole time the box spectacle was going on, AJ drew Lisa close, kissed her and pinched the envelope from between her fingers. She giggled at his excitement as he opened it. The contents of the envelope were two plane tickets to Toronto, together with two tickets to the Maple Leafs versus the Edmonton Oilers game that coming weekend. He laughed and kissed her again.

"Could be a fun game," he said to her, his eyes sparkling.

"Especially if we bet on it."

"I like that idea, but you know your Oilers are gonna lose anyway, so you may as well just admit defeat now."

She thumped him playfully, "I don't know if I want to sit with a smelly Leafs fan," she told him folding her arms across her chest.

"Well, that's a good thing, since they're my tickets and I get to choose who comes with me!" he joked.

"My name is on the plane ticket," she retorted as he stopped her with a kiss.

She didn't know how things were going to turn out; she didn't know if they'd have their happily ever after ending that she wanted so very badly. She didn't know if the Leafs would, in fact, beat her beloved Oilers. Nor did she know for certain that they'd make it to her next birthday as a couple. No matter how much she wanted things to be normal, AJ was still married and that challenge lay ahead of them. But, right then and there, in that instant, as they stood entwined in each other's arms, she knew she wanted to marry him, that she wanted to spend the rest of her life making him as happy as he made her. A wave of pure happiness overwhelmed her. As if he felt it too, AJ pulled her tighter and kissed her.

"What about box number five?"

Jeremy. Again.

"Oh, Wait." AJ said, startled by Jeremy's interruption, "what about box number five?"

"Sure," she told him. Her cheeks were hot. This was it. The moment he would realize he was in love with a complete nut job.

He opened box number five. Sitting on top of the tissue paper, lay a book. The cover of the book was a collage of pictures of the two of them from her first trip to see him and from their time together in Ireland. He smiled widely as he lifted the book out of the box.

"What is it?" he asked her with a puzzled look.

"Well, it's a book." She began. "It started off with me just writing a dream I once had about you, and it grew. I tried to stop writing it, but it just kept coming and plaguing me. I just kept writing until I couldn't write anymore."

"What's it about, babe?" he asked her as he traced his fingers over the cover of the book.

"It's our story, AJ. You write songs. I wrote a book. It's about us," she told him. His eyes met hers and she realized she was worried for no reason. He opened the back cover and said, "Hey – why the blank pages?"

"Because the ending hasn't been written yet!" she told him matter-of-factly, as he came across the last page, which read: "To be continued..."

As AJ flicked through the book, he was way too

overwhelmed to speak.

"This has been the best birthday ever," he managed as he struggled with the words. His eyes were filling with tears, and she could tell that she had touched a part of him that no one else had, or ever would. She smiled at him.

"I love you," she whispered.

"I love you too," he told her softly as he turned to the start of the book. The dedication page read:

To my darling AJ,

I want to be the first person you talk to every single day for the rest of your life and the last person you talk to at night before you sleep. I want you to play with my hair, rub my shoulders, argue hockey with me, and kiss me – just because.

Our journey won't be easy, but the best things aren't supposed to be.

I'm game if you are.

I hope this makes you smile to read, as much as I smiled while writing it.

For all the times you made me smile without trying, for all that's behind us and all that's yet to come.

Your puck-bunny,

Lisa.

AJ smiled at her, not bothering to fight the tears. In that moment, as their eyes met, Lisa had never been surer that she really had found her soulmate.

Lisa Millar will return in:

The Good in Goodbye

Enjoy an exclusive excerpt now

Lasairiona E. McMaster

The Good in Goodbye

Three minutes.

You can wait three minutes, Lisa. It's just three minutes. One Mississippi... two Mississippi...three Mississippi...timer on your phone, Lisa...five Mississippi...

She drummed her fingers on her thighs.

Christ woman, you wait longer for your toast to pop.

Calm down.

She sat, fully clothed, on the toilet. She was sitting as far away from the "The Sticks", which she was handling as one would radioactive material, as her small bathroom permitted. Beads of sweat trickled down the back of her neck and fear gripped at her stomach. Deep down, she already knew the answer. Her boobs were bigger, she was bloated and achy, and her usually, set-your-watch-by-it period was late. Two weeks late. While many of the symptoms felt like her period was on the way, she had a feeling in the pit of her stomach that it wouldn't show.

Flights mess with my cycle. I'm stressed out. Lisa tried making a mental list of the reasons her period could be two weeks late.

Crap. I'm totally pr-

"Shit!"

Her thought was interrupted by an urgent need to vomit.

And let's not forget the nausea, she thought as she quickly stood up, spun around, opened the lid and spewed the contents of her breakfast into the toilet.

Why do I even bother eating?

Since when do pregnancy symptoms appear so early and so strongly?

The three-minute timer on her phone sounded as she vomited a second time.

"Ugh." She groaned as she kneeled on the floor hugging the toilet bowl with both arms, her head resting on the seat.

Aaaaand once more for luck. A hat-trick of vomit and it's not even 8 o'clock. Good job, Lis.

Pulling herself up off the floor, she turned on the faucet, splashed water over her face and grabbed blindly at a towel before straightening up. She breathed deeply.

Ok, this is it, this is when your period arrives and you realize you're being an absolute fool.

She picked up the stick and slowly turned it over.

"Pregnant," the screen read.

"Are you sure?" she asked out loud. Stunned.

She grabbed the second stick. On this one, two lines were displayed.

Two lines is pregnant.

"I can't be-"

She frantically swiped up the third stick and was met with a plus sign on the tiny screen.

"Fuck."

Author Note

This book has been in the making for well over a decade. I first started it back in 2005, when I 'met' the real-life AJ, fell in love with him and was inspired to write this work of fiction about him, his friend 'Jeremy', my best, friend and myself.

AJ encouraged my creativity, loved my writing, and it really wasn't long before I was pulling all-nighters, just to get the words out of me and on the screen. I couldn't sleep. I was totally inspired. AJ was definitely my muse, and I couldn't stop writing until the book was finished.

Fast forward to November 2018. I repatriated from India to my home country of Northern Ireland and began a purge-and-clean process around the house – it was there that I found a hard copy, the *only* copy of this work left in existence. I honestly thought the manuscript had been lost forever. Wondering if this old manuscript was a lost cause, or whether my story actually had something to it, I sat on it for a while before sending it to my (very famous author) friend Liz and said, "Hey girl, watchu think of this?" Liz told me to push through the editing phase, bring it into the 'now' (cause who wears gypsy skirts or uses iPods anymore?) and show it a little love, because she believed in this story – and, she said, she was sucked in, despite not being a fan of the lovey-dovey *stuff*.

Without her, this book truly wouldn't exist – so thanks, bitch face.

Anyone who knows my best friend and me, will know right away who the character of Chelsea is loosely based on. Amber and I have been best friends since December 2004. That's fifteen (and counting) years of sharing just about every detail of our lives with each other – and she's only tried to kill me once – that's really not bad going!

Without her, I wouldn't be here – I realize that sounds a little extreme, but in real life AJ never showed up to meet me. I got stood up, ghosted, and I truly thought I might die of a broken heart. Amber held me together (literally, as she was visiting me in Ireland when this happened and I cried on her lap for hours) until I was strong enough to stand by myself. And she's still that person, keeping me together when I fall apart.

I can't ever thank you enough for making me realize I was stronger than I ever believed I could be. Love ewe.

Acknowledgements

To Col, thanks for building me this little work-space haven, and to Lewis for (kinda) giving me the peace to use it.

To my boss, friend and the best chiropractor I've ever known, Dr. Jo, thanks for keeping my spine aligned so I can spend hours at my laptop creating my masterpieces.

To my editor, Cassie – thanks for all your hard work, for the instantaneous replies to messages, the constructive criticism, pushing me to be the best writer I can be, but mostly for being a sarky mare and making me LOL at your very professional editor-y comments.

To AJ and Jeremy, thanks for the memories, and the inspiration. I remember not being able to sleep for days until this story was written, and the editing and re-write process was just as intense.

To my rad team of Beta readers from ASJ's 'Top of the Tops' group. Do you have a favorite jeweler? I sure do. She's an entrepreneurial kick-ass amazing sparkly hero, Alyssa Smith, and she created a secret group for all of their Top Fans on Facebook. I didn't realize I'd meet such an amazing bunch of women on a random Facebook group. Thank y'all for advance-reading my story and putting my neurotic mind at ease that you didn't all hate it, for wanting more, and for encouraging and supporting me daily, in everything, not just my writing.

Lastly, to my friends, readers, reviewers and supporters, if it wasn't for you, these books I write would be gathering dust on my bookshelf. Thank you all.

Keeping in touch with the Author

If you want to read more about me, you can sign up to my newsletter here on my Facebook page, @QueenofFireLas.

I send out the *occasional* new release updates, super-exclusive tidbits and sneak-peeks, questions on what you like and dislike about my books and occasionally even ask for feedback on things I need help with for my books (like what to name a character in an upcoming book or what your favorite romance novel is - other than my own, OF COURSE!).

As an indie author, I live for the good reviews – if you loved the book and feel so inclined, drop me a wee review on Amazon or Goodreads. If you hated it, however, your review function is probably broken and you shouldn't even bother going to check.

ABOUT THE AUTHOR

Lasairiona McMaster grew up dreaming of an exciting life abroad, and, after graduating from Queens University, Belfast, that is exactly what she did - with her then-boyfriend, now husband of almost ten years. Having recently repatriated to Northern Ireland after a decade abroad spanned over two countries (seven and a half years in America and eighteen months in India), she now finds herself 'home', with itchy feet and dreams of her next expatriation. With a penchant for both travelling, and writing, she started a blog during her first relocation to Houston, Texas and, since repatriating to Northern Ireland, has decided to do as everyone has been telling her to do for years, and finally pen a book (or two) and get published while she tries to adjust to the people and place she left ten years ago, where nothing looks the same as it did when she left.

Connect with her on social media Facebook, Instagram and Twitter: @QueenofFireLas

29069366R00201

Printed in Great Britain
by Amazon